CRITICAL ACCLAIM FOR
THE NEON LIGHTS ARE VEINS

"Knight's slangy prose is a perfect fit for characters whose dreams die slowly or explosively."

—*Publishers Weekly*

"*The Neon Lights Are Veins* is a dope-fueled gutter-punk odyssey through a gaudy nightmare version of Los Angeles. With echoes of James Ellroy and Nathanael West, Knight carves out his own bit of L.A. crime-writing turf in this impressive debut."

—Richard Lange, author of *Rovers*,
Dead Boys and *The Smack*

"Nolan Knight is at the forefront of Hard-Ass-Noir. He's the mad hatter of words and dark moody storytelling. He's a creative crime-pugilist!"

—Frank Bill, author of *Crimes in Southern Indiana*,
Donnybrook and *The Savage*

"Nolan Knight has written a dark, dirty and entertaining sewer ride through the neon-lit streets of Los Angeles. Imagine Nathanael West and Darby Crash writing a 21st century noir and you've got *The Neon Lights Are Veins*. Highly recommended."
—Jim Ruland, author of *Corporate Rock Sucks: The Rise and Fall of SST Records Forest of Fortune*, and *Do What You Want: The Story of Bad Religion*

"High action. Very fast paced. A great read. Highly Recommended."
—S.W. Lauden, author of *Bad Citizen Corporation* and *Grizzly Season*

"Nolan Knight's *The Neon Lights Are Veins* is unlike anything I've read before (and that's saying something!). The novel's story is a fast-paced mystery and caper, dragging the reader through the underbelly of the Los Angeles night, but most impressive is Knight's style: in your face and no-holds-barred."
—Steph Post, author of *Lightwood* and *Miraculum*

THE NEON LIGHTS
ARE VEINS

NOLAN KNIGHT

THE NEON LIGHTS ARE VEINS

Crimson Gate Books

For Jenny Jay
A Lovebird
Forever Wild at Heart

ONE

Loveless Gutters

1.

She was swallowed by the streets on Good Friday, searching for a dream that wouldn't have her. Mongo told him over bacon-wrapped dogs at Pink's; her clothes still piled high in their apartment, leaving Mongo to scoop rent. *Must've went back home*, Alvi thought. Couldn't hack it in Hollywood—just like the rest. Once hope waned, they all felt the cold cage of the Pacific.

Too bad this world craved dreamers.

"Fucked up is what it is, Alvi! Bitch knew I needed money for my shoot, and she ups a does this?"

Alvi focused on Mongo's purple lipstick, contrasting a fresh shadow beard in bloom. Took a box of razors to make her female soft. She smashed the mustard bun into her face, fluttering silver eyelashes over glittered mocha cheekbones. His window to speak.

"You act surprised Gabby pulled a *Gabby*. Was bound to happen sooner or later. Ditch whatever she left behind and forget her."

"That's rich, coming from you, loverboy. Should apply that wisdom."

His eyes rolled.

A mother and child attempted to sit at an adjacent table. Soon as the kid began to point at every blue tat bleeding about Alvi's face and neck, mommy scooped him up and bolted.

Mongo continued. "Fuck! She been even helpin' with utilities lately—makin' sure the room stay clean. Vanda gone too. Left the Zimba 'round one for the boulevard, ain't nobody heard from 'em since. You really think they both up and gone?"

He shrugged, scooping dregs of kraut with a spork. "Check the *Times*. If somethin' happened last night—should be there."

A white smocked fry cook approached, lugging a five-gallon gas can with both hands. He dropped it at Alvi's Old Schools.

"Thanks for the grease, man."

"Anythin' fa you, Alvi. Need me to shit in a bucket? Can have that too."

They smirked, rising from the plastic table. Cook rushed to boil nitrates.

"Help me load this into the ride, Mong."

Her stilettos clicked towards the parking lot. "Honey, this queen could crack a nail. Then where would we be?"

"You're payin' double tonight, then." He shook his head, bracing chicken legs before the heave.

Alvi crushed three Parliaments before Mongo was through with her client, some apartment john off Genesee. He gunned the ancient Mercedes down Sunset, sending grey plumes out the tailpipe, filling the boulevard with a stench of stale fries. Mongo counted the cash. Nearly four a.m. and they were headed home. An early night.

They sat quiet, taking in the galaxy of neon teasing wild desire, zooming their peripheral. Alvi had been out here for a decade. Reminisced navigating each night that first year, relying on these dense glowing tubes for guidance. Favorites on this stretch burst with brilliance: Ye Coach & Horses Cocktails/The Saharan Motor Hotel/Seventh Veil Girls Girls Girls. Crossroad's spinning globe was the cherry. Such radiance was soothing; comfort over concrete in a city so cold. When out romping Los Angeles after dark, you were damn sure to meet the other side of living.

* * *

The Hotel Lafayette sat by its lonesome on Beverly, just shy of Rampart. A tarnished glimpse of a bygone era, it housed around forty hard-lucks on a monthly basis. Broken glass and blue neon relics welcomed them through barbed wire. The pinkish brick pile boasted *Bath & Showers $2.50* high on the side in phantom paints. Lord knows what it originally read, eighty years ago. Mongo held the gate as Alvi strained his back, lugging the gas can towards the stairs.

"I'ma freshen up. Swing by in a few."

Alvi nodded, dropping the container to hit up his mailbox. A lonesome letter sat snug in the slot.

Home was at the top, suite 418. Worst part about driving a grease car was straining the waste vegetable oil of any floating debris: onion rings, zucchini, Oreos—depended on the restaurant. Ronnie—the property manager—would only allow the straining drum in Alvi's room, due to the smell. Lugging up four flights was the price for free fuel and so be it.

The studio was nothing special. Walls riddled with previous nail piercings; a microwave and mini fridge capped out the amenities. His clothes were stacked on the floor under a poster of a kid skateboarder, rocking a poolside Disaster. He sparked a cig and hit up the fridge. Half a forty of King Cobra smiled back. Still had some bite, thank God.

He opened the envelope, already knowing what it was. Ma— sent them every week. This one contained Michael the Archangel, lancing a demon down south. A scribbled Post-it clung to the back: *It's not too late, Alvin.* He tossed it in the trash on his way out.

Beside the door hung a stained Polaroid: a bikini-clad brunette, walking up from the beach, water splashing at the camera. Liquid eyes, slender thighs. Alvi put two fingers to his lips, transferring a kiss on the way out. *Angelica*—their honeymoon. Better days.

***

Mongo sat with a handheld mirror, swapping her violet wig for a do-rag. She ran a comb through before placing it tenderly on the floor. A Styrofoam skull helped prop new hair atop the dresser. Bought it special for the shoot: honeycomb, auburn highlights. She'd carefully curled it for tomorrow but now that had to wait. Thumbing a stack of bills, she contemplated how soon to reschedule. Was short another night.

Fucking Gabby.

This centerfold business was pricey stuff. Wondered if Tyra had the same troubles on her way up, paying to play, hustling to make it. Probably cheaper since she was taller—but look at her now! She lit a smoke and smiled, imagining what a Mongo talk show would be like. The photographer said this was how most models got their start. Sure the rag wasn't Vogue but it would be on newsstands throughout the city. Someone would surely see it and discover her. Oh, what a life! Only a few more days and the fun would finally begin. *Heaven.* She wiggled on the chair.

Silver lashes peeled-off easy; she stuck them together. An achy anus from the night's escapades needed attention. She rattled a stickerless prescription vile out her purse. Four thin Xanibars clanked onto a mirror. She searched for a grate, smiling at the thought of that new saucy title—*Covergirl.*

Alvi tripped down the stairway but caught himself mid-stride. Mongo lived on the floor below. First person he hit it off with when he moved in. Didn't shock him that her Christian name was Vance Mongalez. Television helped her escape Twin Falls, enticed by breezy palms and beach bods out west. Soon as the train hit Union Station, he became a she and Miss Mongo was born. Alvi rapped at the door. She called from the bathroom. "Come in, honey. Pay's on the counter."

He strolled in, noticing two white slugs on the mirror, vacuuming each with precision, not missing a grain. Two more Xanies sat beside the grate. He pocketed them and went for the fridge, stealing a High Life. Room was cluttered in rainbow shades of lady wear. Got a kick from the sea of wigs. Could fill the Pantages with all this garb. Technicolor Dreamcoat be damned.

A row of phone sex ads clung above the nightstand. Each featured a semi-nude Mongo in all her glory. The numbers were great (1-884-WET- BUTT). A Dolly Parton portrait was the only other thing stuck on the wall, hair so huge, frame couldn't contain it.

Gabby's things were on the floor in the corner. She really did leave it all behind. *Strange.* He walked over and rifled through, sniffing a few garments to relight the mind. They shared happy times once. He held her volunteer badge for Clean Spikes Now, a non-profit that gave fresh needles to junkies. Her photo stared back at him. A limp black Mohawk hovered emerald eyes and a crooked smile. Had one of those Gene Tierney overbites—nothing to open a beer bottle with—just right. He tossed it back and noticed an opened *L.A. Weekly*, wedged under a leather vest: adult classifieds, six months old. An ad was circled, phone number scribbled beside.

NEW GIRL/INDEPENDENT
Just need a few extra bucks...Wanna hang?
Petite & Pretty Punker, 5'5, 110lbs., Gabby 310-251—

Before he could finish, in came Mongo.
"Whatchu messin' wit now?"
He showed her.
"That's Gabby's. Some new shit she be tryin'. Didn't pan out though. Couldn't afford to keep postin' it, ran only twice—got one repeat customer though." She pointed at the scribbled number. "Some old dude."
"Never took her to any old dudes when I drove her."

"Shit, I dunno—who said you could drink a beer!"

"I did. Extra for not helping earlier."

"Whateva—ran into Doreen. Said Noodles and Vargas stole a pony keg from Bogie's Liquor. Got it tapped in the Zimba. Let's roll."

"You goin' down like that?" Alvi glared at her baggy pink pajamas and filthy duck slippers. Xani dust exploded his skull, loopy.

"Fuck you, motherfucka, in dat beat up ass flannel."

They roughhoused a bit before heading down.

Zimba Room once beamed ghost blue out front, before the place was abandoned and turned into storage. Took up nearly half the first floor. Mongo and Alvi helped Ronnie clean out the joint few years back, making it a chill zone for the influx of patrons forced to live at the Lafayette. Helped prevent sidewalk loitering too. Cops were already around here enough.

A crystal chandelier kept the joint murky. The antique mahogany bar also remained intact, stretching down the right wall with floral carvings and a smooth arm nook. Graffiti doodles plastered everything else: the poor man's decor. Noodles and Vargas were regaling a crowd of four huddled on dumpster couches as they waltzed in.

"He was wearing a trench coat and fedora this time." Noodles mimed the garments.

"Yeah," Vargas said, "like Dick Tracy and shit! Stood in the corner 'til last call, tryin' to bleed into the wall or somethin'. Fuckin' weirdo."

The girls laughed.

Alvi asked, "Who you talkin' 'bout?"

Noodles said, "Kiefer—caught him boozin' at the Ye Rustic again."

"Shocker, right?"

Mongo greeted the crowd as Alvi grabbed plastic cups from

behind the bar and pumped the keg.

Alvi poked Vargas, "What is it?"

"Icehouse." He made a sour face. "Least it ain't warm."

Alvi hoisted the brew in thanks.

Mongo took a seat next to Doreen, a chubby white gal from Fresno. The other three were Lexi, Faye and Elvira. At a glance, anyone could tell that Faye was the only one blessed with a vagina at birth. Lexi and Elvira were husky Puerto Ricans, working hard on the boulevard to buy their true selves. Faye was a new resident. Face screamed foster care but Alvi figured just another runaway. She wouldn't last. For some reason the redheads never got by for long.

Vargas and Noodles slouched on the floor, bright spiked hairdos now lax. Looked like snow cones. Studs and boots shiny too—must've fallen drunk in a fountain again. They lit smokes in unison.

Doreen asked, "Had that photo shoot, Mong?"

Noodles jumped in. "Photo shoot? You tryin' to be a supastar or somethin'?"

Mongo rolled her eyes, exhaling a cloud. "Child, if you haven't heard, I'm somewhat of a celebrity in this *fine* city."

"Oh really," said Vargas.

Alvi chimed, "Know those free smut rags 'cross town—phone sex numbers inside?"

They nodded.

He reached out and squeezed Mongo's cheeks. "This purdy face has graced several hotlines for the *LA Xpress*."

They began to hoot and laugh.

Mongo slapped Alvi's hand away. "Not no more—this week they're putting Miss Mongo on the mothafuckin' cover, y'all!"

Lexi and Elvira bounced with excitement as Doreen gave a monster hug. The boys clapped before grabbing another round. Faye followed like a stray dog. Noodles and Vargas rummaged pockets in search of a roach. No dice. They hurried out to try and score. Alvi had the tap in his mouth, siphoning the flow when Faye's fingertips brushed his neck.

"Love your tats."

He turned. "Been so long—forget I have 'em." Girl's face was uncomfortably close, eyes squinting. *Typical runaway, searching for a protector.*

She stuck out her digits. "We haven't actually met. Faye Green."

Green? He wanted to bust, reciprocating the stale fish instead. "Alvi Drake—pleasure." Before she could continue, he made his way back to the couch. Mongo was starting in about Gabby to the girls.

"The shoot was set for today but I couldn't come up with the photographer fees. Had to reschedule 'cause that bitch Gabby done bailed on me. She's supposed to front half the fuckin' rent. Any you talk to her today?"

Elvira and Faye shook their heads no. Doreen pointed to Lexi. "We saw her last night."

Alvi slouched. "With Vanda?"

"Yeah," said Lexi. "They was out by Del Taco, *papi.*"

Mongo asked, "They say anythin' 'bout leavin'?"

"Nope," said Doreen. "Were actin' all sketchy—barking at each other 'bout a club or somethin'. Figured they was tweakin' hard—left 'em alone. That's the last we saw 'em."

Lexi nodded.

Mongo glared at Alvi. "Where she come from again?"

Alvi shook his head. "Don't look at me."

"You the one dated her when she got into town. Never told you where she's from?"

"Never got a straight answer." He killed the cup and burped. "Prolly back home—wherever that is, cuddlin' her teddies." *Made things easier thinking that way.* "Give it a few days, either her or Vanda will turn up—watch."

2.

Rocco began to hyperventilate, pinned on his back, body smooshed like a marshmallow atop warm gravel. Shouldn't have pulled the corpse so hard out the trunk. Her cold eyeball rubbed waxy against his chin. Searched for strength between the moon and the gutter. *Why did Valley nights have to be so muggy?* One deep breath and he exerted it all. Posturing simply wasn't good enough; had to toss the girl off the overpass before anybody saw. Timed it perfectly till the mishap. The Escalade's bumper helped prop the princess. Freeway was scarce this late an hour; headlights from a lone big rig hovered like fireflies over pond. One final heave and the body began to float, down, suspended in grace until that final *crunch*.

He tried not to peel out, but the engine had other plans. A blank rearview washed relief. Noticed a blood drop, clinging to his nose. Swabbed it with a McNapkin and sped toward civilization. The Hollywood Freeway sang beyond.

Zzzzzzt!

The cell stabbed his heart. Screen glowed Satin.

"Hey, Raymond."

"How's it?"

"We're good." Almost slipped with the mishap details but knew better.

"Meet at the spot in an hour."

"Cool."

The phone clicked dead. "Fuckin-A." He tossed it to the console, squinting, adjusting thick brown specs.

Twirling spotlight towers beamed over Hollywood Boulevard, ushering 101 zoomers to come experience gold-bricked stars of grandeur. Giant tubes blared atop boulevard roofs: Knicker-bocker/Patron/Roosevelt Hotel. The Broadway shrugged a shoulder, uninterested in anyone not gushing over her. Rocco took Vine to Franklin once Capitol Records sprung up, windshield awash with sordid neon. Backstreets brought safety just as boulevards sprang prey. He utilized them, undaunted by sirens of beauty and success, black palms rustling high above.

True city grit stained the Hollywood fringe. Down Virgil, 99-cent stores and *carnicerías* sat darkened between dilapidated homes and cloth-door barrooms. Makeshift taco stands illumi-nated street corners with flood lamps. Their scent of onions and beef sent filthy dog packs into frenzy.

He parked the candy apple beast in a church lot next to King Carne, a Mexican themed market, specializing in fresh flesh on the go. A giant rooftop rooster stood tall amongst flapping American flags. Rocco sat patient, perusing a UCLA brochure, waiting for his uncle to arrive.

At half past three, he showed. A team of cars sped in behind the silver Bentley. Rocco exited, hiding the brochure under a seat.

"Rocco Felix!" Raymond flashed canines, his thin moustache perfectly parallel.

They met in embrace, Rocco careful not to crease Ray's custom herringbone three-piece. Four men exited other imports, clad in empty suits and bug-eyed sunglasses, awaiting instructions. Raymond slapped an arm around Rocco as they headed towards the *pollería*.

"What I say about wearin' those glasses 'round my boys, huh?"

Rocco fumbled to fold them. "Sorry."

"No need, nephew. Just don't want ya lookin' weak is all." He peeled four bills and handed them over. "Grab yourself some prescription sunglasses—somethin' sharp."

Rocco crumpled the cash.

Ray yelled, "Dominic, let's roll through the front—wanna surprise 'em."

A chunky brown lug sped to unlatch the market door.

Thick waves of carnage puffed out the innards, followed by the squawking clamor of caged meat. They waded through boisterous darkness, crammed with chickens, turkeys, ducks and pigeons. Rocco wasn't immune to the stink yet, hand cupping his nostrils to keep down his dinner.

A row of bunnies welcomed them to a festive rear door; thumping bass vibrated the knob. Ray unlatched the lock and punched through, exposing a black lit dance floor surrounded by scantily clad girls, each consorting with a slew of belligerent fellas. The girls' eyes popped, sending whispers of "Raymond Satin" throughout the joint. Rocco stopped at the bar for a Tecate, watching as the crew slithered through the club, playfully paralyzing their prey. Still couldn't believe this was his life now: a carnal underworld tucked in the ass of a meat market. He chugged beer to forget.

Raymond flashed fangs here and there, bumping fists with the DJ and bouncers. His jewelry refracted beams off rotating spectrum bulbs. The new black girl was haggling some half-pint ranchero in a booth. Ray turned to one of his men, and she was whisked upstairs without an explanation.

The barmaid slid Rocco another, completely ignoring other guests. He thanked her for the brew, wondering just how forced that smile was. She was a raven-haired cutie, goblin green eyes, looked like one of those Suicide chicks. Her blurriness had him squinting, eyes on her chest, trying to make out the T-shirt. *Rancid?* She noticed.

"Like what you see, sweetheart?"

He peered back, blushing. "Tell you the truth, if I had my glasses, I'd be in love."

She smiled, slapping his hand. He wanted to talk more, first normal interaction he'd had in weeks, but a single whistle sparked him upstairs.

He excused himself. "'Til next time."

"You betcha."

The second floor was dark and cozy; plush La-Z-Boy sofas armed the room with red leather. Wet bar in the corner, flat screens all around: A guy could get used to this. The girl stood, slouched in front of large, tinted windows, looking down at the party. Everyone crashed on a sofa as Ray circled, tapping her shoulders with a fingertip.

"How's everything at the apartments, baby? Everyone bein' nice?"

"Uh-huh."

"Good."

She jumped as Dom chopped ice with a screwdriver.

"Just making you a drink, sugar. Relax."

Her eyes closed, telling herself, *Don't trip.*

Ray grabbed a Grey Goose magnum and took a pull. Dominic handed the glass over for a pour.

"Here you go, baby. Drink up."

She threw it back.

"That a girl. Now, the reason you're up here's really quite simple. This' the second time I've had to tell you about arguin' with the customers—look, I don't mind you getting the best buck for your bang—but baby, you gotta take him back to the room first. It's just bad business, 'kay?"

She bit her lip, giving a Bobblehead nod. "Sorry, Mr. Satin. It won't hap—"

"How's the drink?"

"Huh?"

"Little strong?"

"I guess."

He took it from her. Some of the boys began to giggle. Ray grabbed a container of cranberry and gave it a splash before snatching the screwdriver, stirring it smooth. Rocco perked, watching the guys, wondering what he was missing. Satin handed the drink back. The girl reluctantly placed it to her full lips. Before she could take a swig, Ray began caressing her ribs with the flathead, scratching the tip down past her pelvis.

"Honestly, I'm not so sure you're gonna remember, JaTonya."

Soon as her mouth pried to retort, he struck, jabbing the tool into the back of her left thigh. Dominic's fat hand muffled her scream. Glass shattered on the floor. Satin held a beat for the squirming to simmer before pulling the shank back out.

"Primo!"

A short Filipino rose at the far couch, grabbing a cocktail cloth to tie off the wound. Raymond tilted his head and blew a kiss, wiping her tears away with a palm.

"If you're gonna be a B-girl in this casita, you gotta be fuckin' *perrrfect*." He gave a playful clap. "Well, baby—now you won't forget." A single nod had Dominic whisk the girl downstairs. Satin grabbed the vodka and lounged next to Rocco.

"Gotta keep 'em scared, Roc—can't ruin the merchandise though. Cut 'em where it can be covered—remember that. It's key to running this kinda business. Who knows? Someday, this place could all be yours."

Rocco nodded, rejecting the idea.

"So, let's talk about tonight. Everything went fine, like you say, huh?"

"Yeah, nobody 'round—freeway was pretty empty. Got her in the truck lane."

"That's perfect. Just wanted to bring you in, let you know how proud I am—you're a major prospect in this organization. I know you've only been on board a few months but, what can I say, I'm impressed—we're all impressed! Shit, I hated dumping bodies too when I was coming up, but hell, you gotta do what you gotta do, nephew." He pointed to his temple. "Gotta separate the mind from the act. Bitch made the decisions that put her there, right?"

Rocco sat silent.

"Listen, there's a meeting set up for Tuesday, three o'clock. Gotta go over a few new things—*big things*—same place as last time, 'kay?"

Rocco wished he could object. If his father was still alive things would be different. "A'course, *tío*. Not a problem."

3.

Wild women. White robes—soiled faces, all clawing mercilessly, dragging him to dirt. Michael the Archangel ignored his cries, hovering on a cloud of writhing demons: newborn baby in one fist, golden sword in the other. He reached for the child but the weight was too much. Climbing, biting—the mob used their nails to rip him limb from limb. Gabby stood over, laughing, pointing. The Archangel roared, hoisting his sword for the final blow. Through bodies, he whimpered: the swine at a regal feast; a Thanksgiving turkey—conscious of the carving. Blade ascended, its glimmer his only solace before everlasting dark...

Alvi burst from the cot, panting in rhythm with every brain throb. Three quick pills got him back in bed. Nightmares were getting more vivid. He tried to forget, counting minutes till relief washed over, tingling his skull back towards sleep.

Two days had passed without word from the lost girls. Missing person reports had been refused; newspapers couldn't spare the ink. Alvi washed up in the sink after straining a fuel batch, trying to forget everything about Gabby. Their few months had drawn aftershocks: the hole in his wallet still warm, one in his chest still numb. Had great eyes though, like Angie. He missed waking up beside someone; that foreign pillow scent was comfort. Wiping a rag over his buzz cut, down his face, he paused in the mirror, glaring at the cursive *ANGELENO* above his left eyebrow.

Had he finally hit bottom or broken straight through?

He flared a Parliament before diving under the cot to retrieve pristine vintage skateboard decks: three Vision Psychos, couple Alvas, a Roskopp Big Ugly and a Gonz. He carefully leaned each on the wall, one at a time, snapping shots with a camera before carefully loading them back. Decks like these were a hot commodity for collectors. Big bucks when mint. Clinging onto them was a godsend, kept him afloat the past few years. Still had boxes back at Ma's in Torrance too. Sometimes the past carried rewards.

A jelly jar atop his dresser harbored a slew of pastel pills: Vics, Xanies, Percs—few Oxies. He fished for three Vicodin ES—*coffin cuts,* he called them. Popped them dry, getting dressed. He loaded the camera into a Thrasher backpack along with an eighties era complete. Shit was gorgeous, rigged with Tracker trucks and Slimeball wheels; thing could fly. Its graphic featured a rat nailed to a cross, screaming RATBOY SAVES! He slung the pack over a shoulder and grabbed the gas tank before heading downstairs.

At the third floor, Mongo's door was open, music seeping out.

I'm just a soul who's intentions are good...

He dropped the tank in the hall and went by. Sitting in front of the mirror, she brushed knots out of an electric blue bob.

"Yo."

She spun.

"Headed into Hollywood—wanna roll?"

"Nah, working out the room today." She thumbed at a California flag draped out the window: a calling card for repeat customers, passing by. "Got my big shoot tonight."

"Cool." He leered at three fresh slugs, grated atop the mirror.

She sighed. "Just one, okay."

He sped over.

"Think the girls might hit up the New Bev this week, catch whatever's playin'. You down?"

He nodded, crinkling sinuses, sucking back snot.

Mondays at dusk made Hollywood Boulevard tolerable. The influx of black socked tourists was at an ebb, creeps and hustlers taking back the night. Alvi surfed sleek terrazzo sidewalks with top speed precision. He cruised by souvenir shops, windows blaring celluloid gods, ironic t-shirts, Oscars for lesser folks. Stripper stores had freak mannequins busting out of cartoon lingerie. He carved through gold stars, ollying milk crates, screeching the occasional power slide. A frontside Big Spin through Chandler Square made him one happy burnout. Pills coursing made him even happier. He bombed Cahuenga, arms aloft, embracing the downhill rush: one with the city.

The Megastar Hostel sat just north of Selma on Schrader, a cube cluttered with world flags and film roll accents. Alvi popped out the board, catching it mid-air without looking. A pair of German girls huddled at the front desk, machine-gunning questions to a green haired stocky dude in shades. Alvi waded through their backpacks. Bootsie didn't budge. Peering around Boots' shades, Alvi could see he was fast asleep; the Germans remained relentless with their inquiries.

"Bootsie!"

The dude burst, almost falling back off the chair before taking notice.

"Alvi! What the fuck, man? How goes it?" He came around the desk to trade skins.

One of the pale girls said, "Excuse me…sir?"

Boots gave her one finger, smiling at Alvi. "So, what's up?"

"Cool if I use the computer to load my eBay shit?"

"Sure thing, sucka."

They walked down the hall, leaving the girls to their brochures. Boots told his latest tourist story: two plump Norwegians with insatiable assholes. *Filthy fucker.*

The ancient desktop was occupied. Boots ordered two Italians to bail, allowing Alvi to sit. The camera uploads took all of five minutes, and with three more, he was back in business. Before clicking out, he pulled up the *Times*, checking for Gabby, just in case. He scrolled headlines.

MAN CHARGED IN MACHETE ATTACK

DRUNKEN OFF-DUTY OFFICERS DISCHARGE FIREARMS DOWNTOWN

MEDICAL MARIJUANA DISPENSARY RAID IN WEHO

GRIFFITH PARK BRUSHFIRE CONTAINED

The next one caught his eye.

OFFICIALS BAFFLED AT I.D. OF BODY PARTS ON 5 FREEWAY

He read on.

> SUN VALLEY—Remains of a 20- to 30-year-old female were retrieved earlier this morning on the northbound Golden State (5) Freeway. Initial reports indicated an animal being struck; however, Los Angeles County firefighters determined the remains as being human, according to the CHP collision report. It is unclear whether the victim jumped off the Laurel Canyon Boulevard overpass or if she walked into traffic during the early morning hours, Easter Sunday. The body was struck several times by vehicles, dismembering the remains for nearly a mile. The identity of the victim is currently pending.

Alvi froze, imagining the horror. *One night you're partyin', next you're freeway paste.* Another lost angel. He zombied through the hallway, almost passing Boots before saying, "Thanks."

Boulevard bulbs pulsed. The El Capitan battled Mann's Chinese for maximum wattage. Alvi lumbered under the debauched carnival of lights past some jerk in an Easter Bunny suit, fishing gutters for butts. A brawl poured out some club across the way. He stopped at The Cave, lighting a smoke under its tattered bikini marquee, marinating. *Hell are you, baby girl?* Be nice to know she was still breathing. He shook it off. She'd turn up eventually. Life would suck on a familiar level. His hand trembled after cashing the cig on a dildo display case. First things last, he needed an uplift of spirits.

The Frolic Room's flamboyant signage was Alvi's favorite in the whole city. Rods glowing blue, green and pink, crisscrossed behind thick yellow letters. Thing was nearly junked once. Disney had rented the Pantages for some shit-show and decided it clashed with their rat image. Luckily, drunkards banded together, waving broken bottles at City Hall. Best dive in town.

A large Hirschfield mural spanned the side wall, depicting yesteryear celebrities in a hedonistic heaven. Alvi plopped on a stool in front of W.C. Fields. Place was empty, still early. Lady tending bar loaded the icebox.

"What'll it be, Alvi?"

"Hey, Dita—Maker's rocks."

Juke spun, "You Can't Put Your Arms Around a Memory."

"Busy, busy?"

"Fixin' to be." She slid down the stiff.

He killed it with two long slugs. Without words, there came another.

"You seen Gabby 'round lately?"

She planted wet palms on the bar. "Oh, 'bout a week ago.

Sat in the corner with some old man. Bought her drinks all night—good tipper."

"Get a name?"

"Yeah," she smiled, "Cash."

"Hardy-har." He popped three Percs and guzzled.

"Why you care all the sudden? Still got those puppy dog eyes for her?"

He paused, face serious. "No one's seen her in a few days. Thought I'd be a nice guy—ask 'round."

"Nice Guy Alvi?" She poured another. "Why go and ruin a good thing, huh?"

He snorted. "Wash some fuckin' snifters, will ya."

"Now, that's more like it."

He tossed the hooch up and in.

The front door swung open, boulevard washing a rainbow about the room. A giddy young couple walked in, their clothes bleeding with glittery skulls. Alvi thought, *Either Rancho Cucamonga or Rancho Palos Verdes.* Soon as they caught wind of him slunk over the bar, they froze—as if a gorilla was petting their poodle. Dita smirked as the lovebirds feigned interest in her autographed eight by tens.

When the door swung upon their exit, Alvi could see hoards spewing up from the Metro Rail stop across the street: loners and partygoers out for a taste of sin. He thought of that time, stumbling off this very stool and careening down into the Metro's guts. Just wanted to see where the subway would take him; a midnight vacation through time and space. His pickled brain imagined a vortex in one of the tunnels, one that could suck his twisted soul into a peachy parallel universe. Only pleasant dream he'd had in years. Sanctuary would've been welcomed— almost palpable…but the coffins killed that holiday. He awoke to a conductor shaking his shoulder. Car's floor was wavy and brown, reminded him of that frosting atop a chocolate Zinger; apparently, he'd passed out on it the entire ride. Not a single passenger dared disturb his slumber. *What if he'd been dead—*

not just on the inside?

Angie hated it when he touched the hard stuff. Said he turned into a werewolf. They almost had it all back then. If only it wasn't impossible to have another go. Hell, if she could see him now...Coffins helped though. *Had to keep numb.*

Gabby was his first romance since that love. She was much younger but had seen plenty of bad stuff—made her sharp. Recklessness played a factor in her fulfillment; never felt like he was enough to tame her. Regardless, she was a companion through this lonesome abyss. Made him feel the world again, see beauty. Held his head in her arms whenever he'd snorted too many downs or went cold turkey. Even told her about Angie once—only person he'd ever opened up to, albeit ever so slight; promised she'd never tell a soul since it cut so deep, and he believed her. Began to believe everything she said, even when Mongo and the others told him not to.

Should've known the BIG news wasn't on the level but couldn't believe it was a lie. *Why would she pretend something like that...after knowing about Angie—his torments?*

Of course it wasn't planned; still saw her condition as a blessing—some sick yet glorious sign from above. *What a sucker.* Mongo said she'd done it to buy a few more weeks with his meager finances. Played it cool ever since, pretending he knew all along. *Didn't matter.* Eventually, the snakeskin of denial shed off. Gabby still had his heart on a meat hook; could bleed every drop, if she wanted.

Bourbon burned the insides just right.

Final contemplation: Say the girl hadn't done him wrong. Gabby was no Angie, but helping her might be possible—if she needed it. One thing was certain: Couldn't sit back and watch this time.

He slid the glass to Dita and blew a kiss goodbye.

4.

The Escalade roared around the west wing of campus, dodging geeks on scooters and broads on bicycles. Rocco parked amongst a row of student apartments. An academic cocktail of virginal scholars and beach bunny athletic types romped towards the University in flip-flops and Bruin garb. Rocco brought a backpack this time, not wanting to be pegged as an imposter like last week. He filled it with granola bars and Mountain Dew, in case he got hungry.

UCLA was the Monica Vitti of college campuses: lean, tan, Romanesque—hypnotic to the human eye. Rocco fell in love with it, last week aboard. He kept track of time, hitting up the student services kiosk for more department pamphlets. Being a college boy wasn't an option anymore, but a kid could fantasize. Of all the families in the world, had to be shit into this one.

The Powell Library sat near the heart of the grounds. Checkered floors and eccentric brick arches made it an ancient basilica for the brain. Easily the last place to expect a meeting of corruption. Rocco hurried through the first floor, remembering to take off his glasses. He launched through the study room door, a minute till three. Satin stood behind a flimsy podium, jotting huge letters on a dry erase board. His lugs gazed on, seated at a table with notebooks and pencils: a perverse course in crimi-nology. Rocco grabbed a chair as Ray began, pointing at three words on the board.

"Money, power and monopoly—that's the goal, gentlemen—in that order. So far, the first has been attainable. The casita has proven to be a huge success—best in the city by far. In just three years, we've netted over ten million, thanks in part to the high-end clientele coming the past six months. That clientele has proven itself helpful in more ways than one. Their satisfaction with the services has sent word trickling up—*way up*." He sat on the edge of the table, next to Dom. "Had a meeting last week with, let's just say, a highly influential Angeleno. We tossed around some ideas and came to an epiphany, one that will enable these." He got up, underlining *Power* and *Monopoly*.

The room throbbed. Ray let them simmer.

"Who's our main competition right now?"

"Nobody," said Dom.

Satin grinned. "Seriously—who?"

The guys grunted, "Fitzie's."

"Yeah, well *fuck* Fitzie's—that corral of bush pigs ain't chompin' on our leftovers no more! I got news for ya—in a few weeks, there ain't gonna be no Fitzie's—ain't gonna be no more competitors—at all. This partner has promised to see to it, and I believe him." He paused. "Soon it'll be just us, gentlemen—at the top."

Primo raised his hand.

"Yeah?"

"You gonna tell us who this new fool is or what?"

"Not yet. He's hosting a little get together Wednesday night at the Ritz—wants us all there." He paused. "There's a bit of a catch to the deal though—on our end. This new associate is held in high regard within the community and because of this, he can't be seen gallivanting 'round with a bunch of hoods."

The guys smirked.

"That means we're gonna be playing a certain roll, specifically for the public—I'm not exactly sure to what capacity or extent this will be, but whatever it is, I'm sure it'll be worth it. It's the whole reason for this party—our proper introduction to his circle."

The boys began to mumble at each other. Ray clapped two dry erasers, bringing them back.

"First on the agenda though, we're hauling a shipment for him, coming up through Brawley."

Primo asked, "What exactly?"

"All I know is that we need a U-haul sized truck, and it's going down Friday. The rest I find out at the party."

Rocco zoned out, daydreaming this were a real classroom.

A lazy-eyed Mexican spoke up. "Who's picking up this drop?"

Satin smiled. "Good question, Freddie. As you all know by now, a little mishap occurred the other day—one of the B-girls thought it'd be smart to try and blackmail me—"

Primo looked confused.

Freddie leaned over and whispered, "One dat said she had a picture of Satin—from *dat* night."

Primo nodded, tuning back.

Satin continued. "Nevertheless, the problem got resolved and had to be disposed of. Rocco Felix stepped up and made that happen."

The gang panned towards Rocco.

Cold stares snapped him back into focus. He put down his granola bar and leered at Ray, not sure what they were talking about.

"I want you to make the pick-up, Roc. Now, I know this is *big* but you can handle it. Kang will go with you to help load the truck."

Across the table, a mutt in a track suit rolled his eyes.

"Think you're up for this?"

Rocco perked on the seat, clearing his throat. "Sure...just tell me when and where."

Satin smiled before touching on the importance of sharp attire for the party, concluding with, "That's all for now, guys." He grabbed the eraser to wipe the board. The words remained: tall, black, prominent. Satin double checked the marker, muttering under his breath, "Fuck, itza Sharpie."

The Glendale Galleria was packed with loitering teens and Armenian housewives, out for anything gold. Place reeked of Wetzel's Pretzels. Rocco sat in front of a mirror, trying on loud sunglasses to no avail.

"How do those feel?"

He shook his head at the spray tanned clerk. "Pinch my nose. Lemme see those."

The clerk reached behind the case, pulling a pair of white Gucci aviators. Rocco slid them on and checked the mirror. *Ridiculous. Ray would be all about them.*

"I'll take these." He handed over his prescription.

"Give us an hour and they'll be ready."

He hung back in the car, rifling through business administration pamphlets and liberal arts studies. Each program bent his mind in refreshing ways. He reclined the seat and shut his eyes, envisioning dorm room summer nights, intellectualism sandwiched by beer pong and togas. All those great things the movies had promised. But how to get out this life and back to his own? Become that teacher he planned on…Before that night—*the slaughter*—before Uncle Ray took him in after everything crumbled, his life a reeling slot machine, spinning, grinding— before reality hit and decisions were made, his bags already packed for him. Ray seized the family business, cementing Rocco's fate. He buried the hurt with his forearms, forcing the swell back below. Just months aboard his new life and already trying to leap off.

5.

Mongo stepped onto Wilshire from out a slinking red bus. She leaned against The Wiltern's emerald façade, utilizing its green and red tubes to analyze her make-up for the umpteenth time. Under this art deco marquee, she'd pretended being in OZ once—back when she first crawled into town. Crashed behind the ticket booth for three weeks in a Rainbow Bright sleeping bag; OZ made the stone-cold floor much more glamorous. Sunkist beaches weren't really *everywhere*. If only that girl then could catch a glimpse of her now: cream soda curls covering lush violet contacts—on her way to a motherfucking photo shoot!

See children...the stars were *calling*.

She unfolded a paper wad from out her clutch, checking to make sure she was at the right address. Powder blue neon: Los Altos Hotel & Apt's. Place looked classy. Dipped fingertips into the courtyard fountain, admiring mini palms and pristinely carved foliage adorning Spanish walls. Water cascaded out a figure's hoisted barrel; reminded her of that statue she'd given mother for Christmas that time—one daddy used to smash her elbow when she didn't make the baseball team. She had saved loose change for a year to buy it. When daddy caught her choreographed routine to "Borderline"—same gift shattered across her skull. Scar was still tough and pink; never quite receded into her hairline like that doctor said it would. *At thirteen years-old, how could she have guessed the refinery had been shut down? How could she have been anyone but herself?*

She buzzed room 506. A single *click* invited her to the next leg of living.

The unit's door was slightly ajar, a shrill voice beckoning inside.

"Come—come, sweetness! Make yourself at home—there's champagne on ice in the living room. I'll be out in a jiff."

Place wasn't as grand as she'd imagined two seconds ago, knocking on the door after walking through intricate wood carved columns and gold flake. Could feel noble ghosts brushing up against her the entire trek up.

Oh, well.

She placed the guy's four-hundred-dollar fee onto a folding table, ones used to pile hotdogs for kid birthday barbeques. Walls were smooth and creamy, devoid of images. Figured a photographer living in this manor would have pristine examples of their work throughout the place.

Must be an eccentric. Shit—beat Alvi taking her phone sex pics in front of a bedsheet in the Zimba.

She pulled out her compact and applied another layer of lip gloss. A toilet bowl gurgled. Two beach chairs sat around a plastic lunchbox holding a bottle of André.

Maybe this wasn't where he lived? Yes, it had to be. This was his studio! Right?

She waited to hear a faucet splash—an old habit from living amongst strangers for so long.

Nothing.

"Hello—hello!"

Mongo spun to see a swarthy man, reptilian skin, rather old. His checkered button-up had lost its sleeves. A pencil thin goatee hugged his lips. His glossy fingers shot out.

"Sammy John—it's a pleasure to finally meet you in person. You. Are. Stunning!"

Mongo forced a giant smile, gazing at the hand before extending her bejeweled acrylics.

"Miss Mongo, honey. Pleasure's all mine."

"Smut is simply a dying art form, my dear—a dinosaur blocked in ice—a baby seal on the wrong end of a club—you see?"

Mongo swilled her third glass of André, palate akin to stomach acid. Place wasn't exactly Sammy's after all. Mommy lived here till the day she croaked on a cocktail olive, dead center amongst partygoers over to watch the Academy Awards. Sammy recalled the day in disgust: her glistening low-cut dress, that phony laugh, ruby toenails she'd made him slather with three coats. He proceeded slandering as if mother's ear was to a wall in the next room. Thanks to rent control, he could afford to use the spot for shoots: made for good impressions on wayward youth.

Mongo had only changed outfits once so far and wondered how many Tyra would don in a normal sesh. Pouting grape lips at Sammy, she draped her bones over a stuffed jaguar, hoping all her ribs were defined. In the world of dirt merchants, Sammy was top of the heap...back when *Deep Throat* had America to the balls. Between snaps, he'd regale her with story upon story, strange tales no one would ever find boring but, somehow, cloaked in halitosis, they became dry and endless; Mongo could only feign smiles.

"Oh, I'm sure the poor gal would've met a fate far worse than blowing her brains out. All that beauty was beyond fucked after crashing her Vette—but my dear, this was the *nineties*. We all wanted to blow our brains out!"

Xani rails during bathroom breaks made the tales tolerable. Mongo exhaled a deep sigh, hands on the sink while scoping her face in the mirror. No matter how soft and colorful, those strong pesky features were all that she could focus on: wide nostrils, a dense brow—jawbone cast in iron. Most days she would avoid mirrors for as long as she could. If only the others knew...or did they? Could they see through these blemishes she'd despised since birth? What would they think if she told them that once upon a time she ate saltine crackers for a month thanks to a teacher remarking on her athletic build? Would they judge her for scraping fifty-grit across her upper lip, trying to halt natures curse in middle school? Knowing those at the Lafayette, they wouldn't think a damn thing—too busy struggling with their own lost wars. That's what she loved most about Los Angeles: you could be anyone *and* no one—all at once. She sneered at herself upon hearing Sammy call out.

He was fidgeting with his camera at a corner window, glancing down at the street, irritated. Mongo placed a hand on his shoulder.

"Mongo—could you be a doll and tell me when this delivery guy shows up? I want to upload these images to see if we got a definite *cover*. Fucker was supposed to drop off the new *Xpress* layout earlier—I need to start formatting the photos."

"Sure thang."

"Thanks, sweetness. Just keep an eye out for one of those Hippie busses, 'kay?" He pointed. "A Volkswagen—should pull up right down there."

Mongo peered out at electric wilderness blanketing cracked streets. The glow evoked serenity from up here. Loveless gutters couldn't be seen through all the flash and glimmer. City's halo played tricks on the eyes: *landscape gently breathing*. Squeaking breaks broke her trance. An ashy Volkswagen trembled curbside. She whistled.

Sammy opened every door for her on the way out. Two tenants on their way to fine dining clenched jaws, exchanging quick glances. Sammy took notice.

"Some folks just can't contain themselves 'round true talent, Miss Mongo."

Mongo roared.

Out the courtyard, Sammy leaned in for a hug, pecking Mongo on the cheek. The VW loomed like a sickly fly on the corner. A quick, "Ciao," and he turned to approach it.

Mongo cleared her throat. "When can I expect the issue on newsstands?"

Sammy stammered. "Oh...it's really an intricate process that I wouldn't dare bore you with right now...*buuut*—let's just plan on it being there faster than you'd expect." His palms smacked. "I'm sorry but I really must attend to this matter—it being time sensitive and all—"

"Of course...I undastan." She bit her bottom lip. "It's been a pleas—" Before she could finish, Sammy's back was already three steps away. She stared at the VW, driver hidden behind a square windshield reflecting the world.

High heels clopped down Wilshire, careful of uneven sidewalk. She conjured grand details to relay when the girls asked all about the shoot. At a crosswalk, felt eyes searing the back of her skull; turned, only to see those blank headlights, still on the corner. She smirked, goose pimples tickling both forearms.

Hell, some bitch must be tramplin' my grave.

CVS drugstore (Western and Hollywood).

Faye Green wet her lips at the variety of selections: a cornucopia of candy bars and fruit chews, all ready to bore her teeth out. At least that's what she thought. Prescription glasses were the last thing to break before leaving home, some gaudy European disasters everyone had told her looked marvelous; they crunched under her heel like Frosted Flakes. Hated the way she looked with them on but couldn't quite stomach the thought of a contact wandering up behind her eyeball. Had managed so far since coming here, slowly getting used to the blurs of city life. Soon she would be able to recognize new friends afar by the shapes of their skulls. Could always call her folks to send a new pair but they'd just come swoop her back into their world. Happened twice before—that's why this time she ran farther.

Her palms began to sweat, itching to grab a Snickers and

wolf it before that snooping register bitch would notice. She continued to browse, as if she had money to spare. Thought for sure dad's Rolex would've pawned for way more. *Least she got something.* By next week, she'd be on her ass.

Uncomfortable customers gave awkward glances. Could feel their looks. *What—you like these freckles?* A pack of Circus Peanuts hung before her nose; she carefully read their ingredients *(Gelatin?).* What else was she supposed to do? Doreen's clients usually lasted fifteen minutes, five of which were spent removing and jumping back into their clothes. Most of the dorks met her on the boulevard beforehand—but not this one. He managed this dump; the office, his means of discretion. Doreen said he had a tiny prick and couldn't go most the time. *Easy money.*

Faye couldn't wrap her brain around that life. The money— of course. The deeds...Sex had been anything but exhilarating for her. First goes weren't even of her volition. That Fourth of July spectacular her parents made a big deal of each year. Aunt Lacy wasn't even her *real* aunt—just some sleaze that went to high school with her stepmom. Powerless upon the side lawn, she could still hear the slapping...their moans: Lacy was pantiless in a star-spangled sun dress; had Faye's shoulders pinned with both knees while "Uncle" Jim grunted, "SSssshhh," thousands of times—whiskers scratching *everywhere.* Could recall the exact moment her body went numb. Some flag flapping, Freedom Fries, cowboy song (for the troops). She'd focused on fireworks bursting overhead; a far-off Roman Candle was her scream. Didn't know alcohol could do that to a person. Hadn't even drunk more than a cup of Lacy's Patriot Punch. Maybe it was her fault. *Maybe it wasn't.* Three whole years and she still couldn't tell father why apple pie made her puke. Just another cloud in a sky of issues that forced her to leave home, again.

And now she was here, under fluorescent bulbs, reading (and smelling) greeting cards for the bereaved.

In this time of overbearing struggle—

"I'm done, bitch!"

Faye smiled back at Doreen, air-humping a Doritos endcap.

"Did you pick out candy?"

"No. Gonna spend my dollars on burritos, girl."

"Dollars? Bitch anything in this place is ripe for the pickin'!"

"What about her?" She pointed to the register girl.

"Who?" Doreen craned. "Dat's a life-size Sandra Bullock—a DVD display!"

"*Really.*"

"Weren't kiddin', huh? Them eyes be *way* fucked."

"Not that big a deal."

"Listen—fool runnin' this bitch ain't gonna say shit 'bout nothin', 'kay? Got a picture of his wife and keeds on the desk. Told me shit's cool—fo' reals."

"Alright."

They meandered back to the junk food aisle.

Doreen counted her cash before tucking it up into her bra strap; stretch marks wormed across her gut. Hand shot out with a twenty. "Here, Faye—take it."

"Nah, I couldn't."

"Girl, I know you broke."

Faye eyed the bill and clipped it with two fingers. "Thanks, Doreen. Didn't need to do that."

"*I know.* Also know how hard it gits when you first roll into this city. Should really consider giving this here a go. What I be tellin' you? Hustlin' makes the world go 'round."

"I couldn't just sleep with anyone—no offense."

"Bitch, please. My grandma always told me I could do anything I put this here mind too. You ain't no different."

Faye grabbed three King Sized Snickers, four Cup-O-Gold's and some Laffy Taffy. "Just ain't my bag, Doreen. Good looking out though. I'll figure something out."

"You know Miss Mongo can hook you up with clients that don't even be into straight sex—fetish stuff. High-brow bitches."

"Like what?"

"I dunno—nothing too freaky. Dat bitch Gabby used to bust it. Told me she hardly took off her underwear."

"Yeah—I dunno."

"Alvi be the one driving you to appointments."

Faye's cheeks caught fire.

"Yeah, I thought you'd like that. Should go talk to Mong."

Automatic doors swished upon their exit. Sandy Bullock received a middle finger from Doreen. They leaned against a mural of an Aztec goddess near the bus stop. Doreen sparked a spliff.

"So, what's his story, Doreen? You know much about him?"

"Child, in these parts…you only know as much about someone as they want to let on. Sure, Alvi's nice—easygoing. I can see why you lovestruck. One thing I do know, personally, I've never had or known anyone who's had a problem with him. Seems true blue—fo' reals. But like I said, some people speak the world in L.A.—but Alvi…Alvi don't say shit."

6.

Alvi stood out front of the Lafayette, swabbing a nose bleed, waiting with Gabby's *Weekly* for three young *vatos* to get off the payphone. Just wanted to give the scribbled number on her classified a call—see if this "old man" picks up. No biggie. *Just a few coins to dispel his curiosity.* A harmless deed that might shed light on things...or might lead to nowhere. Either way, that would be the end of it—hands clean.

Another two minutes and the bangers lumbered back to the corner, commencing their narco slang. He dropped change into the slot and punched worn cubes. Sun gleamed off the box's tarnished silver, band stickers baking its backdrop. Four rings brought a muffled voicemail.

Hey, you've reached Chester. Prolly workin', so call me at...

Alvi scrounged for the pen in his jeans, jotting the number just before the beep.

Click.

He dropped more dimes. One ring this time.

"Swami's Barbershop—Swami speaking."

"How late you guys open?"

"Close at six."

"Cool. Chester workin'?"

"He's on lunch. Wanna leave a message?"

"Nah, thanks."

Alvi hung up. Knew the place, off Sunset in Los Feliz. Got a cut there, way back. Could swing by the shop…if he wanted.

Chester?

The phone began to ring. Knew better than to pick it up, corner thugs sprinting towards him.

At the front door, he bumped into Ronnie, a likeable leathered wall of muscles. Was pushing sixty and still a workout rat. Face was tattered with scar tissue from pro bouts at the Olympic, way back when. All those absorbed combos had his mug slumping like a Shar Pei.

"Rents due, Alvi."

"I'm workin' on it, man. Don't stress."

"Yeah, yeah. Ain't you I'm stressin' 'bout. Seen Vanda 'round lately?"

"Nah."

"If you do, send her my way—owes two months. Got a feelin' she skipped."

Alvi thought fast. "No shit? I let her borrow my good jacket—few weeks back. Think I can have a look in her unit?"

"I'm on my way out—Maribel can let you in."

Alvi jabbed his pec. "Thanks, man. I'll have rent too—promise."

Maribel stood in the doorway, taking a penny to some scratchers, all three hundred pounds of her cracking the door jamb. She was a sweetheart come Christmas, rest of the time just barking orders at Ronnie. *Matrimony.* Alvi figured her closet was like Superman's, only filled with the same-colored sweatpants.

He ransacked while being watched, not quite sure what to look for. Anything that suggested her and Gabby's whereabouts would be nice. Maribel's wheezing was atrocious. Room was practically empty, not even a toothbrush. Soiled laundry and pink hair extensions littered the floor. Skid marked panties had him move to the closet. A Day-Glo negligee hung lonesome on a wire hanger, plastic high heels scattered the floor: pole grinding garb.

"Hurry the fuck up, Alvi! News is 'bout to interview that woman whose monkey ate her face."

He bounced up, trying to see if anything lined the top self. A shoebox, packed with random papers. He tossed it under an arm. *Could have something.*

He rushed by Maribel's soulless glare.

"Find it?"

"Not the jacket, just some—um…shoes she borrowed." He pointed to the box, heading downstairs before Maribel's uni-brow could tilt.

The drive-up Vermont was as good as it got during rush hour. Alvi dodged K-Town kamikazes and pizza sized potholes. He placed Vanda's box on the back seat, contemplating how to handle this Chester. A red at Beverly had him scoping the scene. Children pushed strollers as heat beat the elderly. Some shoeless Joe sat at a bus stop, peeling EKG stickers off his chest.

Commotion broke.

A swarm of cops brought down an immigrant, selling her fruit on the sidewalk. The corner preacher saw his opportunity with onlookers, amplifying his megaphone. "Chillren—*CHILLREN!* De *DEBIL* jus' land on my showler! He an' he *DEMONS* don' *LIKE* de word a *GOD*—but chillren—*CHILLREN! I DON' KAYERR!*"

Ah, that Los Angeles sunshine.

Signal burst green.

During day cruises, Alvi kept his eye out for ghost signs: ancient, busted neon that property owners didn't touch out of respect. In a city famous for its cannibalizing, sights like these were a rarity. He caught a new one up past Macho's while circling for parking. It read Sarno's; Pastry Cakes tracked vertically down the side, topped by a birthday cake. Angie told him about these relics: tracks from L.A.'s neon boom. They reminded him of her. Secret shrapnel through the heart of their city.

Swami's wasn't your charlatan, salon-style shop. This mother was the real deal. Opened as a barbershop in the twenties and never faltered. Paper said some fucker tried to turn it into a Quizno's, but thanks to Swami, the neighborhood retained some class.

Alvi headed past the candy cane spiral, into the lair of man. Ricky Nelson crooned. Smut rags and nickel pulps cluttered the magazine rack; Lawrence Tierney and Killer Kowalski sneered from mint green walls. He focused on each of the white-smocked barbers. Combs bathed in Barbicide beneath certifications. Clung to the third chair's mirror read *Chester Mims*, a creased portrait smiling back. He profiled the flat-topped duffer, gaunt and frail, carefully scraping a straight razor down an Adam's apple.

Same fella.

The shop's chalkboard had eight names awaiting cuts, giving Alvi an excuse to bail. Now he had a visual on Chester. Place closed in a few hours anyway. Could catch the duffer afterhours. Face to face. *A quick chat—that's all.* Alvi walked out, saying, "Catch ya later," before heading towards Vermont.

Four Dresden Room highballs and it was almost closing time. Alvi grabbed the car and parked across Sunset. Day fell to night, the store's blood red BARBER SHOP beamed below white scissors. Each of the barbers exited, hanging back till Swami locked up. Chester made *adios* rounds. Alvi was halfway out the car when a bolt hit the brain: *Maybe Gabby was holed-up at this guy's place?* Slid back in and started her up, waiting. Chester hopped into a sawdust Rambler and headed east. Alvi held for a beat, then launched behind.

He was careful to keep distance; traffic on this stretch was oddly low. Trash skipped concrete like tumbleweed. The Rambler sharked along, brake light busted. Neon washed hypnotic.

GOOD LUCK
VISTA
CIRCUS OF BOOKS
COCKTAILS

Swarms of beardos frolicked amongst unkempt ladies in mom jeans, steam from their java clashing with clouds off their smokes. The Olive Motel loomed eerie on the left. Alvi blinked for focus. More tubes ablaze:

TATTOO
LOS GLOBOS
SUN LAKE DRUGS
LIQUORS

The Rambler glugged past Burrito King, down through Echo Park. The Jensen's sign was dead: once blipped a bowler, tossing a strike. Chester lit a smoke; Alvi did too. He wondered how far they were headed. Figured downtown, hopefully no freeways. Traffic picked up as droves hit a Dodgers game late, nearly thwarting the tail. Chester pulled into a glowing purple fog: The Paradise Motel. Alvi glided by, parking at the lot's far end.

Chester flicked the cig before entering his abode, room fifteen. Once the light turned on, Alvi could see his silhouette through torn curtains. He sat there, watching for over an hour. Around nine, a skinny creep rapped twice at Chester's. The door opened and a deal was made—money for goods. Alvi was done waiting, chemicals in his body beginning to take their toll. The transaction sparked an idea.

Get down to the shitty gritty.

He hopped out.

Two knocks sparked a gravelly voice. "What's it now, Leo?"

Alvi coughed, "Gave ya the wrong stuff."

"Ah, shit."

Slapped his face for alertness. Playing some tough guy wasn't the plan but that hard stuff in his liver coupled with all those downers had clouded the mind. Soon as a chain lock unlatched and door cracked, that fucking *werewolf* took over. A foot wedged the base as he pushed inside, knocking the old man onto a slumping twin. He slammed the door. Chester was shirtless, leather belt strapped to a bicep. Alvi tried not to act as scared as he felt, heart pounded by Kong.

What the fuck just happened there?

Chester rattled, "Ain't got nothin', man—don't hurt me."

Alvi scoped the room. TV spouted Dodgers, up three in the sixth. Spoon, spike and swab were at the sink. Blood spurts tacked a wall by the toilet. No Gabby. No girly stuff in the closet.

"Where is she?"

"You a boyfriend or somethin'?"

"Somethin'—where she at?"

"Who we talkin' about?"

"Gabby!"

"I—I dunno. Haven't been with her since last week. She in trouble?"

Alvi shrugged.

Chester recalled the face tats. "You're the one in the shop earlier, huh?"

Alvi ignored the question, noticing the duffer's hands in the air, trembling like Ali. Didn't seem startled from the situation—must've been rolled before. Something didn't look right though, probably just needed his meds. "Ain't gonna hurtcha, Chester. Just need a few words—that's all." Alvi tossed a Hawaiian shirt off the floor, pulled a Lucky out a pack on the dresser and grabbed a chair by the tube. "Go on an' get straight. I'll wait. Then we talk 'bout Gabby."

Ten minutes later, Chester emerged, buttoning the shirt filled with blooming Polynesians. Color had returned to his face, eyes droopy—back to normal. "So, what's going on with her?"

"That's what *I* wanna know."

Chester opened a drawer and pulled out a fifth of Old

Overholt, handing it over. "Ain't got cups." He sat across the small table. Alvi took a pull. Chester began. "Met her through the classifieds, same way I meet all the rest. Didn't think nothin' of it at the time, just wanted some company. Sittin' around a barber shop all day can get dauntin'—*machismo*. Don't got no family. Payin' for a girl's time is what I do. After meetin' Gabby—she's the only one I wanted to be 'round from then on. Somethin' different about her. Used to bring me baggies of fresh rigs from where she volunteered—showed love. Daughter I always wanted."

Alvi scoffed. "When's the last time you saw her?"

"Wednesday. She come by askin' for some money—five hundred. Took her to the Frolic for drinks."

"What for?"

"Cop a buzz."

"No—the cash."

"Her band had another show come Sunday. Needed new microphones."

Alvi knew of Gabby and her "band." Came into town for glory like the rest, figured a band was the quickest way to it. Couldn't play an instrument but she was determined to sing. He sold a box of Salba decks for that band and never saw an instrument or heard a damn lick. He passed the bottle.

"You believed her—gave her the cash?"

"A'course. Watched her sing the week before at Silverlake Lounge—second gig."

"*Really?*" This was news to him, along with everyone else at the Lafayette—there being an actual band.

"Yeah, she was pretty good too. Not so much singin' but screamin'—you know the type?"

"What's the band's name?"

"Oh geez, gimme a sec." He reached back into the drawer and pulled out a *Weekly*. "Right here. Little play on words, I guess— chick band." He pointed to a concert scroll for the Echoplex. There on Sunday, underneath Kill Dads read, GalAvant Gardes.

They had the night's first set.

"She's gonna be at this, huh?"

"Why wouldn't she? Should've seen how excited she was to be opening up for that Dads band."

Alvi scratched the bridge of his nose. "Know she doesn't have a phone but is there some other way you can reach her?"

He shook his head. "Without that classified, she just contacts me, son."

Alvi rose. "If she swings by, tell her Alvi Drake's lookin' for her—sorry for bustin' in."

"Understood. I'd bust through doors for Gabby too."

"You goin' to that show?"

"Plan to."

Alvi nodded.

"Hey, if you want, I got more dope—clean rigs."

Misery craved the miserable.

"Nah." He took out three coffins, popped them and swilled rye. "Got my own devils. See ya Sunday, man."

Vanda's box was filled with random receipts and medical papers from the Hollywood free clinic. She'd caught the clap, infections here, ointments there—nothing too shocking. Alvi had it all splayed on his cot, nipping at a King Cobra, stuck in a perma-haze thanks to a few Oxies. Wasn't till the last pile that something of substance came to light. Tucked under a flap was a picture reel snapped in one of those curtained kissing booths. There were three girls in each of the four squares. Heavy make-up; looked like Halloween. Regardless, two stuck out: a mummified Vanda and Gabby gone Goth. He'd never seen the third girl, a Latina, dressed up like *Mi Vida Loca*. Their faces played different in each shot: smooshed, kissy, cross-eyed, laughing. The white bar in between each read Cha Cha Lounge.

He rifled some more, a newspaper clipping on a missing girl dated last summer. *Where is Erma Rios?* Birds chirped out the window, sun kissing the palms up and under. He clipped both finds next to Angie's picture, transferred a kiss to her lips and hit the sack. Tonight was gonna be another long one.

7.

The silence between gasps was soothing; Rocco did his best sidestroke, splashing and kicking like a dolphin to wave. The giant pool was all his this morning. A lavender marine layer blanketed the sun as he toweled off, taking in aromas of dense foliage on the grounds. The Bunker Hill Towers had its perks.

Through the yard, Rocco could hear pops and grunts coming from the tennis court. Wondered who Ray was losing to now. He wrapped the towel around his shoulders and headed over.

Raymond tossed his racket, sending it skidding across the court, miles from any lime ball. The white gentleman celebrating on the other side outweighed Ray by a good fifty pounds. The sweat drenching his sleeves showed that he worked hard for the win—hard as Ray had let him.

"Great game, Raymond. Beating someone ten years younger never gets old. Tomorrow—same time?"

Satin acted exhausted, "You got it," looking at Rocco, pointing to his conqueror, "Watch out for Judge Mahoney, Roc. He's a beast on this court too."

Mahoney and Satin slapped backs while exiting the cage.

"Hear you're escorting the D.A. to the ball tonight. You gonna put out?"

"Suck a dick, Raymond. Better yet, make it two."

Ray laughed. "See you there, champ."

With the judge a good distance away, Rocco asked, "Is that who's throwing the party?"

"No—he's small time. It's good to get in with the whole city though. Never know when you might need a favor."

A team of lawyers sat in the West Tower lobby, rapidly texting on plush beige couches as valets brought their cars around. They acknowledged Ray, standing as he walked by, lingering behind cold hands and plastic smiles. Rocco put his head down and pressed for the elevator.

The day consisted of chauffeuring Satin to high-end shops, tailors and his jeweler on Broadway. Lunch at Morton's had them high on champagne, chomping New York strip. One of the few days where he and Ray got some face time, still on duty but keeping his hands clean. If only this lifestyle could sustain without stacking bodies. Rocco took the opportunity to address something weighing on his mind.

"Uncle Ray…the night that my dad—well, has anything else came up about what went down? Anything new?"

Satin coughed into a crisp white napkin before addressing with earnest. "Like I told you, nephew. My stepbrother was a man of many secrets. Unfortunately, you and your mother—" He made the sign of the cross. "—knew that firsthand."

"Tell me what you remember again?"

"We were all out drinking, ended up at the casita—your father had brought one of his girlfriends—there were so many, was hard to keep track."

Rocco's brow scrunched. He could never forget that body found beside his pops'. "Erma—the girl in the car, remember?"

"Oh, that's right—sweet girl. I guess they danced for a while, partied some more. Told us he'd be right back, and they left. Rest of us were upstairs 'til morning, playin' bones, foolin' with the girlies—didn't even know somethin' was wrong 'til later, when Hector didn't answer his cell, missed the meeting he called."

"But who would've wanted to off him like that? Could it have been a cartel—I heard he used to run dope back in the day?"

"The man had many enemies, Roc. What can I say? This type of business runs high risk for high rewards. You see *me*. I'm lookin' over my shoulder most of the goddam day."

Rocco nodded. "Just wanted to know if any new info has come to light. Been reading the papers."

Ray's dropped his fork. "Papers want to crucify anyone involved with *any* lead they come across. I wouldn't put too much thought in any of the shit that makes print. Look, the police are still workin' the case—last I heard they had some angle on Fitzie, that's all."

"You really think *Fitzie* coulda done somethin' like that?"

"I dunno—but if the cops had somethin' new, they'd go public with it. The rest is all speculation, right?"

"I guess."

"Believe me, *mijo*—I promise whoever murdered Hector is gonna get theirs, tenfold…by *us*."

Satin's suite was nothing glamorous, a simple two bedroom, comfortably furnished with a wet bar and Wurlitzer. Rocco wasn't complaining, just glad to have a place to stay. He flipped through the juke for Sam Cooke, punching "A Change is Gonna Come" while Ray slid into pearly new digs. A seven and seven helped soothe the night's nerves. Was the first time he got invited to one of these big shot parties. Ray emerged, draped in a vanilla three piece with a gold tie and hanky. The almond sized nugg on his pinky could buy a yacht.

"That's not what you're wearing, right?"

Rocco looked down at his two-tone Tommy Bahama. "What?"

"Shit, looks like you're about to serve me a pulled pork sandwich."

"It's all I got."

"Shoulda said somethin' earlier." He grabbed the phone and dialed. "I got a guy—runs numbers. Has a tux rental front. Might have somethin'—shades are workin' though."

Within an hour a suit arrived. Rocco froze in the mirror, not quite filling out the purple sharkskin two-button. Ray had him ditch the tie and go straight bone, unbuttoned twice. Not what he would've picked but he wasn't fitting the bill. He threw on the shades as they headed down to a stretch Hummer, waiting with the crew.

Figueroa was filled with the guts of a Lakers game. Overweight couples in athletic gear cluttered newfangled eateries at L.A. Live. Children sported jerseys featuring their favorite criminal. The limo waded through, pulling into the Ritz, a bulbous blue tower where white gloved valets ushered them towards glamour.

Rocco stuck towards the back of the pack. The boys were sharp as usual, acting hard. With Satin in front, a visiting Midwest family could have pegged them for a bible-thumping boy band.

Two elevators shot them to the lounge. Signs proclaiming *Closed for Private Event* welcomed them to the bash. Prying through doors, the eight-man mob paused for attention. A few glanced before returning to scotch and gold flaked hors d'oeuvres.

Rocco took in the downtown panorama sweeping the room, undaunted by the caliber of attendees. Only one he recognized was Liván Marin, the Dodgers Cy Young ace, over by the piano. The rest of the room exuded wealth or rank, mostly white, sidled by knockout women with upgrades. Ray played to the room, regaling them with Judge Mahoney's wicked backhand, miming his own unworthy strokes to break ice. Rocco grabbed a beer and sat at a far table, taking in the skyline with wonder. Skid Row loomed east of towers lit like Keno boards, begging for scraps. *How could such beauty be so cruel?*

The night rolled on, crowd cutting loose, tossing bills at the piano boy to play something wild. Ray had vanished into an adjacent lounge while the rest of the crew lingered by the curtain, surveying the party like secret service. Rocco watched as Liván slid his fastball grip up the skirt of some honey. The curtain parted; Satin waved them inside.

The room had a commanding view of the South Bay, planes floating towards LAX like falling stars. A puny Latino canoodled with a sultry blonde by the window. Rocco recognized her, Mindy McCann, local weather slut for KCAL 9. The Latino's hand cupped her rump, slipping a little tongue. Satin drew their attention to a suit across the table; the man had questionable eyes over a dustpan 'stache.

"Guys, this is Van Holt—think of him as the Mayor's right hand."

Holt rose, nodding to the room.

A slap on the ass sent Mindy out through the curtain, leaving the Latino's full attention on them.

Holt said, "I'm sure you all know this man, Mayor Vicente Reynaga."

The Mayor glad handed, one at a time, more than pleased to meet their lowlife acquaintance. Rocco had only seen this plastic grin on TV or newspapers, embracing terminal children, playing for the cameras. Wondered if he was as stiff in real life. Reynaga patted him on the shoulder before taking a seat. Behind praying hands, he began reciting a premeditated address.

"Gentlemen, it is no secret that backdoor brothels—are scouring this fine city. Heat is raining down on City Hall to take action. The papers are flaming torches my way. I cannot ignore this demand any longer, and as your Mayor, I have accepted and embraced this challenge." He gave dramatic pause. "The Commissioner is calling for an immediate crackdown on these sex lairs, and I've given him the go ahead. The fact of the matter, gentlemen, is that we plan on busting each of these facilities before months end—around forty—every last one, all taken down by the swift strike of justice." With that, he rose quietly and parted the curtain, rejoining the gala.

Satin flashed canines as the boys sat confused.

Holt commenced in mouthfuls.

"Obviously, the Mayor can't talk firsthand about the details of this operation as any implication by outside individuals could relinquish this opportunity before it has even begun. He will therefore have no further dealings of any kind from here on out. *I* am your superior and cannot stress confidentiality enough. Mr. Satin here has guaranteed this, understood?" The room nodded. "I'm aware of your enterprise and quite impressed on its growth within the past year—the numbers don't lie, gentlemen. As you may or may not know, several of the Mayor's friends and colleagues are all regulars, speaking very highly of their experiences at your club. What I've proposed is a twofold arrangement. One: the crackdown omits your club and permits the openings of five more throughout the Greater Los Angeles area, locations to be chosen by us. Profits from these new clubs will be split accordingly, manned by both our team and yours to ensure a secured investment." He took a pull of Perrier. "Two: in return for this approved expansion, we reserve the liberty to employ the services of, well, all of you. It shouldn't be a surprise that the casita business is not our only underground enterprise. Such services shall be basic in nature, drop-offs and pick-ups of various products, mostly. The first of these being on Friday. Ray will cue you in on the details." He rose, buttoning his coat. "It's been a pleasure, gentlemen, and we're thrilled to be on board. I have high hopes for this expansion and so should you." He made for the lounge. "Mayor Reynaga will be introducing you shortly. Please come out when you hear his address."

As he parted the curtain, Satin pointed directly at him. "*Power.*" He pointed to them. "*Monopoly.* This is it—the next level. When I tell you shit's gonna blow up, it always does—and this is no different. In a matter of weeks, with the city's power behind us, we'll be untouchable."

Rocco stared out the window as the boys began to clap, giving Raymond fist bumps or hugs in celebration. *How could they not think this could all end badly?* He wondered how long a teacher's degree would take, ballparking a timeframe he'd have to partake in such antics.

The sound of applause caught everyone's attention, forcing them to straighten their ties. Reynaga's voice beckoned. Rocco was the last to enter; all eyes from the party were fixed, porcelain. Reynaga stood behind the piano with a glass of champagne.

"Ladies and Gentlemen, this evening is a joyous one indeed. It is a celebration for this fine city along with these fine gentlemen you see before you. Raymond, will you come join me?" Ray flanked. "As of late, illegal gambling has run rampant across our city and it has been my mission to eradicate it within county lines. As you are aware, I have created task forces to combat each and every aspect of illegal gaming and now I stand before you with my latest effort." He placed his hand on Ray's shoulder. "This is Raymond Satin, owner of King Carne, a market near mid-city accommodating only the freshest of organic meats." He pointed to the crew. "These are his employees," rifling through their names as if old friends. "Together they have made a successful business out of their passion, hard work...perseverance. Now they have volunteered for a new cause, one that is very close to their hearts. You see, their store is the first to have taken a stand against illegal cockfighting, refusing to sell to all those involved along with rescuing some of the poor feathered victims of this war. The city has been sup-plying King Carne with the names and profiles of this under-ground network's most devious criminals. Through their store's compliance, over the past year alone, they have helped the city put away or deport nearly forty of these heinous individuals." A wave of applause resonated. "A public press release to honor these efforts is forthcoming, but for now, ladies and gentle-men..." He hoisted up his glass. "A toast...to the city's new Cockfighting Task Force."

Ray played to the applause as the boys tried their best at modesty. Rocco stood bashful before haunting elastic grins.

And just when he thought the craziness had peaked...If he wanted an out now, he was going to have to create one.

8.

Hitting Hollywood after eight meant shit parking. Alvi rode his skate. He clung to the rear of a celebrity tour bus, trying to contain speed wobbles between lights. Better than braving packed sidewalks. Flash bulbs snapped out the open roof, catching Superman and Marilyn posing with three gutter punks, begging for beer. Alvi let go before Cahuenga, shifting up the curb, launching into the crosswalk. Night air bit his cheekbones. Three twink prosties smoked out front of The Spotlight as he veered around the corner, down Selma.

Boots was lively this time, tossing two backpacks outside, bursting with clothes. "If you don't pay, you can't stay. Ain't that right, Alvi?"

"You got it, man. Computer free?"

"All you."

Alvi hit the hallway as two Guatemalans rushed out and began hassling Boots.

"Listen up, motherfuckers! I'm only saying this *uno mas* fuckin' *tiempo*. This is *America*. You don't pay, now you're trespassing on private property. Legally, I can shoot you in the fuckin' face! No *dinero*—then *Blamm-O!*" He pointed towards the front desk. "I'm getting the gun, okay? *Pistola!*"

Bootsie sprinted inside, sending the foreigners to scoop their bags and dash down the sidewalk.

Alvi checked his eBay. *Ka-chiiing!* Each of the decks had sold higher than expected. Rent was covered along with a few hundred to burn. He transferred out his PayPal and then Google'd Erma Rios. A slew of articles came up between petty porn sites, those expected when searching for females. He clicked the legits.

She was a Whittier runaway, working the streets till her disappearance. Said she was last seen entering a black Beamer at Santa Monica and Mansfield. He scanned through the rest, each reading similar, spanning weeks. The second wave had articles on a vehicle fire in Inglewood, the insides harboring remains of two undisclosed individuals. Alvi pressed till paydirt.

Officers disclose the remains as belonging to that of a male, Hector Felix (51) and one female, Erma Yesenia Rios (22). Further tests are pending as to the exact cause of deaths...

At the edge of the article were two pictures: a Mexican with a thick handlebar moustache, the other of Erma. It was a high school snapshot: black hair, brown skin, barely a smile. He fished in his pocket and held up the Cha Cha Lounge photo reel to the screen. One in the same; mystery girl no more. He printed the articles and slid them in his backpack.

Sleeping through daylight still had Faye Green flustered; body couldn't adjust. Huddled on two flattened sofa cushions in the corner of Doreen's unit, she awoke to warm rays of sunshine blasting through towels draped over the window. No matter how hard they tried, room wasn't dark enough. She rubbed sleep from her eyes and slouched against a wall smudged with handprints.

Barely snoozed for three hours.

One of the apartments below had their TV cranked: some soap opera theme song—one her stepmom would have on, vacuuming those glorious rugs. As if that had startled her. Doreen snored worse than a chainsaw; blamed it on a deviated septum. Girl passed the buck on just about every hiccup in life. Faye sensed something crawling by her foot; cringed once realizing it was a cockroach, climbing through a pizza box. Shiny bastard scurried once Doreen's nostrils growled. She'd heard horror stories about the bugs burrowing into ear holes or even worse. Doreen had a new story for her every day. Last night, with fixed brown eyes, she regaled a slow one about her best friend who'd met his demise hopping a train through Salinas.

Feet slapped down the hall; it could only be Miss Mongo. Got in about the same time every morning. Rest of the rooms at this end of the floor sat vacant in decay. She tiptoed to the door, careful not to stir Doreen as it shut behind her.

Vast boulevards helped Mongo through somber nights. After the dud of a shoot, she strolled for hours—uninterested in johns, just their attention. Few horns stroked her ego. Swatted nails at an old man, melting behind the wheel of a rickety Ford. Work nights she might've entertained an offer; tonight she was an everyday stiff, off the clock, wasting life. Watched dawn break from the Lafayette steps; far off skyline a glittery gold. Soon as concrete began to bake, she lumbered upstairs. Had barely tossed her heels to the floor, about to close the door, when a sudden, "*Pssst*," down the hall caught her attention.

Faye approached in whispers. "So, how'd it go?"

Mongo waved her inside.

"Hand to baby *fuckin'* Jesus—this place was vintage Hollywood glamour, girl! Gold everything over marble floors—crystal chandeliers big as the Liberty bell."

Faye had yet to blink, cross-legged on the floor. "No way!"

"*Dead* serious. Miss Mongo walks into that studio and *BAM*—hair and makeup bitches be swarmin'—racks upon racks of pure elegance to wear—I'm talkin' straight Tyra stylie, baby. Did I already mention we went through a whole case of Moët?

Faye nodded, flecking purple polish off a big toe.

"And, honey...this professional photographer—Sammy John," she chuckled. "Not only is he the absolute best in the biz, fool's downright Hollywood royalty—his momma won herself the Academy Award!"

"An Oscar! What movie?"

"Huh?"

"What movie was she in?"

"Oh...she ugh...lady was a costume designer, I think—wasn't in front a no camera."

"But what picture was it?"

Mongo bent over to remove her wig, thinking hard. The Wiltern flashed in her brain. "*Wizard a OZ.*"

"Whoa. That's heavy."

"Yea-huh, that's what I said. Listen, if it was me sitting down there hearing all this crazy shit from you—*pssht*, I wouldn't believe it." She lit a cigarette, stroking coconut oil into her bald scalp. "Cross my heart, girl. Me as Liz Taylor—all night long!"

"That's amazing, Mongo. *So* cool. I mean, everybody wants to be loved."

Girl's last words floating about held Mongo silent, deflated. Face turned sour as she puffed menthol. "Yeah...well, can't let it get to my purdy head now." Grey plumes slithered out her lips. "What is a *star* anyways, huh?"

"How you mean?"

"What exactly *is* a *star*?"

"I dunno. Someone famous, adored by the world and stuff."

"Nah, honey. A star ain't nothin' but an itty-bitty light in the middle of a dark, dark place."

Faye's grin began to fall.

Mongo dropped her smoke into an empty beer can. "Enough about me, girl. Whattabouchoo? How you diggin' L.A.?"

"I love it so far. It's way different than I expected."

"Ain't gotta say that *once.*"

Faye came out with it: the real reason for her visit. "You know, Doreen was telling me that Alvi might be able to take me 'round to some of Gabby's fetish clients."

"Oh, really? You hard up fo' cash?"

"You can say that. Can also say that I'm beyond curious about sexless johns."

Freckles formed words on Faye's face, spelling out everything for Mongo. Wasn't all about the money. She'd seen the way the girl acted around Alvi. Wasn't the first to go mush for the boy. Gabby sat in the same spot, saying the same shit. Setting them up came around to bite her in the ass but whatever. Not like she was sending Faye out on a romantic evening. *Could use some of the money off those clients.* "Stand fo' me."

Faye twisted up from the floor.

"Ever hustled before?"

"No—got taken for twenty dollars playing Galaga once."

"'Kay, don't be tellin' me *that.* Let me see what you look like."

Faye peeled off a pink beater and slid down plaid boxers, not knowing where to place her hands in the buff.

Mongo studied her curves and had her spin. "I'll make some calls. First you gotta trim that firecrotch—shave your legs. Got any make-up?"

"Lip gloss."

"Well, we got our work cut out then—but you'll do fine. That juicy ass along with Miss Mongo—best damn beautician this side of Western...*sheeit.* First, gotta take you to the free clinic—make sure you right—grab condoms and stuff."

"Okay. They got an eye doctor there?"

"Prolly. Why?"

"Lost my prescription glasses along the way."

"See what we can do, girl. Dis place look better fuzzy though."

Faye stepped back through her shorts. "What about Gabby?"

"What about her? If she ever pops back up, wants these clients back—don't even trip. I'm gonna slap da taste out that ho."

"And Alvi won't mind—you're sure."

"Nah—not when I'm done with you."

Faye bit her bottom lip, taming a smile.

Mongo sashayed down Beverly, across Rampart, making her way to Original Tommy's. Alvi asked to meet for dinner. A bright square blinking *World Famous Hamburgers* twirled clockwise above. She adjusted her wig, ignoring the lasered stares of fifteen fatties in line. Alvi was perched at a makeshift counter, sticking out from the shack. Two chili burgers steamed before him.

"Ooh-wee! Dat's what I'm talkin' 'bout."

Before she could grab the sucker, he shot the photo booth scroll in front of her face. "Ever seen this before?"

Mongo studied the shots closely. "Nah. What's this from?"

"Dunno, found it in Vanda's room."

"You broke into ha room?"

"Maribel let me in—figured there might be something telling us where they went."

"And this is all you found, some funny pics—why you all interested in Gabby all the sudden? I should be the bitch huntin' her down. You hate that girl and got every reason too." She lunged into the burger.

Alvi shrugged. "Past is the past, Mong."

She spoke through a mouthful. "You feelin' okay, honey? That cunt lied to you—strung you along for months, using you for rides—money. Soon as she dumps yer ass, turns out the bitch ain't even—" She forced a swallow, composing herself with a fist to the mouth.

Alvi shushed her to quiet down.

Voice softened, "Wasn't even pregnant after all, Alvi. Never was! Now, that's cold. Hell, I just need her to ease the rent, but you—you need her like another kick to the nuts."

"Regardless, somethin' feels off 'bout her leaving like this.

You know who that third girl is in the picture?"

Chili dribbled down her chin. "Who?"

He took out the articles from his backpack, splaying them out for her. Mongo's eyes skipped.

"Another dead streetwalker. So, what?"

"Maybe there's a connection?"

"Like what?"

"I dunno, she went missing too—I'm just saying. Shit's weird."

"You in Hollyweird, honey. Shit's normal."

He picked at his burger, trying to arouse an appetite. "I spoke with Gabby's old man client."

"You what?" She rolled her eyes. "You gone crazy, child. The bitch left, like you said, prolly home with her teddies and shit. Why waste ya time?"

"Don't you wanna know what he said?"

"Not really."

"She's in a band."

"Bitch, please."

"A *real* band. They got a show this Sunday. This dude, Chester, said she's supposed to be there. Why would she wanna blow town then?"

Mongo soaked fries in mustard; three pearl press-ons were missing.

"I'm going, if you still want that rent?"

She burped as a fry cook lugged Alvi's tank over.

"*Gracias, amigo!*" He turned back to Mongo, waiting for a response.

"I'll go witchoo, but I think it's bullshit."

"Might as well make sure, right? Help me lug this tank back down the street."

She took a napkin to her face. "Mm-mm."

"I paid for that burger!"

"Sheeit!"

9.

The club was popping tonight. Rocco stood at the upstairs windows, peering down on the decadent crowd, pawing at lurid ladies of glamour. Black Tie Night. The girls dressed to impress as if trampling red carpets. Local athlete celebrities grinded the dance floor. Judge Mahoney and some colleagues ordered bottle service from a booth, pointing at women, immediately ushered over. Rocco put his hand on the glass, taking in the party's pulse. That raven haired barkeep was working a client in the corner, sleek in a black satin dress, hair draping the right ear like a perfect wave. With the new custom frames, he could tell for sure she was something else. He saw Raymond heading up the stairs, three goddesses in tow. The door flung open.

"Shit, Rocco. Didn't know you were up here already. One sec." He turned to the girls on the stairs. "Just a moment, ladies. Don't go too far." Closing the door, his attention clicked back. "Have a seat."

Rocco hit a couch. "Pick-up still on?"

Satin tossed a Tecate, pulled a set of keys out his coat and tossed them over.

"It's a standard delivery truck. Primo took it from a warehouse in Vernon. The plates are legit." He pulled out a map from his back pocket and opened it on the glass coffee table. The route was already highlighted yellow. "A Walmart Supercenter, off the eighty-six. The connect will be at the far end of the lot—one of those Jumex juice trucks. Pick-up's at four thirty. Everything's square—moneywise. You tell 'em *Señor Holt says, hola*—they transfer the goods into our rig."

"What are they transferring?"

"Holt was vague. I didn't press. Our job's just to make sure it gets to L.A. Listen—after shit's cool, head for Holt's Glendale warehouse." He handed over a one-page Google map. "We'll be there, waiting. Got it?"

"Yeah."

"There's one other thing that's come up. Before you make the pick-up, you have to dispose of some cargo on board—three of 'em."

"Bodies?"

Satin nodded. "Kang knows a spot by the Salton Sea. Made a few deposits there before, shouldn't be no thang—sorry to have to spring it on you like this."

Rocco exhaled. "Not a problem."

Ray rubbed his head, messing a slick black do. "Kang's waiting in the rig, better get on. Dump might take a minute."

Rocco headed for the door, pounding the beer before braving the stairs. Never a dull moment with Ray in command.

The drive was uneventful, listening to Kang snap jerky the whole way. Half Korean, half black—most of the crew talked shit on his unique face. Not Rocco. Didn't know enough about the guy to trade barbs behind his back. Had a strange look that made him unstable; *Blade Runner*-esque. He guided Rocco off the eighty-six at Desert Shores. Bodies banged the bed sidewall.

Night had swallowed the earth, forcing Rocco to squint, slapping on his geek specs. Place was a shoreline wasteland; blackened sea still as a drum of oil. Skeleton homes and wreckage stuck in the dirt. A rusted-out school bus, halfway in the soil, sent vibes of the atomic age. Only three lights glowed up ahead—two-bit shanties.

Kang: "Stop the truck."

Rocco grinded the beast to a halt, confused. Kang's almond eyes scanned the desolate perimeter, making sure nothing was alive.

"My brother lives out here—he cooks. Got a backyard with everything we need for the situation."

Rocco nodded. "Sure, no sweat right?"

"Yeah...kinda. Keep on—park behind that first shack."

"Wait—what you mean *kinda*?"

"Love my bro and all, but we don't get along too good. Ain't nothin' big. Be back on the road in no time."

Rocco checked his watch, two-thirty.

Before they pulled around the frail brown box, two shirtless men in oxygen masks leveled shotguns their way. Rocco could tell which was Kang's brother. Other guy was pale as an egg, practically albino. Both had shoulder length braids woven with colored cords; looked ready for Burning Man.

The shotgunners rushed the doors, forcing them out with their hands to the moon. Rocco followed orders while Kang paid no mind, kicking his brother in the gut before snatching the gun with zero effort. He tapped the barrel to the mask. His bro slid it off, telling the white boy to be cool.

"Been awhile, Marky."

"Not long enough."

Kang helped him up, handing back the gun.

Marky said, "Who's the beaner?"

"That's Rocco. Gotta make a dump."

"Shitter's clogged. Me and Roach been pinchin' loafs out by that speedboat over there."

"*Make* a dump—got three this time." He tossed an envelope from out the rig. "Satin says thanks."

"Oh, shit—cool. You know what to do."

Kang turned to Rocco. "Let's go."

The stiffs were wrapped in tattered moving blankets, couldn't have been dead for more than half a day. The first was a male, big boy—least two-forty. Took both to carry the fuck out back, laying him on the ground beside a large blanket of sheet metal. Kang pulled the steel aside, exposing a large metal dumpster, buried in cracked earth. On three, they heaved the lard-ass in. The other corpses were women; one was in her sixties, the other barely out her tweens. Rocco stared at the young girl, mocha hair still silken, vibrant. A shattered nose kept her from movie star status, dried blood down to her chest. Rocco didn't want to know what they had done to deserve this. *Could anyone deserve this?* They tossed the ladies atop the fatso. Marky and Roach spectated from lawn chairs, munching baloney rolls.

Kang put on gloves and pushed over a large barrel on wheels; had a gas pump nozzle. Rocco watched from a distance as Kang carefully poured its contents into the hole. Sordid steam rose towards the stars. Marky and Roach slid their masks back on. The smell was horrendous, fresh charring flesh. Rocco plugged his nose, coughing and headed for the porch.

Marky laughed, speaking through the mask, "Don't even ask, yo. Shit's craze. Does the job every time."

Kang ran from the smoldering pit, shirt up over his nose, waving Rocco inside.

The four of them sat on crates around a feltless poker table, enough crank on top to fuel a truck stop. Kang and Marky stared at each other in disgust while Rocco watched the albino go rail for rail; a human anteater. Marky finally spoke.

"We're headin' up to El Lay for that Cuddle Fest rave. Shit's gonna be real. Should roll out."

"Nah, visit Mom while you're in town though."

"Hospitals bug me out."

"Why don'tcha call her no more? Keeps askin' about you."

Marky smirked. "Doesn't occur to me."

"Why you gotta be a little bitch?"

Their eyes hammered. Roach chuckled, gripping his dome as if the drugs were gonna launch straight through.

Rocco headed towards the door. "Time to roll."

Kang ignored him, eyes still daggers. "Your boy here don't speak too much, huh?"

"Roach knows his roll. That's why we get along so well—like brothers."

That did it.

The men lunged, exchanging glancing blows. In seconds, it became a bad grappling match. They rolled out, into the backyard. Rocco made for the truck, focused on the importance of what lie ahead.

Kang eventually emerged, dabbing a busted lip with his sleeve and climbed in. Rocco could see Marky and Roach, inside, on the floor. Their bellies bubbled exhaustion.

"Sorry 'bout that. Got somethin' for the road." He held up a Ziploc with fine crystal, stuck his face in and sniffed. Rocco was reluctant to taste but took a bump to yield Kang's bitching. The dust hit with high voltage. He embraced it, thinking, *Bet this' how doctors get through med school.*

They were back on the road, gunning south, doing ninety and right on schedule.

Brawley was a sleepy farm town, just north of the Mexico border. Rocco didn't need directions from the freeway: The Wal-Mart sign was a beacon amongst crops. Couldn't remember the last time he blinked, listening to Kang machine gun stories, each as meaningless as the next. They pulled in five minutes early. The lot was filled with hordes of RV's, trailers and vans. They were taking advantage of the store's overnight welcome; a new sprout of community, thanks to hard times. Their Jumex truck was tucked at the rear, just like Satin said. Rocco sidled beside it, cab to cab. Three rancheros peered back with dead eyes. Rocco rolled down the window.

"Señor Holt says, hola!"
The men swiftly exited their rig to unlatch the rear. Rocco could see pistols in the back of their jeans. Kang unlatched the cargo door, and the men began transferring medium sized boxes, all labeled Jumex. Within twenty, their rig was near full. Rocco slammed the door shut.

Few more bumps and they were headed back. Kang brandished a switchblade before the freeway onramp. Rocco was beyond wired, didn't know what to think.

"Pull over."

"Why, man—why?"

"Gotta inspect the merchandise."

"Fuck that. Ray didn't tell us to mess with it—doesn't even know what the cargo is."

"Nah, fool. Believe me. We gotta check it—few years back, me and Freddie picked up some bootleg booze for the club and didn't check—pulled into town with a shipment of tap water. Ray was fuckin' pissed."

"That was different—you knew what you were picking up."

"Don't matter. Gotta make sure we got *something* in the back."

Rocco merged onto the shoulder, flaring hazards. They opened the rear, twitchy. Kang took the blade to a box. Inside, under a layer of peach nectar canisters were dense bricks wrapped in heavy black plastic. Kang sliced one, scooping the blade, analyzing the residue.

"Mother fuck!"

Rocco shivered roadside. "What is it?"

Kang placed the brick back, careful to re-cover everything. "We gotta go."

Back in the cab, Rocco asked again. "The fuck was it, man?"

Kang's eyes couldn't blink. "Black tar—Xalisco—a shitload."

Rocco started the engine, surprised, anxious to get to the warehouse, praying for smooth sails between here and L.A.

With a heroin load this size, one blown tire could bring the heat down hard.

10.

The girls were packed in the Mercedes, singing to a Madonna mixtape Mongo snuck onboard. Alvi swooped them up after dropping Lexi and Elvira on the boulevard for a joint.

Faye asked Doreen, "What's that smell?"

"Ya uppa lip, doll."

Alvi overheard. "That's the smell of freedom, Faye—waste vegetable oil—car runs on it." She looked puzzled in the rearview. "Got two gas tanks aboard, one with diesel to start the engine—other with grease. Once the grease heats," He pointed to dashboard switch, "I flip this sucker, and we're cruisin' for free."

The concept flew over her head, face scrunching. He refrained from further logistics, gliding into a metered slot under a jaundice marquee.

The New Beverly Cinema was a revival house in the core of a Hasidic neighborhood, just west of La Brea: a magnet for cinefiles, stragglers and degenerates alike. L.A.'s last true Grindhouse.

Tonight's feature was spelled in crooked block letters, a salvaged seventies' exploitation flick entitled, *Gone with the Pope*. Admission was cheap, real buttered popcorn was cheaper. The gals grabbed seats dead center as Alvi hit a nearby liquor store for tallboys. When he returned, the place was packed, pitch black, reeking of reefer. He lit his joint and peeped from the back. Memories of nights here with Gabby flooded the brain. All those uneasy silences at their start. She'd squeeze his knee during *Maniac* or always comment on Linnea Quigley's nipples. He thought about that Christmas Eve, their first kiss, smoking out on the bus bench during a Lubitsch intermission. She wanted to ring life dry: cute babies, a dog named Georgie. Jesus, those green eyes. He snapped back when the gang hollered at a racially charged zinger and fetched his seat.

The flick was surreal. Nowadays, you couldn't make one about kidnapping the Pope and asking a dollar ransom off every Catholic in the world. Beat the hell out of empty remakes. Alvi waited for the girls to go potty. Two teen boys entered the men's room with backpacks. After five minutes, they emerged in full Hasid garb, exiting to Beverly in panic mode. Alvi dug it. *Strays in all packs.*

Doreen scored coke off a client. They piled into the car for bumps. A Parliament recessed filter was the spoon. Faye only squinted with concern. *Zip—zip—zip.* Mongo's cell chirped; she saw the text and shouted for joy, lime wig shimmering like a radioactive pom-pom.

"The new Xpress is out, you guys! Alvi—take us to a newsstand."

He fired up the ride and coasted up La Brea. Barely after midnight and his body was thrashed.

The stand sat just past Santa Monica. Alvi bought smokes while the girls scrounged for the new issue, gnashing teeth, looking everywhere for Mongo's face in full blown color. A trio of grunts got his attention. Mongo stood, teary-eyed but stoic. Wasn't on the cover. Just another plastic blonde, pouting puffy lips.

Doreen rubbed her shoulder. "It's prolly on next week's issue, girl."

Mongo agreed, sifting to the Specialties page, making sure she still had the phone sex ad. It was there; triple the size of all the rest (1-866-FO-BALLS). Relief washed over.

Alvi pulled out a cig but had lost his lighter.

Faye told Mongo, "Things could be worse."

The Indian clerk tossed Alvi some matches. A paper strung-up caught his eye. The *Times*. Smack-dab on the cover, thin column.

Officials Identify Victim Found on 5 Freeway…

He scrolled, eyes bouncing for a capital G. A sharp V grabbed him instead.

19-year-old, Vanda Maples…

The smoke fell from his lips. Mongo took notice.

"What is it, Alvi?"

He stared at her, then back at the paper. "Vanda."

Doreen lunged, "What," pulling it from his hands.

"She's dead, Mong. She's *dead*."

TWO

Black Palms, Blank Hearts

Brief Sidebust...

Albuquerque, New Mexico—A Friday, 10:48 p.m.

Colton adjusted his Stetson before cranking the clutch into third, gunning the Mustang up Eubank, swerving through minivans like good ole #3. His single-chamber Flowie sent a high-pitched squeal from the engine, drowning out the non-stop barrage of questions coming out his two little princesses, perched in car seats behind: Lottie Mae (4½), Shasta (3). Where we headed, Daddy? We want pancakes! Hold yer asses, ladies. Gotta pick up yer Uncle Jackie first. Then pancakes, Daddy? He threw the Cobra back into second, letting the exhaust do its job. Jack was out front of T.D.'s Gold Club: a medieval titty joint, Amateur Night banner slung across its turret. Was nearly the same height as his brother, small build with tiny feet; what more could you expect from a Chinese family tree? Jackie tilted his camouflage trucker to the little ladies before hopping in shotgun, taking the last drag off a Winston. Shit, Colt—took you long enough. You know me, always anxious to save my big bro from the tank. Daddy! Yes, Lottie Mae? She tapped Shasta, and both girls screamed in unison, PANCAKES! Jack smiled. Pancakes fuck-er—pronto. Colton cursed in whispers. Jack smart-assed, What, being a single pop ain't what it's cracked up to be? His breath sang bourbon. Ever find out where the old bitch went? Lottie Mae overheard. When's Mommy coming back, Daddy? Shasta cried, I want Mommy! He turned to Jack, See what the fuck you done? Jack put his paws up in surrender. Girls—girls, sim-mer down! Your Mommy ain't coming back—she's gone, okay?

Is she in heaven, Daddy? Yes, Lottie Mae, Mama's on that gravy train upstairs. Shasta began to bawl. Jack took over. Now, don't be sad, ladies. Your Mama loved you mighty hard, just loved herself a bit more. Colton pulled into the Village Inn parking lot, screeching to a halt. Don't go tellin' 'em that, asshole. Why not— it's the truth? Colt turned around to face them. Your Mama caught the dreamer's bug is all. She's an angel now, watching over you—alright? The girls nodded, anxiously awaiting syrup slathered cakes. Jack chuckled, reflecting on what really transpired. Colton forced the trucker bill down to Jackie's nose. You're payin' your own way tonight. That so? Betcher ass. How 'bout we make it interesting? How so? Three consecutive donuts 'round that there sign post, I'll pick up the whole damn tab m'self. The engine whined to life; a Ford built ricer. Buckle back up, girls. Daddy's gettin' you some free fuckin' pancakes...

11.

Her knuckles crashed against the window sill, eyes tearing, newspaper to the floor. Gabby gazed out at the rooftop rooster, wagging its giant ass between Old Glories. Two tears fell before she forced composure. Vanda was reckless. Satin didn't play. *Told her not to do it.* She distanced herself before it went down. What kind of friend would usher her into such a mess? Two tears were all Vanda would ever get. Gabby brainstormed, unfolding twin sheets of paper, each with identical images—blackmail photos that had sealed Vanda's coffin. Her first thought was to destroy them. Vanda had her hide them, in case... *Well, now it was.* The pages were dangerous but she might be able to use them, to escape or afterwards. First—had to find a way out that didn't rip her to bits across warm asphalt.

The room was tiny, crammed with bunk beds and a bath, making it more of a cell than a studio. Satin had all his girls like this, situated dorm-style in a brick apartment complex behind the casita. Most of them were free to come and go, long as they made their shifts, dolled up accordingly. Everyone made their shifts—guaranteed. Satin ran backgrounds on each after they began working for him exclusively. Dangled a grand at their face to make them wet. They all got off. Fear management from then on. The whereabouts of relatives were a constant reminder during weekly meetings. Shifts were met so families remained safe. Satin made sure all his B-girls had loved ones.

Gabby's freedom got fucked thanks to Vanda. Now she was on lockdown, escorted nightly to and from the club, sans pay. The money was shit anyway, not even close to what she hustled on the boulevard. Bartending earned her a bit extra; skills she'd honed back home. Ray promised *mucho dinero*, that's what he told her and Vanda when they started. Pure bullshit. Each of their up-front cash was spent within days.

The first couple weeks were fine, allowing them to romp the Lafayette and their regular haunts between club shifts. Nothing more than a side cash secret. Then Vanda's plan came to light; her intention all along. Gabby never saw it coming. For all she knew, Erma had died in a blazing car wreck. Footsteps resonated in the corridor. She re-folded the deadly images and shoved them deep through a slit in her mattress.

The door unlatched, opened by Freddie; his lazy eye lingered left. In walked her roomie, some black chick from Watts, ass like a giant pumpkin. Must've done something to Satin to earn that limp. *Or not.* Seemed like a sweet enough gal. Been only a few days, but they got along alright. Freddie re-locked the door behind her.

"Hey, JaTonya. How's the leg?"

"Betta, thanks." She eased into the bottom bunk with a grimace. "Wasn't dat infected after all." Mascara bombing Gabby's cheekbones got her attention. "Girl—what's wrong?"

Gabby glanced in the mirror over the sink and washed the smudges off. Her black hair had grown in on the sides; she missed the Mohawk. Time spent here flew fast. She shot over and peered out the door's glass square, making sure Freddie had bailed before picking up the paper and handing it over.

"Where'd ya get dis?"

"They slid it under the door this morning."

JaTonya's eyes bounced through the article.

Officials Identify Victim Found on 5 Freeway...

"Who's Vanda?"

"My friend—used to work here."

"Dat's straight horribo."

Gabby sniffed. "Give you one guess who's responsible?"

JaTonya jerked. "Nah?"

Gabby bit her lip, nodding. "Read that last bit."

Since identifying the body, officials have been unable to locate the whereabouts of her father, Irving, mother, Stella and younger sister, Yvette. Anyone with knowledge of their whereabouts is strongly encouraged to contact local authorities.

JaTonya handed it back.

"All that shit Satin threatens us with—it's for real."

"But why? What she do?"

Gabby sat cross-legged on the linoleum floor, fiddling chipped pink toenails. "When I took the job, was 'cause I needed the cash—told you about my band and all. Vanda told me about this place—thought, *A grand up-front? Sheeit.* So, I went along and everything was fine, then she told me about this dirt she had on Satin. Guy supposedly killed a friend of hers—Erma. She'd followed the case in the papers and stuff. They pointed the finger at Satin 'cause his brother was killed beside her—found both of 'em in a burnt-out car near Hollywood Park. Cops didn't have enough to book him though."

"So?"

"So, Vanda didn't care if he got jailed or not. Just knew the guy had money—least that's how the papers played it. Told him she had proof of what happened—a picture Erma texted before the shit went down. Threatened to take it to the cops, unless."

"Did she really have it?"

Gabby hesitated, knowing better. "I dunno—prolly not. She was stringing him along, saying it was stashed with some friends who were expecting her in a few days. Told her not to mess with him, but she wasn't scared. That was the last time I saw her." She pointed to the paper. "He called her bluff."

"Dat's why *you* in here den?"

"We were friends. Satin thinks I might try and get brave too.

Told him I barely knew her but he still tosses me back in here every night."

"Damn, girl, dat's some scandalous ass shit right dere. Whatcha gone do?"

"Only thing I can do. Try and get the fuck out this bitch—hit the road, fast enough to warn my family of the harm headed their way."

"Where dey at?"

"Huh?"

"Where ya gotta run to?"

"Oh—Shit City, U.S.A."

JaTonya was in the bathroom re-dressing her wound as Gabby sprawled on the top bunk, catching a power nap before another long night slinging drinks. In her hand, the severed arm of a powder blue plush toy. White stuffing jutted out from where it once connected to an animal body. She clung to the binky, rubbing its round fingers while refraining a thumb suck. What a habit that was to kick. Her eyes were closed but the mind wandered. She put the paw to her lips, smelling. *Was it all just a big mistake?* She could feel fame in her core. Everyone knew she'd been blessed with talent. Destiny brought her here. Hollywood beckoned—begged. Couldn't work another day at that Chili's, shaking pussy ass cocktails for fat fucks, wondering what could've been as they regaled her with droll hunting ditties. Life had fastened concrete boots that were dragging the soul.

Everyone back home would laugh at her now. They'd roar soon as she ran back into town, tail between her legs—for their own damn benefit too. Why preserve *their* being—*their* livelihood? What'd they ever done for her? Should let them rot in their obesity. If Satin wanted them, he'd have them. Just like Vanda. She could move on though, give another go at another band in another big city. San Francisco was okay. Chicago could happen. Hell, NYC was at the top of the list. Could do it—blow town—never look back, again. She rubbed the binky on her neck, one more whiff before sliding it back into a pocket. God, it smelled good. Never could come to hate that newborn scent. Only thing that could send her homeward bound and she damn well knew it.

12.

Alvi and Mongo trekked towards Hollywood. She clasped his shoulder as he towed her on the skate. The line had already formed. Thirty men, women and teens mingled in trance, trampling stars. A truck painted Clean Spikes Now was being unloaded in an empty parking lot. Boxes packed with paper sacks were placed onto fold-out tables. Mongo proceeded to hobnob through the queue, inquiring familiar faces on Gabby's whereabouts. Alvi singled out the head of the operation, introduced himself, asked to give a hand—name was Kip. Couldn't stop staring at the guy's frosted bangs as he spewed the Gabby predicament.

One by one, junkies slunk past the tables, grabbing sacks filled with alcohol swabs, tourniquets, needles and OD pamphlets. Kip gave the skinny on Gabby, constantly tucking bangs behind an ear while they distributed disaster kits.

"Nice girl. Was hoping she'd show back up. Been a few weeks now—could use the help."

"She tell you about any plans or anythin'?"

"No, just her usual band promo. Why—what's the deal?"

"Nobody's seen her in a while. Last person she was with just made the *Times'* front page—dead."

"Jesus." He paused from passing another bag to look at Alvi, scooping locks for full view. "You think she's—"

"Dunno yet—she have to fill out any paperwork to volunteer for you guys?"

"Yeah, everyone does. Basic info."

"Mind if I have a look."

"Sure, under the circumstances." He tapped the co-ed beside him to take over the station. "We're not supposed to do it, but I ain't one for rules."

Alvi smirked.

Kip pulled out an accordion file and began rifling through the G tab. "Here it is."

Alvi looked it over. Basic indeed. Data listed: Gabby Gretsch, age twenty-four, address was the Lafayette. N/A was scribbled on all other incidentals. At the bottom of the form was, *Your reason for volunteering?* She'd put down, *Need some good karma.* He gave it back. "Thanks."

"No problem. Keep us posted on any news."

Alvi obliged before skating towards Mongo, pacing under the Fonda's concert scroll. Acrylics in the air told him her queries came up short. He skidded beside her. "Gabby *Gretsch* ring a bell?"

Mongo's purple brows peaked.

They had a layover at the Frolic. Dita let Alvi behind the counter to use the phone. Mongo sipped a Bloody Mary, waiting. A pack of bikers huddled around the elbow of the bar, zoning out at the Dodgers on a flat screen. Place was quiet. No jokers. No juke.

The small tube spouted a scrambled Angels' game in progress. One patron paid mind. Mongo sized him up: eyes a bit glassy, gold rings—looked right Christianly. He erupted at the screen as she speared an olive.

"No way! No freaking way!" He pointed at the shit tube. "Did anyone see that? Guy was safe by a mile!" He cupped a hand to his mouth, "You're blind, Blue!"

Dita humored his excitement with a halfhearted smile and

resumed dunking pints. The guy approached the runt of the pack, thinking him less the brute, tapping his denim vest.

"Hey, pal. Check this replay, will you? Tell me if the runner's safe or not?"

The runt's eyes remained on the TV. Mongo laughed.

The guy begged, "Someone watch this, come on!"

A burly one grunted, adjusting on the stool. Mongo snorted, tapping her toes on the floor. The guy swayed back to his seat.

"Might I ask what's so funny, my dear?"

"You in the wrong muthafucka, right here. It's the Angels, honey—nobody gives a fuck."

The pack snarled, nearly showing teeth. The guy dropped a buck tip and hit the door.

Alvi hung up the phone and grabbed a shot glass. "We're good, Mong. What'd I miss?"

Mongo and Alvi headed towards Wilcox. Tickets for Gabby's show were twelve dollars more than they wanted to pay. Luckily, Noodles and Vargas were considered cream of the scene. Could pull strings.

The boys agreed to meet them out front of their new place. Ronnie had banned them from tenancy at the Lafayette due to an accumulation of dramatic events, the last being Noodles attempt to end it all with a swan dive off the hotel's rooftop. Vargas had also tried offing himself the year before, hanging from a fourth-floor balcony like a rabid bat for hours into the night. They would blame it on LSD or PCP but everyone didn't buy it. Seemed like every year depression would grab hold and one of them would lose it, creating a stir which climaxed with firemen and police—ultimately capped by a seventy-two-hour psychiatric hold. Rest of the time they were stand-up kids; everyone enjoyed their presence in the Zimba: always good for a laugh. Both fled Yuma; cousins ostracized for hair colors unapproved by that ancient text feared by all who lived there. Got tired of being the town's main suppliers for annual book burnings or CD smashings. *Born against.* Just wanted to live in a smaller intolerance swamp—anywhere with live music seven days a week. L.A. crackled outstretched neon and cradled them home.

The Mark Twain was a side street dump, accommodating vagrants and druggies with hourly to weekly rates. Vargas and Noodles sat on the front steps, puffing a doob. Mongo quickly got into rotation.

Alvi said, "You guys still friends with that Echoplex bouncer?"

Vargas let out a plume before passing the pinch to Mongo. "Yeah—why?"

"Need tickets for Sunday's Kill Dads' show. Figured you two could help me and Mong get in."

"Shouldn't be a problem," said Noodles.

"You two gonna be there?"

"Nah—downtown. Bronx play La Cita."

"You ever heard the band, GalAvant Gardes?"

Both boys shrugged, wagging heads.

Vargas said, "Why?"

"They're opening—Gabby's supposedly the singer."

Vargas bugged at Noodles before they both started chuckling.

Noodles said, "Better take earplugs."

Vargas: "Think you can spot us a coupla forties for the favor?"

"Sure—right now?"

Wild grins washed.

Noodles said, "Mickey's, man. None of that King Cobra piss you sip."

Mongo passed him the J. Two hits, and he skated towards Sunset.

Faye propped a leg on the toilet, careful with the razor as she groomed naughty bits. Mongo emphasized that most johns liked it soft and sleek, even if she wasn't up for sale to these fetish clients, all folks liked something nice to look at. Most men's preferences didn't matter though, she wanted it perfect for Alvi—just in case.

Earlier in the day, an excursion to the Sunset Free Clinic had forced another reality of her new world: a waiting room filled with sickness and lethargy, faces composed like aged driftwood, petrified features beaming life stories, gazing through pamphlets, out windows or at the Sparkletts tower in desperate need of water. She signed in; anti-bacterial sanitizer pumped into a palm once the pencil had dropped, lemon scent masking the room's stagnant breath. Every seat was occupied so she sat on the dusty floor amongst patients, chewing a dampened sleeve. To pass the time, she tried making out words on slanted health signs taped to every wall.

Faces on the nurses were cold and harsh—not quiet driftwood, less dark...maybe teak. Faye didn't feel any judgement coming from them, just a dead silence accustomed to folks gone completely numb. Invasive questions had her snickering and bashful, fiddling with a tongue depressor which they allowed her to keep. None of the doctors saw patients on first visits. She would have to come back to have her eyes checked. Vials were drawn; bloodwork results would take a few days. When asked where she could be contacted, she gave the Lafayette's address and said she could return for the results. Driftwood stares followed her out the doors onto Sunset; knew she was a fresh transplant, flesh still rosy and soft. She held her breath until sucking in hot boulevard air. Snack break raucous came from a playground across the street as she boarded her bus. Halfway home, remembered that she'd forgotten to ask for condoms. Didn't know why she would need any but those were Mongo's orders. She'd ask around for some, doubting a swift return to that wretched dispensary.

Red speckled cream rinsed from out her thighs. She walked to the mirror, admiring her innie, smooth as a scoop of French vanilla. Twirling, she inspected the rest of her freckled physique. There were slight rolls on her back and gut. She pinched them before jumping up and down, seeing how soft she actually was.

The chunks were just where they counted. Had been awhile since giving herself a good once-over. Tits were up, rosy rotary dial nips; ass a tad bigger. Normally she would've been petrified but figured a guy like Alvi would dig squeezing beach ball handfuls. She bent over and spread cheeks.

Pretty adorable.

Unwrapping the towel from her head, she let fiery locks lay. Hands on hips, she wondered what this Gabby girl had that she didn't. She'd seen a picture, some Joan Jett wannabe—nothing special. Maybe she knew some world class sex tricks, a former gymnast or something? She snarled and reached for a cosmetics case.

Applying makeup still felt new. Back in Portland, her father wouldn't allow it—*'All this whorin'-up'*. Stepmom agreed, too scared of her own opinion, soul too black and blue. Lucky for her, Mongo gave a crash course the other night, letting her borrow a Dolly Parton portrait for future guidance. She'd been way off beforehand, relying solely on gloss and glitter. Another peek at the headshot and she continued; a new face for her new place. Layers of radish red lipstick solidified that independence she'd longed for. The Greyhound trek was worth every stolen penny. Now, there was only one desire left. She sat, admiring a beat before puckering and smashing a kiss on the bathroom mirror. In lipstick, she scrolled, *FAYE LOVES ALVI,* dotting the *i* with a puffy heart.

Alvi and Mongo coasted to the Lafayette on fumes. Another envelope from Ma glared back at Alvi in the mailbox. Another Archangel crumpled as he headed up with Mongo. At her floor, Ronnie was cleaning out Vanda's apartment with tin trash bins. Alvi tossed Ma's prayer into one.

Ronnie saw them and asked, "Want any of this shit?"

They both shook heads, walking straight past.

Mongo dolled up for the night ahead. Alvi waded carefully

through Gabby's belongings this time, searching for anything that could further clarify this *Gretsch* business. Nothing but rock shirts mixed with random trinkets and makeup kits. Got a surprise in her denim jacket: two string bikinis. He held them up, sniffing.

"What'd Gabby need these for?"

Mongo finished applying silver lipstick and looked. "Fuck if I know. Maybe she gone to da beach?" She grabbed the mirror and grate, rapidly turning four bars into dust. "Told you, they ain't shit there. Awready went through it twice."

Alvi stuffed them back and rolled up a dollar, awaiting rails.

"And what do you think you're doing, child?"

He floated a warm grin. "It'll be an advance."

"Tell you what—let you vacuum three if you do me a solid."

"Sure—what?"

Mongo smiled. "I'm glad you said yes, 'cause I awready promised her you'd do it?"

"Ah fuck—who?"

Mongo handed him the mirror and walked down the hall. By the time he upped a pair, she was back with Faye. Both stood before him, smiling to high hell. Faye was cleaned up; face that of a young Angie Dickenson. *Angie*, he thought. She grasped her wrist with a fresh manicure and knocked her knees. "Heya, Alvi."

"What's up, Faye?"

Mongo: "Tonight you'll be drivin' Miss Green to a few appointments I've set fa her. She's in dire need of some scrilla, and I got a few harmless foos that be willin' to help her out."

"That so?" Alvi pulled in the final rail, pinching his septum.

"Fa show! Look at her!" She stroked Faye's copper locks. "She all purdy and *shit*—fuckin' red hot!"

Alvi scoped, up-down. "Looks nice."

Mongo winked at him. "I'ma hit the boulevard with Doreen. You two have fun now."

Mongo left before Alvi could argue, knowing damn well this was more than a favor. Faye remained, blue eyes fluttering over bosoms crammed in a deep red V; skinny jeans and heels worked overtime. He figured, *What the hell? Could use a break from all this drama.*

The ride up Western was silent. Faye bit cuticles as Alvi dazed on in medicinal bliss. Stan's Peepshow beckoned sleaze between Mom & Pops. The 101 remained sedate, headlights and brake lamps stagnant for miles. Tape deck spun: *Love...is leaf-like. You and me, baby.* Alvi turned it down a notch.

"Who's the first john?"

Faye dug deep into her cleavage, mining for Mongo's scribbled note. He tried not to stare, adjusting his rearview, implying attentiveness. She handed it over. He sneaked quick peeks every other second.

"Just two appointments?"

"Guess so."

Alvi scanned the names. Knew the folks. Harmless clientele. "Two looners and a wammy—you know what you're in for, right?"

"Mongo briefed me a bit. No big deal, just a little weird. Never heard of this kinda stuff before."

"Yeah well—takes all kinds. Ginger and Don are good people. Used to be Gabby's clients."

"Which ones are they?"

"The looners—balloon fetishists. Mongo told you exactly what they like, right?"

"Um, the guy's a popper...his wife likes it when you inflate and strip?"

"Pretty much—he's more of a loon than she is. Gabby used to rub the balloon all over Ginger, once it got to its peak. That's when Don liked to *pop*. Said it made 'em wild, usually brought a good tip too."

"I can do that."

"They're in the Los Feliz Hills. Should make it on time."

Faye lipped a strand of hair. "Honestly, I'm a little nervous about the second guy. Mongo said he's big into *pies*?"

"Yeah—not real ones though. Monty likes shaving cream pies. Your typical WAM john likes to cover girls in strange textured stuff—you lucked out that it's only shaving cream. Could be a helluva lot worse."

She stuck out her tongue.

"He'll prolly have you rinse off with milk or beer afterwards—in the shower. Put your clothes somewhere far from the plastic lining—trust me."

"Lining?"

"Yeah, he throws it down all over the living room. Likes it *wet and messy*, just not on the furniture, you know?"

"This what all the girls do for cash—fetish stuff?"

He couldn't lie. "Well…at first. Usually big money entices them to broaden their horizons, so to speak."

She stewed for a beat before giggling. "Geez, if daddy could see me now."

Alvi did a deep dad voice. "Young lady, I'm so disappointed in you—don't you know pie and balloons are tools of the Devil?"

She cracked.

"Where 'bouts you from anyway?"

"Portland was the last stop, once pop got out the service."

"Army brat, huh?"

"Shut up."

"That's cool. Portland's cool too—Skate City."

"You been there?"

"In a past life. Used to hit Burnside twice a year. Awesome trannies."

"Can't seem to get enough of those trannies, huh?"

He choked. "Transitions—when you skate from ramp to ramp…"

Her doe eyes lacked interest but he could've kept on and on. She wouldn't have stopped him. Angie was the same way. Gabby too. Just another tick some women had that made him love them more.

Griffith Observatory sat like a jack-o-lantern atop darkened hills, high above monster homes. Faye touched his arm, thanking him for doing this again before heading out, up the driveway. Alvi watched as tall wooden doors opened on the Spanish abode. Front yard bushes belonged in a zoo. Faye stopped and doubled back, leaning through the car's window.

"Mongo told me to bring condoms for some reason—but I forgot. Do you have any?"

He opened the glove box, handing her a sheet of four golden squares. "Won't need 'em for what your clients want. Just always good to have some. Never know what kinda propositions could be headed your way." He dug back into the box. "Here, take this too—can keep it."

Pink pepper spray; she took it from his palm, nodding a final time.

He watched as Ginger welcomed Faye into their home before waving at him; could've passed for a librarian. He returned the greet, leaning over to smell lingering perfume on the passenger seat.

The wammy lived a few blocks south on Rodney: seafoam apartments up tile steps. The street provided a view of tree tops in the distance, all silhouetted by big city lights. Alvi sat in wait, staring up at the blackened palms long enough to imagine he was marooned on a tropical island. Like needle to record, the city began to serenade. Honks of nearby vehicles doubled as exotic chirping birds. The rustling of a can collector's cart became an ocean. His pretend paradise. If it wasn't for Faye tapping on the window, he could have drifted for days.

She sunk inside, hair wet but clothes dry, holding a thirty-two of High Life out to him.

"The champagne of beers—what's the occasion?"

"Leftovers."

"Thanks." He held the neck, pinky out. "I'll drink it like a debutante. How'd it go?"

"Alright. He added raw eggs to his repertoire."

Alvi made an *ew* face.

"That's why it took me so long—couldn't wash it outta my hair." She smiled, "What do I owe you? Made one-thirty tonight."

"Not bad for a newbie. Usually the girls give me whatever they can, pills or pot mostly. Don't usually take their cash." He hoisted the brew. "You can forget about that though. This one's on the arm."

"That don't seem right, Alvi?"

He spouted greasecar logistics again, emphasizing free fuel. She shrugged, still puzzled, giggling away awkwardness. They agreed to never speak of it again. He found her company oddly satisfying. Most of the girls just sat in back, fixing their make-up or powdering their brains. After *this* client, Gabby usually wanted to stakeout Danzig's house on Franklin—just for a glimpse, hoping the Misfit would take out his trash. He watched the way Faye stared at Hillhurst Liquor's happy green tubes. *What the hell?*

"You like neon?"

"Only since I moved here. They're everywhere. Something hypnotic about 'em, you know? Make me feel like a moth or something."

Instead of heading south to Virgil, he swung a left on Sunset. "Wanna see a few of my faves."

She lit up, ear pasted with a dollop of cream.

The Mercedes cruised down Caesar Chavez, looping first through Chinatown so Faye could see radiant pagoda rooftops; dragons snarled here and there. All the while, he carried on about the Museum of Neon Art and their salvaging of derelict city signage. She sat in wonder, imagining the modern downtown in its original glory. Only a tarnished glimpse remained. Alvi continued, pointing out odd illuminations, rarely acknowledged by the living. Most of them were burnt out, rusted, clinging to rooftops like Harold Lloyd.

Broadway beamed lonesome letters of once gaudy words. Arrows flickered—all pointing to perdition. He told her when the neon boom hit, this stretch harbored more luster than Times Square. They gazed at blue and white diamonds, winking out jewelry store windows. Theaters, bars and eateries blitzed from all angles. The busted string of radiance was superb, fluttering high above bleeding streets. They took in the soundtrack: a single saxophone wailed under a dingy marquee, charming flotsam from one crime to the next.

He took her to the giant JESUS SAVES, grinning a hellish red, then onward to Felix Chevrolet.

Back on darkened side streets, she pressed. "You got the dirt on me—now, gotta tell me yours."

"Nothin' much to tell." He hit a shortcut down an industrial corridor, peppered with gentlemen's clubs.

"I wanna hear it anyways."

"Born in the South Bay—Torrance. Moved out here a long time ago—back when you were rompin' grade school."

"Hey, I ain't *that* young."

"Please."

"Where's Torrance?"

"Not far. Know where Redondo Beach is?"

"Think so—you lived by the beach?"

"Not on it but close. Could skate there."

"Why would you ever move—that's my dream, a nice little beach house. Could learn to surf—stroll barefoot everywhere. You surf?"

"Nah—scared a sharks. It was great though, growing up there. I just...had to leave."

"Uh oh, what'd *you* do?"

He shot a glance. "Nothin'—I—look, there's the sign on your right."

She leered, a bit uncomfortable, wondering if she'd said

something wrong. *Enough with the prying.*

Alvi gazed at the glowing feline: tall, strong, triumphant. Oh, the stories he could tell Faye. Stories he hadn't told anyone at the Lafayette. Highest of highs, lowest of lows, to which extent, only a dead girl knows—*Angie*. He craned and munched coffins. "Where to now?"

"Back through Broadway!"

He made a loop. Skyscrapers stood sharp in the distance, keeping the heavens at bay.

Night kept them till dawn. She playfully sent punches his way, trading barbs on a rainbow of topics. Her ironic last name touched a chord. They waltzed around moments, laughing and living amongst the toxic gleam of the city. Such moments, when present, strangers couldn't help but become friends. That's how he wanted it. *Friends.* Last time Mongo set him up was with Gabby. His new heart was still growing. To be out the shadows of loneliness, even for just a few hours, was good enough.

13.

The tall metal ladder teetered thanks to a gimp leg. Gabby had a few of the girls hold it in place while she loaded the bar's top shelf with bottles of Chivas. Out the window, she saw the Escalade pull into the lot and park under the neighboring church's white cross. That cute guy got out—one of Satin's boys. She watched as he fumbled, switching optics for shades while heading to the rear entrance. Climbing down from the ladder, giggling, she said to the girls, "New guy's here." They grinned.

The club didn't open for another hour, so when he sidled up to the bar she ignored him on purpose. He sat, waiting, watching as she hauled a booze box from out the *carnicería*. She was fumbling with a ring of keys, trying to re-lock the door without dropping the load. Rocco approached. "Lemme help." He grabbed the box from out her arms.

She swiped hair from over an eye and smiled before punching the key. "Thanks. How you doin' this fine day?"

He slid the box atop the bar. "Couldn't be worse."

"I hear that." She hung the keys on a hook above the register. "Killer shades."

"Thanks but...not really."

She sang, "*You wear your sunglasses at night.*"

"What's that?"

"Just a bastardized version of a shitty eighties song."

"Oh."

"Now, don't *I* feel old?" She sensed something wrong. He wasn't as charming as their last flirt. "Tecate?"

"Mmm…" He scanned the bottles, noticing a box strewn on the floor. "Chivas-rocks."

"Comin' right up." She filled a tumbler with ice and poured heavy. "Solving problems are we?" She smiled. His grin took a second too long. "Oh shit—I'm sorry. I don't even know you—didn't mean to pry."

"Ah nah, it's nothing. Had a really long night, that's all. I'm Rocco by the way—Rocco Felix."

Their hands met.

"Gabby Gretsch. So, you're the new guy 'round here?"

"Yeah…I guess."

"How you like workin' for Ray?"

"It's got its perks. Not exactly what I planned on doing with my life but welcome to the club, right?"

"No way, buddy. B-girl bartender was what I told *my* high school counselor."

He smiled.

"There it is," she said. "I won him back!"

He took down the glass.

She poured another. "So, how'd you land this job?"

"Nepotism—Ray's my Uncle."

She paused, the bulb in her brain gaining wattage. This boy just got a lot more attractive. "You don't say?"

He let an, "Unfortunately," slip under his breath.

"Least you got the looks in the family."

He choked on an ice cube.

She wet her lips, thinking, *This just might be the ticket.*

Those images were tattooed on Rocco's brain. The blood crusted nose of that teen raked his eyeballs over and over like a penny slot. *My god, the smells.* Satin gave him tonight off. Was in no condition this morning, pulling into the warehouse with Rat Fink eyes. Ray reprimanded Kang for giving him too much synthetic charge. As if the tweak was what really fucked him up.

Rocco slouched over the counter, rimming his sixth whiskey. *Separate the mind from the act.* Not a chance. He stared around the room as Gabby bounced back and forth, sliding drink after drink to eager customers. Place was filled out, even for a Saturday. He stared on at the chorus of girls, barely clothed, ready to bang. All shapes and sizes: big tits, small tits—white, black, brown, yellow. No shame. No regard. Each girl strutted the *wild side* in plastic pumps or stilettos.

Suddenly, two giant mounds rested behind his neck. Felt like warm bags of sugar. He peered over his shoulder for a glimpse. A freak-tittied fortysomething with sandy hair smiled back. She gyrated the twins, sending the shades up his skull. The world was a blur of pink freckled flesh.

"Come play with me, sailor?"

Gabby came over before he could respond.

"Daphne—he's with me, okay?"

The beach balls slid off as Gabby shot daggers.

"My savior." He smiled.

"Don't mention it. She's bad news." Gabby mimed plunging a syringe into her neck. "Pretty sure she's got something crawlin' downstairs too."

"No doubt."

"'Nother drink?"

The Chivas had him bold. "Maybe later—tonight, after you get off."

She played coy. "I'd love to, Rocco—really. But I don't see it happening anytime soon—not because of you though. I like you."

She didn't have to say it. "It's Ray, right?"

"Got me on lockdown."

"What? How come?"

She shrugged.

"Lemme see what I can do."

"No, I don't wanna get you in trouble."

He shushed her. "Lemme just see what's going on, okay?" Ray had taken the crew up to a party in the hills. Still, someone had to be on hand, watching over the girls and security. The light was on upstairs. "Be right back."

Freddie was in front of a flat screen spouting Coffin Joe. Both hands gripped domino tiles. The girl Ray stabbed the other night sat across the coffee table, shirtless, black tipped utters pointing to crooked toes. She was locked into her hands as well. Freddie's good eye remained on the tiles while he spoke.

"What you doin' here, Roc? Supposed to be takin' a load off."

"I am—just tyin' one on too."

Freddie flipped a three-two, empty cubes at both ends. "Fickle nickel!" He looked at Rocco. "You want next game?"

JaTonya penciled the score and slammmed her last tile. "Tension, busta. Domino!"

Freddie's eye scanned the tiles, frantically adding. Ten on top of his stash. "Fuck!" He stood and removed his beater, ribs so defined, could hit them like a Xylophone.

Rocco said, "Strip bones, huh?"

"Yup."

"No thanks."

Freddie flipped the train of tiles while JaTonya penciled another house, smiling.

"That's smart, dog. Bitch got two houses on me already. What you want then?"

"Figured since I'm here, could help close up—lockdown one of them girls for ya." He raised an eyebrow.

"Shit, need to get that dick wet, huh? I feel you. Which one you want?"

"Bartender down there—Gabby."

Freddie stood, tossing him keys. "Not my type, but ass is ass, right? This one's her roomie—me and her gonna be busy tonight too." He winked. "Love me some dark chocolate. Take your time—Ray'll be in tomorrow, 'round noon." He grabbed JaTonya's left breast from behind, pointing the darkened tip at Rocco, stroking her braids. "We'll be up here all night, homie."

"Cool."

"Have fun, ay."

The crowd began to die off downstairs. A handful of girls slouched in booths while the rest rode wannabe stallions back in their rooms. Gabby was getting chatted up by an old man in a cowboy hat. Rocco recognized the guy from his TV commercials, always petting a tiger amongst used cars. He went around the bar and grabbed Gabby's hand. She recoiled before realizing.

"Come on," he said.

They strolled, hand in hand, through the church parking lot. Gabby figured he was going to have her out in the car. She welcomed the lust, tingling at its prospects. He opened the passenger door for her, running around the hood. The Escalade growled to life. Rocco switched shades for specs. She found it cute.

"Nice car—expensive."

"It's Ray's. Lets me use it after I drive him around all day." He checked the stereo clock. "Looks a little too late for that drink."

"It's okay. Just glad to be outta that place for once."

"You hungry?"

"Starved."

He pulled out onto Virgil. "Good—I know a place."

She put a hand on his knee and smiled, wishing she had more than three dollars in her pocket, enough to run out at the first red light, find her way to the train station and onto the next big city. But that way he looked at her—the same way fools drooled over Marilyn—had her knowing that the time would come, sooner than later. She leaned over and kissed him on the cheek. "My savior."

***

Since '24, the Pantry Café had never once closed for business. Rocco told her how the doors didn't even have locks, but she didn't believe him. Striped awnings welcomed them below dim tubes. Place was packed, catering the last call rush. They took a spot at the counter. The cook's face glistened with grease, cracking eggs one-handed. Breakfast wafted their way, mounds of bacon and hash browns simmering on the flat grill, waiting to be munched.

"Ever been here before?"

Gabby shook her head no, taking in the time warp decor. They opened menus before two fresh mugs of coffee. He instigated the get-to-know-you process. She clammed on details, claiming Hollywood as home. He grew up in Long Beach, an only child, played ball for Wilson High, mother and father both gone now. She put on the rebel front, talking about the GalAvant Gardes till their food came. He scarfed Portuguese sausage and eggs. She slathered French toast with syrup, careful not to speak with mouthfuls.

Rocco said, "Well, you know how *I* came to work for Ray. How'd you get involved in all this?"

"My friend...Vanda." A piece of bread flew onto his shirt. She covered her mouth. "Oh my god!"

He laughed, wiping it with a napkin, dwelling on the name she just dropped. Never knew the girl when she was alive, but the name *Vanda* was rifled out Ray's mouth enough times for him to know exactly *who* she was. Couldn't forget the way her eyeball rubbed waxy on his chin that night—how she floated to the Freeway like a deep-sea mermaid. He forced a smile, hoping the morbid visions didn't seep from his eyes into Gabby's. "She got you all wrapped up in this?"

"Said it was quick money, and I bit. What can I say? I was broke. Needed cash for the band."

"She tell you 'bout what she tried to do to Ray?"

"Look at you, sounding like your uncle." She smirked and lied. "No...found out what happened to her though. Everybody knows—was in the papers. Whatever she did must've been major. Whole family's gone missing—mom, dad and sis."

Steaming bodies blipped back into his brain. *Last night's cargo.* She kept on.

"Put me on lockdown too."

"So that's why, huh?"

"Ray thinks I know what her plan was or something. Shit, I barely knew the bitch. What'd she try an' do exactly?"

"I dunno specifics. Ray said she tried to blackmail him or something. As far as what happened to her, I know as much as you do." He thumbed his chest. "New guy, remember?"

They stared blankly as a waiter splashed fresh toppers.

She switched modes, licking syrup off a finger. "What's the plan now, handsome?"

He fumbled keys, anxiously trying to get inside her room. She unclasped his belt, hands sliding south. The door flung. She let up, strolled over to the window, twirling her shirt in the air. The moonlight cast contours of tiny handfuls. He closed the door and came towards her curling finger. Gently cupping a breast, he smashed into her lips. Tongues wrestled, noses vacuuming each other's scent. She pried off his shirt, clawing at his chest before slithering down for more.

He picked her up before gushing, looking at the bunk bed, wondering how this was going to work.

"Mine's the top."

He threw her up and used the ladder, junk swinging—*baaad* naked.

The bed was too small, dipping with each moist thrust. The cadence was off but she kept moaning. His shin cracked the rail, a hearty *thwack*. Her eyes went wide, catching his pain. She rubbed his shoulder to stop. Suddenly, he shot out of her and leapt to the floor, limping in circles.

"Cramp?"

He nodded.

Her bare feet slapped linoleum. "Come here."

He weathered the hurt, watching fingers fall out her mouth and strum downtown. She spun in front of the window.

He pounced.

She kissed him over the shoulder.

He propped her leg in the air, hand hitting imperfections at the back of her thigh—deep scars. *Fuckin' Ray.*

She cringed the moment he slid back home, pressing hard against the glass, fogging over the image of that goddamn rooster in the distance. The inside of her lip bled from biting, one of those things that brought her back to adolescence; that lousy first fuck, during recess. *Only one way to beat all of life's bad things: learn to love 'em.*

14.

The Echoplex was tucked in an alley off Glendale, a cave-like concert hut whose clientele fluctuated between B.O.'d hipsters and B.O.'d Rastafarians. Tonight reeked Punk Rock. Last time Alvi came here was for the Masque's 30th anniversary show. Surprised Gabby for her birthday, taking her to see a slew of vintage bands. She was beyond thrilled, rifling off everyone she recognized, like he didn't know. *Adorable.* She had her moments. Three weeks later, they were through.

Mongo wore one of Gabby's denim vests: patches, buttons, studs—all Frankensteined askew. Wanted to blend in. As if the Sunkist wig wasn't enough. They approached the entrance. A simple, "We're listed," spawned VIP badges. Noodles and Vargas came through.

The innards were a darkened mess, forcing their eyes to adjust. They scanned the cave for Gabby, pushing through teams of fisted youth to the rear bar. Alvi chatted with the barkeep, her tongue spliced like a lizard. Didn't know shit about Gabby or the band. An obese kid in boxers flung sweat off the stage, spastically growling, blood trickling down his chin. Mongo tried jiving with the chords to no avail. A tornado of elbows, boots and bald heads swarmed the pit. Alvi kept scanning and caught a familiar face: Chester leaned against a side wall, chomping ice with droopy eyes. Alvi screamed once the song scratched, waving him over.

"Heya, Alvi."

They shook hands.

"Seen her yet?"

"Nah, they go on next though." He turned to the bar. "'Nother scotch an' milk."

"Ugh," said Alvi.

"Got a ulcer, kid. Ain't that bad—smooth."

Mongo cleared her throat.

"Chester, this is Mongo—Gabby's roommate. Mongo—Chester."

"Nice to meetcha."

"So you da old dog Gabby be runnin' wit?"

He smirked.

Mongo sipped beer through a straw, sizing him up, scoping his thumbs.

They stood for a while, trading concert tales. Chester told them how rock was dangerous back in his day. They humored, carrying on like old buds until the stage lights came back. Amplifiers reverbed as three slovenly girls strapped instruments. The crowd gazed in silence. Guitar, bass and drums—sans singer. She wasn't there.

Mongo turned to Alvi. "Told ya. So much fo' rent."

Chester said, "I don't get it. She was on cloud nine about this gig. Somethin' ain't right."

Alvi watched as they tore into a brutal rendition of "We Got the Neutron Bomb."

Mongo said, "What we do now?"

"Wait—talk to these girls. See why they're missing vocals."

They flashed badges to an earpieced lug guarding the backstage door. He nodded before letting them walk through. Mongo was expecting extravagance but found nothing special. Groupie types leaned on strewn equipment, smoking and drinking throughout the corridor. Alvi caught wind of the drummer, walking out a rear exit with a high hat. He followed her while Mongo searched for complimentary booze. The girls loaded gear into a cargo van in the alley. Their liberty spikes were wilted, beaten into submission by on-stage theatrics. Alvi dangled his badge to help out.

"Great set in there, ladies."

Bassist: "Really? Shit felt flat."

The guitarist scoffed, shaking her head. "That was embarrassing."

Alvi said, "I guess you guys sounded a little better with that other singer—whatsherface?"

Skinhead drummer: "Don't get us started on Gabby Gretsch, man."

"Why, she bail on you guys or somethin'?"

"Missed practice all week without even a call. Said she was gonna grab us new mics for the show—shit the bed on that too. Fuckin' flake."

"Fuck that cunt," chimed the bassist.

Alvi agreed. "Gabby Gretsch her real name or what?"

"Stage," said the guitarist. "Like, I'm Barbie Wires." She pointed to the drummer, "That's Christian Reich," then to the bassist, "And Courtney Heights-Cox."

He smirked. "Why Gretsch? You guys call her that?"

Courtney shook her head. "Was big into Rancid, you know? Tim Armstrong plays a Gretsch Country Club—least that's why she told us. We wanted her to be Syd Precious."

"Any you know her real name?"

The three shook heads or raised shoulders.

Alvi began to load the kick drum when another van pulled beside. The girls began to leer as the Kill Dads unloaded their gear, heading towards the stage. Alvi knew the singer, Punch Roberts: skateboard legend, SoCal punk pioneer. Sold a bunch of his decks for rent over the years.

Punch noticed Alvi while rushing inside, "Good to see you ain't dead, Rat! Look like hell!"

Alvi patted his stomach, "Went Vegan."

Punch gave a salute. "My ass!"

That peeked the girls' interest.

Barbie said, "How the fuck you know Punch? You in a band or something?"

"Used to skate with him, as a grom—back in the day."

"That's so fucking cool, man!"

Alvi shrugged and turned to go back inside.

Courtney barked, "Hold up." She held out a blue paper square. "If we'd known the bitch was gonna flake on us, woulda made different flyers for our show next week. Should roll out."

He scanned the small sheet: four band names, an address. Behind rude lettering was a picture of Gabby, gazing back in a slight profile shot, Mohawk wild as her makeup. Barely recognized her. "Cool. Nice to meet you girls." He went to fetch Mongo. Found her at the bar with Chester, hoisting a Keystone sixer. "Free beer!"

Stage lights dimmed as he told them what the girls said. Mongo handed the flyer to Chester.

"Gretsch is bullshit. We're back at square one on the name."

"Forget it," said Mongo. "I'm done with the bitch."

Alvi turned to Chester, somberly shaking his head at Gabby's picture in disbelief. Could see the guy's heart slice in two. The Dads grabbed gear to start their set.

"Chester, if she comes back, you can reach me at the Hotel Lafayette—on Beverly." The old man nodded, handing back the flyer, returning to his drink. "Come on Mong, let's bounce."

As they passed the stage, the band started in. Out the speakers came, *We'd like to dedicate this first song to that fucker right there!*

Alvi could feel the blatant stares; few hands patted his head and back. He tried to ignore them. *Shit!*

Mongo took notice, sending a shocked O-face.

Let's hear it for the skate god—Ratboy Drake everybody!

The audience roared as shrieking chords and pounding beats shook the walls. Alvi put a hand up in gratitude, pushing Mongo out towards the parking lot, straight through the front door.

Her barrage of questions was endless. He paused before starting the car.

"You a big celebrity, *Ratboy?*" She laughed, slapping his shoulder. "Why ain't you tell me, foo'?"

"No—it's just…" He stammered, relinquishing all of it—the past life.

"Just what? Betta tell me everythang."

Everything? The engine puttered. "Let's go somewhere first. Tell you more over drinks."

Alvi parked the Mercedes on Grand, just shy of 9th.

"Why you gotta take me into downtown fo' a drink, Alvi?"

"Come on."

She followed as he crossed to the Stillwell Hotel. Neon climbed its corner like a giant white slug. Below sat Hank's bar, tucked in the lobby. They marched under green awnings. Place was brighter than your typical dive, still cozy. Red tiles sandwiched aged wood finishing. Above the ancient cash register read, *Hank's, the last of the great neighborhood bars.* Only vital signs were three tepid goldfish. They took corner stools before a bubbling juke. A walking pencil emerged from an adjacent room. Soon as he noticed the customer, his bucket of ice slipped, thudding the floor.

"No fuckin' way—Rat!"

Alvi approached for embrace.

Mongo watched as the two monsters hugged like combat vets.

"Long time, Guy."

"Shit, man. How the fuck you been. Startin' to get bad thoughts 'boutcha."

"Been okay, man. Livin' off Beverly, you know? Rampart."

Guy's head bobbed before glancing over Alvi's shoulder.

"That's my friend-slash-neighbor, Mongo—Mong, this' Guy Blisko."

Guy wiped a wet palm before extending, sizing her up. "Pleasure. You a rockstar or somethin'?"

"Nah, baby. I just sparkle."

Guy smiled and marched behind the bar. "What'll it be, huh—the yooj?"

Alvi nodded. "The hell is everybody? Could barely grab a seat last time I was here.

"Oh, you know—*the glamorization a downtown.* Sparkly new bars for all the loft yuppies. Sports pub 'cross the way don't help neither." He scanned the shelves and clapped once. "Got some more Maker's in the cellar. Don't go nowhere!"

Mongo waited for Guy to turn the corner. "Fuck's this, Alvi?"

"Used to be home, fourth floor single—before the Lafayette. Guy brought me in; let me stay on the arm—folks own the joint. Grew up together—skated on the same team."

Guy re-emerged, snapping red wax off a fresh bottle. Triples slid down in deep tumblers. Guy poured a third and held it out. "To old friends, huh?"

They clanked glasses and swilled.

Mongo fanned her cheeks as the burn trickled down her core. "So, you a pro skater like Alvi here?"

Guy smirked. "Shit—twenty years ago. Rat ain't never talk 'bout me?"

Alvi chimed, "Mongo just found out 'bout *Ratboy.*"

"*What?*"

"When I left here, decided to keep it under wraps, you know? Needed a vacation from everythin'—from *myself.* Thought I could become a new person or somethin'. Fuckin' stupid, right?"

"What was wrong with Ratboy Drake? Shit's your livelihood, son. Everythin' you ever worked for. What—you embarrassed now 'bout bein' a legend?"

"Don't use that word."

"Eat shit. It's true."

"Was just out there skatin', man—just like you. We never thought 'bout fame back then. Just having fun, right? While it lasted."

Guy filled another round.

Mongo sipped this one. "Tell me 'bout Alvi back then—got me beyond curious, hun."

Alvi shook his head. "I gotta pinch a loaf."

They watched him exit into the lobby.

Guy pulled up a stool. "Met in kindergarten—back in T-Town. Think we startin' skatin' 'round…seven or eight—stole two surfer's boards when they were paddling out at Burnout." He chuckled. "We were blue collar babies. Askin' for skateboards at Christmas just wasn't in the cards, you know?" Amber fluid danced past his lips. He burped and reached for the bottle.

Mongo waved a hand over her glass, good for now.

"So, yeah—we got pretty good pretty fast. Think we were twelve when everythin' took off. Had a big crew back then. Skateboardin' was really startin' to blow up. Used to ditch school all the time to hit up anythin' we could get our hands on—pipes and pools mostly. That's how he got the nickname."

"Ratboy?"

"Yeah." He smirked. "Most pools we'd skate were near Rat Beach. Alvi found most of 'em—he was a fiend, man. Could smell concrete like a bloodhound. Made sense though, he was the best out a all us. Just *fearless* when it came down to it. He'd try and pull shit that seemed impossible just for the fuck of it. Still haven't seen anyone so reckless on a board.

"Didn't take long for him to get sponsored—was the first out a all us. Told Santa Cruz he wouldn't skate for 'em 'less I was on the team too. That's Alvi for ya. Loyal—friends first. You seen his board?"

"One with a rat Jesus or somethin'?"

"That's the one." His eyes moved to the far wall before

pointing to a bright deck on a trophy shelf. "That was my model."

Mongo analyzed its unique shape and illustrations: Mud flap girls, gargantuan breasts, beer cans spelling BLISKO.

They laughed.

He continued. "Seriously, the next ten years were a blur. Travelled the world together. Time of my life, man—sex, drugs and *Rock an' Rolls.*"

Mongo squinted.

"Uh, a Rock an' Roll is when you hit the lip of a ramp and—"

"Don't worry, babe. Just keep goin'.'"

"Yeah, well—shit was good. Money was rollin' in—each had our own signature shoe, man—Vans. Fuckin' surreal. Alvi bought his Ma a house with the dough. I helped my folks invest in this dump."

"Sounds pretty gravy to me?"

"It definitely was a blast but there was a downside for sure. Dropped out of school really young. Couldn't really grasp the concept of the amount of money that was coming in, you know? I lucked out by having parents who invested for me. That wasn't the case for Rat. He ever talk 'bout his Ma?"

"Nope."

"Well, Rat's Pops was killed in a crane accident on the docks—Mona, his Ma, was pregnant with Rat at the time. Sweet lady when I first met her—kinda quiet, always reading gossip rags with her boxed wine. Figured havin' a son as wild as Rat just wore her out, you know? Wasn't 'til the money came pilin' that I saw who she really was.

"'Member this one time, we'd just flown in from Brazil and Mona was supposed to grab us at LAX, right? We were beat as fuck, just got off a six-week tour, practically zombies from all the flights and partyin'. Anyway, no Mona—never shows up. We grab a cab and on the way, Rat asks the dude to swing by Rebo's—this Redondo haunt she used to hang most nights. Soon as we pull into the lot—*BAM!* A shiny red Corvette: leather interior, chrome wheels, the works. License plate read

RATS MA. That was the first time I ever saw Rat cry, man. Shit was heavy."

"So what, she spent all his dough?"

"Practically—took her to court once he turned eighteen and, like, divorced her, you know? I dunno any other way to put it. Was kinda curious if he'd mentioned anything about her to you. Last I heard, she'd cleaned out the couch and found Jesus."

Mongo's shoulders hunched. "Why'd you guys stop, then—if the money was that good?"

Alvi walked back in.

Guy cracked a Bud. "Hear that, Rat? Your pal here wants to know why we quit."

"The Dark Ages?" He craned to Mongo. "We didn't. Skatin' quit us."

A customer in a disheveled suit walked in and sat at the far end. Guy went to serve.

Mongo remained blank. "How you goin' git fired from a life a leisure?"

Alvi reflected. "The whole scene just rolled right over us. Evolution. Street skatin' got big in the mid-nineties and we couldn't really adapt so, we got kicked out the back door. I mean, we tried to evolve but…"

"But what?"

"I guess the drugs didn't help that work out. Lost our sponsors, friends—everythin' dried up. Don't get me wrong, everyone was on somethin'—speed hit the scene really hard. Some of us just went pro on that shit instead; from *Skate and Destroy* to just plain *Destroy*."

Guy approached. "Talkin' 'bout *The Spiral*, huh?"

Alvi nodded in his drink.

Mongo asked, "You two let that stuff get in the way a ya dream? I could never let somethin' get in the way for me."

"Nah," said Guy. "We'd already lived the dream. The thrill of it," his hand fluttered, "had all passed. Needed a new kick and it was all right there, waitin' for us. Everywhere we went, anythin' we wanted for as long as we wanted it. 'Specially if you were with Rat here—fuckin' Master a Ceremonies."

Alvi smirked. "And look where that got me."

"Shit, don't act like you're the only casualty a that war. Rest a us fell pretty far too."

"Yeah, I know—but I'm still fallin'."

Guy topped Alvi's glass. "What was it you used to tell us—whenever we'd get down, thinkin' we was gonna get booted off the team?"

"Make your destiny—try harder."

"That's it. Remembered that nugget while doin' my stint upstate. Hit the bottle once I got out but steered clear a the rock that locked me up in the first place. Now, I ain't top a the world or nothin', but shit, Rat—looks like it's time to take some a your own advice."

"If only it were that easy."

"Easy as you make it."

"Partyin' ain't my problem."

"Shit's always been a problem. What's the thrill nowadays?"

Mongo said, "Women."

"Oh," Guy rolled his eyes, "I get it. *Angie*." He turned. "Hope you ain't still tryin' to save every gal comes 'round, man."

Mongo choked. "Angie?"

Alvi lit a smoke.

Guy went to grab it from his lips. Alvi smacked his hand.

"Ah, fuck it. Smoke away, dick."

Mongo grabbed Guy's forearm. "Wait a sec. Who dat?"

Guy's eyes scanned the room, fixating on the bucket, now still with water. "Look at that. Gotta re-stock some ice. Rat can tell ya 'bout all that mess. Done talkin'."

Alvi puffed away till Guy was gone.

Mongo lasered his profile.

He exhaled upward. "Angie was the wife."

"She the one in dat picture?"

He tapped ash on a napkin, nodding.

"Sooo?"

The juke spun at random: *Sheeeeee—had to leeeeave…*

"So, nothing. *Was* my wife—now she ain't." Alvi tossed a scrunched twenty from out his pocket onto the bar and took the smoke outside.

Mongo headed for the restroom. "Whateva den! Be like dat. Best not leave without me, *Ratboy!*"

Alvi lit a fresh grit with the previous butt's cherry, waiting in the car. Mong wanted to know about the skate life and now she knew. The rest wasn't for her. *Rest wasn't for anyone.* He gazed at the tattered hotel tubes, humming like a madman in the 2ⁿᵈ Street tunnel. Maybe if he'd told Guy the truth all those years ago—moment he showed up with bags under that same dreadful *bzzzz*, the perception of his marriage would be different. Not better, just…different. He took a long drag and remembered why he decided not to. A pity party was always pathetic. He tranced at blue lips of smoke, wafting before him, pretending it was the old soul waving a white flag, drifting, drifting…

Those eyes. That party at The Pad. Could have gone to Frog's to catch The Descendents but didn't. What if he had? Would they have crashed into each other somewhere else? Didn't even know who he was. First one not to call him Rat in years. Everyone assumed they flew blind; it was obvious they were hitched from the get-go.

Ditching the South Bay made sense. Demons were on the rise again. Angie always had a thing for the old haunts of L.A.— could feel the city in her bones. Found a place in Koreatown: The Gaylord Apartments. Was best for her, he remembered. Whatever kept her well was the only option.

That day at Langer's. Spicy mustard splashed about her cheekbones, pastrami flying out his mouth. Hand in hand around McArthur Park as the sun dipped behind billboards, glistening spring drops about the lake. She snapped shots of busted rooftop neon, just as they sparked. Wanted to do a book on them. He'd drive boulevards till she was satisfied with every snap. That smile. That giggle-snort-giggle. Her happiness was his; the city, their Eden.

Angie on that ladder, clinging Art Deco wallpaper behind a white cradle. She'd heard the phonecall; he didn't have to speak. Money was money. The right thing to do. Who'd have thought his era of skating would be back in demand: deck re-issues, shoe reproductions, etc. Nostalgia spun gold. Had to cash in.

That day, flying in from Japan. One cold kiss. Bags under her eyes. The city was only kind when they were together. "One more tour to go and that's all, honey. Gonna fly me back before the third trimester." He couldn't have known what lie ahead…right?

Tour hit a snag in Toronto. She wouldn't take his calls. Landlord said she wouldn't answer the door but could hear her inside. First sight of the apartment was startling. Shattered glass floors, cradle busted to tiny bits. No sign of her. No note. Just scarlet spotted toilet paper crumpled in every room. Hospital calls brought bubkis. He went to take a piss and saw. Demons on the floor: a charred bottle cap, gunk swabs—crusted life blotting tiles.

Those creaking wood steps to the roof. She was in a Ratboy T-shirt, nothing else, babbling to the green GAYLORD neon. Her thighs were crusted crimson, gut skinny, arm bitten with scabs. Reality hit hard, expelling air from his lungs. He wanted to know the whys and hows but the mind went void. Mumbles of abandonment came as she collapsed, eyes swimming, rambling in his arms: "It took him! Took our baby! It's a beast with a downtown heart, Alvi—living and breathing—the streets are arteries." Her eyes rolled; the light was fading.

Tossed her in the tub but she still took the turn. He slapped and shook. His soul watched at a distance, paralyzed with fright. He held her as she faded, water raining upon them: a cold blanket of death. One final whisper…

"The neon lights...they're veins, Alvi. The Neon Lights Are Veins."

A hard tap came at the window, startling the cig from out his fingers. He fished for it around his crotch, cranking the handle.

Guy tossed the crumpled twenty at his face. "Know this shit ain't good here, man. Look—didn't mean to piss you off. Sorry."

Mongo slid in shotgun.

"Ain't you, man. Been on edge lately."

"Yeah, Mongo just told me 'bout your friend. Shit's fucked. Hope you find her."

"We'll see. Thanks for the hooch."

"Anytime—hey, you remember the old Malibu Castle?"

"In North Redondo?"

"Yeah, I had that miniature golf birthday there that time."

"What of it?"

"Just went belly up, man. Me and the boys are gonna bust in and skate the moat—once they drain it. Gonna be killer—you should come."

"I dunno."

"You gotta. All the old crew's rollin' out."

"Yeah okay, you know where to find me now. Just give me a heads up."

Guy gave a chimp grin. "Fuck yeah—holdin' you to this, ya know?" He reached through the window and met Mongo's nails. "Was nice meetin' ya, doll. We'll be seein' each other. Keep this cocksucker in line, will ya?"

Alvi lurched the car forward, forcing Guy to pop out after a few steps. A middle finger in the rearview brought a smile as he gunned the wreck towards home.

15.

The frozen eyes and frothy mouth didn't hold their attention as much as the syringe jutting from a dug-out vein, zigzagging from the girl's left nipple. Satin and Holt's heads gave Labrador tilts, studying the monstrous bust riddled with track marks, matching the girl's arms and neck. These bricks of Xalisco tar were no fucking joke. Holt's guys had already cut the load six times with sleeping tablets and coffee grounds. Ray gave a complementary hit to Daphne. Knew she was hooked. Came into her room to see how great the shit was and found her like this, naked on the floor, thumb still glued to the plunger. Holt wanted a gauge on the potency, and that's exactly what he got.

"Have to cut it some more. That's a good thing—more profit."

Ray squinted at Daphne's chest: giant squid eyeballs. "With fake ones that huge, why jam needles into 'em?"

Holt knelt down to inspect the lopsided anomalies. He poked the right one. "A fix is a fix, Ray." He rose, open palm at the door. "Shall we? Mayor will be here shortly."

Ray secured the deadbolt.

They exited the apartment complex, heading to a stage set-up in front of King Carne. A large banner hung behind a podium proclaiming, C.T.F.: Cockfighting Task Force. News vans cluttered the adjacent parking lot. A half dozen camera crews polished lenses and white balanced; reporters looked over notes in caked makeup, laughing. Satin's crew wore matching polos featuring a giant rooster on the back. Cursive names covered their hearts. They loitered at the entrance of the store, awaiting his arrival. Holt sped towards a limo, pulling up in the distance. Ray approached Dom.

"He inside?"

Dom nodded, "Just like you asked."

Ray turned to see the Mayor waving at the media, porcelain veneers glistening in the sun. Inside the store, Rocco poked fingers through a rabbit cage, taunting a bite.

"Rocco Felix!"

They embraced with a half-hug handshake.

"Wanted to see me?"

"Yeah, how you feelin'?"

"Good—hunnerd percent."

Ray handed an envelope stuffed with three large.

"What's this?"

"For the pick-up. Holt was satisfied—wanted you to have it. Kang got his own cut."

"Thanks."

"Gotta 'nother one for you—give ya heads up in the next coupla days."

"More dope?"

Ray nodded. "Oh—one more thing." He took out the apartment key from his pocket. "Girl in room 56—you'll see. Be careful. Wait for nightfall, after all the media leaves. Drive her here." He brandished directions. "It's up in Griffith Park. Holt's guys will be waitin' for you. They'll be handling these little formalities from now on. Looks like your days of dumpin' just went bye-bye."

He nodded.

"Know which apartment that is?"

"I'll find it."

"It's in the same building as that bitch you was with last night."

Rocco paused. "Freddie told you?"

"Ain't no thang, nephew. Can dip into all the pussy you want in here—just not *Gabby*. There's a reason she's on lockdown, hear me?"

He played it off. "Yeah, didn't even think about that. Was drunk, she was there—you know?"

"No worries. Just slide that dick into somethin' else."

They smiled. Rocco turned to leave. Ray's words stopped him.

"Girl that Gabby came here with tried to rat me to the cops. Too bad she didn't know they've been in our pocket since I took over the casita."

"What you mean?"

"Holt approached me months ago—guaranteed the po-po would look the other way, long as we accommodated some of the Mayor's business buddies. I agreed and look at us now...approaching untouchable."

The door swung open and Dom said, "Mayor's ready for you."

Ray cinched his tie, snapping fingers. "Showtime!"

Commuters zoomed through the Rampart intersection as Rocco leaned against the Golden Lock & Safe shack. Was gonna take about ten minutes to copy the universal apartment key Satin gave to access the body. Figured, might as well have a copy of his own since he wanted to see Gabby again; hell-bent on it. Something about that girl lit a fuse—felt weird inside, couldn't describe it. Maybe if he'd tasted love before it'd be easy.

He scoped the adjacent mini mall, burning minutes. Signs reading *Dentista*, *Lavanderia* and *Panaderia* quickly squashed any intent of a cocktail. School children entered the intersection, holding hands behind a chaperone like a row of ducks. They marched past a vagrant soliciting his booklet of short stories to scared minivans. Rocco fixated on a white seagull, hovering high above, wondering why it made its way out here. *Didn't it know this place was more rotten than toxic sewage shores?*

"Is done, *señor*," said the man surrounded by hanging blank keys.

"*Gracias, amigo.*"

He grabbed them and made for the car, contemplating dinner. Eating wouldn't be an option after another body. Fatburger triumphed.

The apartments were empty: B-girls fresh on shift. He snapped latex gloves and entered 56 with caution. Flies flew from out the mouth of the poor gal. How could he forget those warm bags of sugar? Gabby was right about one thing, Daphne's tracks swirled like a trail of ants. He carefully removed the syringe, placing it in a paper burger sack. Ray called earlier: Holt's crew needed all the evidence. He wrapped her in a blanket; pillow cover over her stone face. Carrying her to the car was a bitch, all awkward and top-heavy. The Escalade was in the side courtyard, next to a dumpster. He slid her in back, just like Vanda and fished for Ray's directions.

The paper said to take Canyon all the way up from Franklin and park at the final gate. Rocco cruised up the residential block, lined with Craftsman's of all colors. The body thumped over wide speed bumps. Foliage grew dense further along, jacaranda pedals making violet carpets. He was wondering how much these houses went for when a sight sunk his gut. A stocky policeman stood at the park's first gate, ushering him with a flashlight. The cop beamed through rear windows as he rolled by. Rocco watched in a side mirror as the guy barked into a shoulder, re-closing the gate. Holt's crew had him scared for a sec.

A patrol car sat in the destination lot. He parked beside it and got out. The young officer in the car met him with a handshake. Name plate read McCorkle.

"You must be Rocco. Already scoped the perimeter. Got a place for her up about seventy yards. We're first on scene—gonna call it in 'bout an hour after we get everything set up. You know if we gotta burn *this* one?"

Burn? Rocco perplexed. "Nobody mentioned that to me."

"I'll double-check on it."

The gate cop wheezed from running uphill to them. He was Sandoval. A call from dispatch said fire wasn't necessary this time. She'd be filed as Jane Doe.

McCorkle walked ahead with the burger bag as Rocco and Sandoval carried Daphne upwards into the wild. A defunct reservoir was to be her OD scene. A giant dragon mural spanned a far wall of the concrete bowl. Sandoval slid down, feet first, body draped on his shoulder. They propped her accordingly, splaying the blanket and pillow case before setting her down. McCorkle forced her fingers around the plunged rig. Rocco emptied the bag: a spoon and burnt matches fell between her thighs. They stood back, checking their work for authenticity. McCorkle and Sandoval smiled at the monstrous bust.

Sandoval: "Looks tits to me."

McCorkle laughed, grasping his utility belt.

Rocco was halfway up the reservoir before they noticed, wanting nothing more to do with them.

A pencil-bunned waitress burped another cup into his coffee mug. Rocco gave thanks without peering up from the English Department pamphlet he was lost in. Each of the introductory courses looked appealing; options for studying abroad torched his brow. The cover featured a thin white girl reading *The Day of the Locust* in the campus' sculpture garden. *Seemed pretty happy.* As he reached for the mug, Daphne's blue skull blipped over the reader's face. He slammed the pamphlet on the table. How the fuck was he going to put an end to all this?

He gazed out the café window, sipping the mug, studying strange accents on the Hollywood Tower apartments; glamorous yet mysterious—a moon-soaked specter. Place flew straight off the silver screen. Its grandeur smudged once Rocco tried brainstorming a way out. Couldn't concentrate—was useless. That shit cop's words pin-balled his noodle.

    'Know if we gotta burn this one?'

    …Burn?

    —This One?

He clawed his eyes, noticing the waitresses through finger slats, staring back behind a wall of donuts. He gave a faux grin and mimed for the check.

16.

Six hands did the job. Alvi held Lexi's shoulders while Noodles and Vargas each grabbed a leg. They had her splayed atop the Zimba's bar. Mongo hurriedly stitched the gaping wound, no longer flapping over Lexi's right eye. Doreen and Faye watched behind the bar, cringing at pools of blood. Elvira kept rattling the incident like a busted string doll.

"A bachelor party—six of 'em. Wanted Greek for their boy. Lexi got in the limo first. It pulled off without me! There was nothing I could do!"

Alvi: "Where were you guys?"

"Santa Monica and Sycamore. They drove 'round with her for an hour, taking turns. Must've struggled. Tossed her out on the corner—where I found her."

Lexi wailed, sobbing as Mongo threaded the needle one last time. Her face was going to need more ice. Alvi dropped three coffins in her mouth, avoiding broken teeth, swabbing her face with a paper towel. Mongo shook her head at him, sanguine hands raised like a surgeon's.

Noodles: "What we do now?"

"What you mean—nothing we can do," said Mongo. "Let the poor gal heal and just be more careful next time out. That's it! Boulevard breeds danger. We all know dat. She lucky it ain't worse—like *Vanda*."

Vargas tossed his beanie and screamed, "I'm over this shit," before heading outside.

Noodles followed as Alvi and Mongo helped Lexi to the couch. Elvira sat beside her with the ice, pressing cubes gently to her swollen face, tears falling onto a torn cardigan. Lexi stroked Elvira's thick forearm with busted nails, letting her know she'd be okay.

Mongo turned to Doreen. "Back in da day, when the Grim Sleeper was killin' hoes in South Centro, we had a code to let girls know dat trouble was brewin'. We'd scream out, *Shit's Fucked!* Then everyone would come beat some ass."

Doreen bobbed her head at the concept.

Mongo turned to the other girls. "Let's do dat, awright? If you in a bad spot, from now on, call one a us—out on the street or by phone, howeva—let somebody know that *Shit's Fucked*, okay?"

Everyone nodded, grimacing at the thought.

Alvi made it to his room after three in the morning. He popped an Oxie, Beam back. Had the bottle stashed under the cot for special occasions. Nothing special about tonight though, just stressed. He tossed his shirt and pulled the flyer out his back pocket, gazing for a few slugs before taping it next to Angie. In his boxers, the bathroom mirror barked. Blue tattoos bled about his chest, ribs and stomach. A crucified rat blurred over his heart. He stood, swilling, wondering what had destroyed that kid in the poster on the wall. Pretended not to know. What if that kid saw the future like this? *Probably best he never had that son with Angie after all.* Was selfish to wish for a family. This world was no place for the innocent.

Opiates bucked hard.

Gabby's picture cried, *Find me, Alvi...*

Angie's begged, *Do it, baby, do it...*

He placed a kiss onto each before crashing the cot, motionless in a numbing daze, anxious for sleep but the mind reeled.

A knock came soon after, snapping him into slight consciousness. "Gimme a secon'!" Took three tries to get up and answer. The walk to the door was like balancing in high seas. He squinted at the hallway light, studying the hazy outline of Faye, barefoot in a long Garfield T-shirt. *Another dream perhaps?* She patted his stomach and came inside. *Guess not.*

"Hope I didn't wake you—couldn't sleep."

"That's okay. Got somethin' for that."

"Can't get Lexi's face out my mind—all that blood."

"That was one of the worst I've seen." He flicked the light and went for the pill jar, fishing an Ambien at the bottom. The light switched back off. He turned.

Garfield was on the floor.

Suddenly, she was there, wrapping strange arms around him, planting a long hard kiss to his rubber face. The act caught him off guard but he reciprocated, squeezing her soft curves. She guided him to the cot—Oxie still grinding him senseless. They groped—licked; felt like days. She moaned commands, breath sweet and minty. Gently mounting, she guided him in, biting his lip once fully plunged. Tight, warm, welcoming. His fingers pinched the base of her rump; she rode, eyes closed, hands high, clutching those fiery locks. He watched her lip curl over and over, stealing one-eyed glances at Angie and Gabby on the wall. *Vixen voyeurs.* He transfixed their faces onto Faye's, one at a time, as she raced to climax.

Angie: *Fuck me, baby! Come on!*

Gabby: *Harder, Alvi, harder!*

Faye began to spasm.

Angie.

Gabby.

Faye.

He struggled to hold his mud through kaleidoscopic bliss, cum spouting in bullet bursts. Lightning struck; all sensation abandoned his crotch, blood flow retreating. He knew not to panic but the opiates were winning. He mustered a magician's will, commanding the cock back to stone. *Work, dammit—WORK!* The dope advanced some more.

Faye stared down, confused at his peculiar facial tics, brushing away beads of sweat.

Alvi went from the ropes to canvas—no standing eight, just a flying towel. Defeat. He tried to ignore Faye's blank expression while slipping into blackness, snoring, beyond mush inside her.

City lights. Abscesses of neon cluttered major arterials—far as the eye could see. A glorified wasteland twinkled to one pulse, coursing in waves. Alvi scanned the panorama, reaching out to pet puss-filled tracks engulfing America's right arm. He could touch 'em—pluck 'em like scabs. Their electricity brought life to his bones. High voltage. He stepped towards them before realizing he was mid-air on a gargoyle stoop, high above Hollywood Boulevard. His arms flailed, teetering on the brink. Nothing around to grab onto; the Pantages' tubes crackled and snapped, lashing out to supply one final jolt. He tumbled, arms flapping dead wings, head first towards those splendid sidewalk stars.

The impact was nil, body slapping the Earth like salami to bun. He stood and dusted his digs: a black tailed tuxedo, spats over wingtips. He paused at names on the stars. New Beverly Cult Dynamos: Timothy Carey, Tura Satana, Divine...

"Hey, Ratboy!"

He spun but no one was there.

"Up here!"

The Frolic Room puffed a cigar, wearing a brown derby.

"Yeah?"

A green tube extended like a charmed cobra, pointing towards the barroom door.

He paused at the fuming signage, carrying on like a curmudgeon cabby, cursing every red light on Vine. The cobra tapped his shoulder, re-directing. He snapped the bowtie and headed inside.

A crashing high hat, hot brass—everything full swing. He

cased the smoky room, clamoring with laughter and clinking glasses. In attendance—the greats: Dietrich, Costello, Keaton, Fields…The Hirschfeld mural was alive—spirits to the moon. Rye now in both hands, he was flanked by Lorre and Harlow. They laughed with their whole bodies as Harpo fondled Mae West, honking to the beat of the kick drum. Life was gay, frivolous. He was pushing towards Chaney and Bela when the music waned. The room clung frozen around him: empty eyes, plastic smiles—a Polaroid of ghosts glaring straight through him.

Movement came hard—concrete boots. Each step more rigid than the next. The bathroom door flung open, expelling a radiant amber cloud. A voice beckoned: sweet, friendly, familiar. He struggled towards it amongst the stone frenzy.

Through the jamb, an exotic gateway. A deep galaxy of celestial light—an outer realm. Strange scenes suddenly conjured then dissipated, ad nauseam: the Easter Bunny instructed Michael the Archangel in dismembering demons, slice by slice; A Black Christ broke bread with a table of Lafayette degenerates. Was this Heaven? He went for a closer look, careful when crossing over, shoving an arm through first. Upon touch, he was sucked in.

The door slammed behind. Floating, he swam through void spectrums. Everything felt cold, a gel consistency, hospital scents. That sweet voice resonated. A woman greeted with open arms in the distance, her aura blinding till up close.

"Ma?"

Her arms wrapped around him. "You are lost, son."

He shut his eyes. "I just need more time."

"It will be too late. Save yourself."

"Dunno how, Ma."

Her arms grew and grew—suffocating; binding taut wires. The more he struggled, the tighter they clenched. Ribs cracked, organs throbbed. And suddenly, she was gone. His clothes now strapped in jailbird stripes. A giant cage slammed out of nowhere—shrinking, shrinking. He tugged at the bars…

Cold sweat. Alone and naked, Alvi clenched his skull, brain throbbing; the nervous system a fireworks spectacular. Five more coffins and back to bed.

Morning came and Faye was gone. Noon had past and he was up, swabbing fingers around his crotch, taking a whiff. Their romp was all too real. He sat up, shaking his head. Knew better than to succumb to lust with another broken girl, especially when he couldn't remember most of it. He fought to stand up, nuts throbbing, weighted like eight-balls. Guess he didn't get off either. Four coffins and into the shower. When he got out, Mongo was rummaging through his jar, short kinky hair matted up like Buckwheat.

"Got any Xanies? I'm fresh out."

"Don't think so. Take whatever you need though." He slid into some pants and lit a smoke. The new tank of gas was settled and ready to be strained.

Mongo popped Norcos and sat on the cot. "What you got goin' tonight?"

He noticed one gold lash still stuck to her left eye. "What you got in mind?"

"Gotta ante up. Looks like you nearly out too. Let's hit up the connect."

He exhaled a cloud, glancing over at Gabby, trying to forget the situation. "Sounds like a plan."

Mongo rose. "I'ma get dressed and call him."

The connect worked at a pharmacy across from Pink Elephant Liquor. That's where he liked to meet up, not wanting co-workers hip to his afterhour activities. Alvi slid into a spot out front, magenta beams washing up the silver coat and windshield. He went inside for smokes and a short dog of Cutty. When he came back, the connect was in the back seat, chatting up Mongo. Name was Burtie—least that's what he told them.

The usual transaction involved Alvi giving Burtie a ride to his apartment off DeLongpre. Pretty low key. While on shift, Burtie pocketed pills here and there to slang on the side; took orders from only a few select clientele. Said skimming was easy with a head pharmacist zonked out on his own doses, fudging inventory sheets accordingly. Alvi and Mongo met him through a mutual acquaintance. Burtie yakked it up about his next big movie pitch, not yet on the page but gold nonetheless. He was a screenwriter, legit in the sense that one of his college buddies scored a directors gig but ditched him just weeks after moving out to help work on it. Regardless, he remained in high spirits, insisting knowing the jerk opened doors.

"And then," He poked Alvi on the shoulder, "Listen to this, dude...the head of the whole platoon—one that charged them up the hill, right—dude was *dead* the whole fuckin' time—got blown up on a previous mission."

Alvi rolled his eyes as he parked out front of the bungalow apartments.

"Well, what you guys think?"

Mongo lied. "Sounds better than *The Dirty Dozen*."

Kid was ear to ear exiting towards the abode.

Inside was your standard twenties-built box: rotting wood, cracked tile kitchen—a bacteria's dream. Burt rummaged through drawers, pulling out vitamin canisters filled with prescription meds. Mongo sat ladylike on a folding chair, smoothing wrinkles on her silk geisha dress. Alvi paced the living room. A frame on the TV held an autographed napkin. Never noticed it before. He picked it up, studying the scribble over circular brown stains. Looked phony.

"Where'd you meet David Lee Roth?"

The kid came back with four large bottles and a box of Ziplocs. "Uh, over at the White Horse."

"Bullshit."

"Hey, man. Would I lie to you?"

Mongo pursed her lips.

The kid laughed. "Seriously, this was about six years ago.

Diamond Dave was on the outs, man. Strolled into the bar when me and my boy were shootin' pool. Chilled with us all night, dude. Told us how Eddie plays that intro to 'Hot for Teacher'—it's really not that hard."

Alvi plopped on a bean bag, smirking.

"So, what you guys want—same as last time?"

Mongo: "Sixty bars."

Burtie poured a heap of Xanex onto a Fangoria issue and began counting. "What about you, Alvi?"

"Take a hundred ES, fifty Percs, fifty Norco—some Oxies, if you got 'em."

"Got it all, sucka. Guys got anything new for *me* this time?"

The rub.

Main reason they bought their shit here. Burtie was beyond curious about their "Street Adventures." Took notes of their stories to use for future projects—wanted to do a big screen piece on "The *Real* Hollywood." Gave a hefty discount the more they spewed. He snatched the pills for free, didn't sweat a few bills, long as the material sang. Alvi and Mongo each grabbed their baggies. They'd already rehearsed the story about Lexi and the bachelor party on the way over. Mongo had a gift for thespian theatrics, always taking the reins. Kid grabbed a crinkled yellow tablet, eager to jot whatever they said as truth. Alvi wondered if next time they'd be regurgitating this whole Gabby fiasco.

Mongo stood, lighting a cig. "Check it. This one's called Bitch Bachelor Party Beatdown..."

Faye sat at the Lafayette's front steps, hugging her knees as a stray lapped gutter water. Her hand reached out to the mangy mutt, thumb poking through a chewed hole in her sweatshirt. Pooch bolted after balking a sniff. She rose as the Mercedes pulled behind a busted Econoline, across the street.

Alvi immediately took notice. "Shit."

Mongo gasped. "That girl thinks the world a you, Alvi. Practically begged me to hook you two up. Don't be like dat."

"It ain't *her*, Mong. She's fine—just the timing's off, you know?"

"Yeah, dat's what I heard 'bout ya fuckin' her too. Timin' was off." She gave a crazed laugh while exiting and hollering at Faye. Alvi trailed in the distance, hands in pockets, wishing invisibility. Mongo bolted through the doors, leaving them in her dust.

Alvi gave a flat, stupid wave. "Hey."

She smiled. "Hey."

Both of them blurted, clashing into jumbled nothing. She giggled.

"No please, go ahead," he said.

"Just wanted to say sorry about last night."

"Why—what for? I should be the one apologizin'."

She stepped down to street level, brushing against him. "Dunno what got into me. Full moon or somethin'. Shouldn't have attacked like that." Her eyes closed and words trailed, leaning towards him ever so slightly.

He quickly pulled out Parliaments. "Smoke?"

Her eyes burst open. He pressed one to her lips and sparked a match. Its orange glow revealed small piercing dimples on her lip, nose and eyebrow.

"Listen—I was pretty fucked up last night. I really like you though—but I just…shit's a mess right now, you know?"

She grinned, gazing off in the distance. "No—totally."

He sparked and took a drag.

Faye re-animated. "Oh yeah! Before I forget, some lady came by earlier, asking 'bout you."

"Me? What for?"

"No clue. Figured she was a creditor or something—told her I'd never seen you 'round here."

"What she look like?"

"Short, older lady—curly black hair."

"Huh?" He flexed the brain.

"Yeah, well—I gotta roll to the liquor store, so...need anythin'?"

"Nah, I'm good. Thanks."

She flicked the smoke towards the street and bolted down the sidewalk.

Alvi ascended inside, jangling keys for the mailbox. The gold tin slot was crammed with coupon ads and a new Thrasher. That was a first. No Ma. No salvation.

Inside the room, he thumbed through the magazine, tossing it on the bed, accidently knocking over Vanda's box perched at the corner. He knelt to gather up the papers and came across an address through a windowed envelope. *Mr. and Mrs. Irving Maples...Whittier, CA.* He reflected a beat and tossed it aside, gathering the rest of the box.

His stack of Erma articles sat crunched atop the dresser. He rifled through, scanning words upon words for that city she'd absconded. There it was—he was right. She and Vanda both hailed from Whittier. Not too big a town. Might've known each other. He looked at the flyer of Gabby, thinking, *You from there too?*

He grabbed the gas tank and headed out. Needed to fill-up before cruising out in the morning.

17.

Holt's Glendale warehouse sat snug in the corner of a dead-end street, trapped on all sides by condemned structures that once employed hundreds. Mayor Reynaga gave a campaign speech on economic reform amongst them, exploiting the visual. That usually did the trick. Throw a suit in a slum and it always made front page.

The place was made of tall, rusted metal, perfect for stacking product to the rafters. Rocco, Freddie and Primo hauled crushed Jumex boxes to the trash bin as Ray and Dom secured re-cut bricks into canisters labeled King Carne. Holt passed instructions on when to come and what to do. Ray had the boys look at it as their rite of passage. They were all in line for a tremendous future thanks to these men. Now was the time to prove they could handle it. Dom backed the flatbed into the loading dock, moon low and smoky.

Rocco said, "We taking all these tonight?"

Ray recounted the canisters. "Eight should do 'til next week. Holt's already got guys lined-up for a couple drums each." He headed over to Dom, telling him to take the load over at daybreak.

Rocco turned to Freddie and Primo. "Why you think Holt wants us to move all this through the shop?"

Freddie's good eye darted. "To hit the streets with it, stoopid."

"Yeah, I know—but why our place? Why not *this* place?" He turned to Primo.

"We don't ask those questions, mang. Neither should you."

They lifted a canister onboard.

Rocco said, "You know, our necks are on the chopping block too—if things go south."

They mean mugged him.

Rocco headed outside. Caught Ray climbing into the Escalade and called out.

"What's up, Roc?"

He leaned through the driver's side window. "What's the deal with all this tar? We're delivering *and* moving it now?"

"Is that a problem?"

"I'm just thinking, is this a smart thing to do—stocking up the store with all this?"

"Listen, nephew. The goods will only be in our possession for a few weeks. Running the H out the store allows Holt's clients to operate freely in the daytime—so he says. We're just a short-lived middleman, that's all. A Mid-City transfer point. Believe me, I don't wanna be messin' with this shit either, but under the circumstances…"

Rocco hopped inside and fired up the engine. "I'm just trying to watch your back, you know."

"Yeah and I appreciate it—but you gotta trust me on this. Partnerships involve give and take—compromise. Hell, Holt said Fitzie's is gettin' taken out this week, kid! We're bangin' on all cylinders! Everything's fallin' into place."

"Okay…okay."

"Your pops used to run all kindsa dope out the store, back in the day, before any casita. Don't have to worry about the cops or nothin' this time."

Rocco nodded, thinking, *And look where he ended up*, as they crept through a graveyard of machines, moonlight sparkling off giant chrome rims.

* * *

Rocco gave a gentle squeeze to Gabby's ribcage as sunrays peaked through the downtown skyline. The view atop the apartments was sublime, just gorgeous tips of the urban jungle, nothing streetside to dampen the mood and kill the fantasy. They'd been huddling on the rooftop in blankets each morning since Rocco made the key, playing it safe not to get caught together. She nestled under his chin, stroking forearms so warm around her. He kissed the top of her head as she watched beams break through buildings, beckoning her towards them, calling to her. *Soon enough*, she thought. Rocco broke the silence.

"Kinda feels like we're in a bad movie, huh?"

"What you mean?"

"You know, *this*, right now—me holding you as we watch the beginning of a new day."

"I guess it has a cinematic feel."

"Not the view alone but, you know, when combined with our situation..." He mimicked a Moviefone voice. "Forsaken lovers, trapped by the confines of a world gone cold."

She giggled. "I wish this were a movie. Then we could write our own ending—do whatever the hell we want—instead a being stuck here, forced to meet like this."

"I hear that."

"Can't just find a way, huh? So it could be like this...all the time." She stroked his thigh.

Rocco reclined, placing hands on cold tar shingles. Crows squawked from a telephone wire. "I wish that too but..."

"Don't you want to grow old, have babies—all that stuff? I mean, that's always been *my* dream. To settle down in a house with cute kids and a dog named Georgie."

He smirked at the picture in his brain.

She looked up and saw. "What you thinking about?"

"Nothing—I mean, that sounds great but it's just not in the cards right now."

"Why not? You're a smart guy—handsome. Could have whatever you want."

He swung his arms back around her. "I know what I want."

"Well, it's yours, honey. All you gotta do is *take* it."

They sat quiet for a bit, his lips rubbing the fuzz on top of her ear.

He whispered. "This is all new to me, Gabby. I—"

He checked his watch.

"—Shoot! I gotta go, baby."

Before he could pull away, she grabbed hold of his arm, spinning on top of him and smashing a warm kiss. He reciprocated, turning it into more. Wanted to stay like this but knew better. Had to make it back to the pool before Ray hit the tennis courts in order to sustain their schedule.

She smiled, eyes bright green planets, pigment trapped by tiny yellow rivers. He explored each with wonder.

"Imagine we're not up here right now, okay? Now close your eyes."

He did.

"Pretend we're far away, rolling on some strange beach in the south of France. We're beyond wealthy without a care in the world. You bring me those flowers I love every day, and I cook your favorite dish—maybe a little burnt sometimes. Only thing that matters out here is you and me—*us*. We're free there, Rocco—a team."

He smiled before opening his eyes.

They gazed into each other some more before she abruptly got up and headed towards the door.

He stood and gathered the blankets. Her back was towards him, wiping an eye in the distance. His gut churned. Would be another twenty hours before they could do this all over again. Each day, the hours grinded slower and slower. If this was for real—that thing everyone talked about—what lonelyhearts longed for—then he had to get busy.

* * *

After the usual string of errands with Ray, he had a few hours to kill. The campus bookstore was filled with unkempt co-eds, unloading used books before spring break. Rocco weaved among them, trying to get in the book stacks for a copy of *The Day of the Locust.* Might as well delve into the curriculum firsthand since attending wasn't an option. Found it. He grabbed a Fodor's guide to France and perused while in line.

Marveling through the sculpture garden, he pondered modern art eccentricities. The catalogue cover guided him to the exact spot. He plopped down at the base of a nude female figure, cast in black. Students and faculty mingled on the grounds. A good two hours of daylight remained, enough reading time to take him away before meeting for the next pick-up. He analyzed the novel's first page, only lasting a few sentences before his mind wandered back to the other book on France. He thumbed through, envisioning Gabby at every landmark, him behind the camera, a finger in every shot. Then a thought popped in his head. *What if Ray was gone for good?* He drifted in daydream, wondering how it could happen before snapping to. How could such a thing even be considered? How damaged had he become in these past hellish months?

The club was empty. Cowboy decorations blasted Ho-Down Night. Rocco could hear Ray's voice coming from the office. Overheard his name, pausing at the base of the stairs, inching step by step, trying not to creak.

"So that's what you're gonna tellim, okay? He don't listen to me—now shit gets real. I want his bitch gutted, nice and slow—"

Rocco stormed the door, catching surprised faces on Ray and Freddie at the couch. Ray smiled.

"Roc, you're early."

"What you guys talkin' about?"

Freddie's eye floated north. "Just talkin' business, son."

"Thought I heard my name. What's up?"

"Must got wax in them ears, nephew. We're talkin' 'bout the club—bullshittin'. That's all." He tapped a drink with his finger. "Prolly heard me say 'On the rocks' or somethin'."

Rocco took a second and nodded, brushing it off. Maybe he was mistaken. Scared him how emotions ran red when thinking about not seeing her again.

"Truck's out back," said Ray. "Freddie's ridin' shotty with ya."

"Any more surprises this time—drops?"

"Just a straight up haul, same spot, same old thang. Better get on. Don't wanna be late."

Rocco turned to head for the door when he caught a reflection of Ray nodding to Freddie in one of the windows. *Something was definitely up.*

18.

A brisk morning sky hovered in pearly grey as Alvi passed through the Eastside, cruising down Whittier Boulevard. A liquor mart, pawn shop and church clustered the same block, greeting him on arrival. Whittier's pulse felt faint: Drab homes yawned to the serenade of busted sprinklers, cars on blocks lie shackled in weeds. A loose Chihuahua darted up the sidewalk, sprinting for freedom in minuscule strides. Even the pets here got the same itch as Vanda. Couldn't blame them.

The Maples' house was a standard one-story wood and stucco. He was careful selecting clothes this morning, donning long sleeves and a Dodger cap to conceal his ink. He parked across the street, glancing at the envelope to ensure he had the right place. He waded through a row of wilting rose bushes, up to the red front door. A doorbell lullaby didn't spark any response. He leaned over the side of the porch, trying to peer through a front window. A voice shouted from afar.

"They're not home!"

He turned to see a tiny blue-haired Latina, standing on the neighboring porch.

"Hi there. Do you know when they'll be back by any chance?"

"Wha'?" She cupped an ear.

He approached her yard. "I was wondering if you knew when they'd be back!"

"Oh, no. They've been gone for days now. You're not the poleese, are you?"

He grinned. "No, ma'am. Just a...family friend. Why do you ask?"

"They've come by every day now."

A kettle screamed from inside, starling the old woman.

"Excuse me, *mijo*." She pierced the doorframe and looked back. "Would you like some Sanka?"

"I'd love some."

The home was cluttered with old lady trinkets, mostly mail-order junk from the backs of Penny Savers. Alvi sat on a brown floral couch, admiring walls riddled with family photos. Most were amateur black and whites featuring chest puffing Chicanos, hardened in front of lowriders. The woman approached with two steaming mugs. She noticed his hands when he reached out.

"Got a lot a tattoos, huh?"

He gave a soft smirk.

"You a jailbird?"

"No—never."

"My sons are."

She pointed to a portrait, resting atop the wood framed TV. Couple of burly *vatos*; the cheap fireworks backdrop suggested Kmart deluxe photography.

She stirred her coffee with gentle twists. "You're a friend of Stella's oldest daughter, no?"

He took a quick sip. "Yeah, my name's Alvin."

She squeezed his hand. "Cecilia."

"I came down here after...findin' out."

"*Pobrecita*. She was always such a good girl—when she was little. Didn't deserve such tragedy."

Alvi gazed solemnly at the floor in agreement. "You mentioned police?"

"Mm-hmm."

"Because of Vanda?"

She shook her head, "Her *familia*. All three of them have vanished. I told them everything I saw but they still haven't a clue. Big shocker, right?"

"What'd you see?"

"Some strange men—three. They came a few nights ago in a real flashy car—silver—one of those you see in the movies, you know? I saw someone pulling into my driveway—lights off. They backed out, parked in front and went next door."

"You've never seen these men before?"

"No. I didn't hear anything suspicious once they were inside either, but no one has seen them since. Something is *wrong*."

Alvi nodded and sipped more decaf.

"This is all because of the streets, you know? It calls to them—these kids. I know it firsthand."

"Because of your sons?"

The old woman's eyes began to glaze. She focused on arthritic hands for strength. "My daughter."

Alvi perked with interest, afraid to inquire. Luckily, she kept on.

"They left together—her and Vanda." She rose and retrieved a gold eight-by-ten from the next room. She kissed the cold glass before holding the frame to her heart.

Alvi wanted to jump out and grab it; Cecilia's movements were painstakingly slow. She handed it over, shaking.

He only needed a glimpse. His eyes met back to hers.

"My Erma," she said. "The streets got her too."

Mint leaves and parsley made love to meatballs with rice. Three flour tortillas helped Alvi sponge *albondigas* broth as Cecilia told him all she knew about her daughter's exploits while on the lam with Vanda. They'd left senior year, two months shy of diplomas. Erma had a thing for Pin-ups; her bedroom plastered with Varga and Elvgren. Cecilia saw the stars in her eyes and got scared, prayed. With her sons in prison, never once did she think that Erma would run away. A daughter would never leave their mother to a cold empty home. At least that's what Cecilia thought. They'd shared one last churchgoing, lighting candles for those sick or locked-up. Erma clutched the rosary she'd had since birth, like always. She gave Cecilia a kiss on the lips before bedtime. The next morning, she and Vanda were gone.

Alvi wiped a napkin and reclined in stuffed comfort. Cecilia walked to her bedroom and returned with a clipped newspaper ad featuring a dolled-up Erma, splayed seductively on a leopard print rug. It was for Cheetahs, a low-rent strip-o-rama on Sunset.

"That was the last evidence I had that she was okay…before." She quickly grabbed his plate and took it to the sink.

"Did Vanda work here too?"

"They both did. Irving was the one who gave that to me. He'd found them working there and managed to bring Vanda back home, but only for a few days. He said Erma ran once she saw him. That was nearly two years ago."

He placed the clipping onto the table. "Do you know if there were other girls from around here that might have left with them?"

"No—not that I know of."

"Does the name Gabby sound familiar?"

Her crow's feet scrunched. "Why?"

Alvi rose from the chair. "She went missing with Vanda too."

The woman grabbed her chest. "*Dios mio.* Is she…also?"

"I hope not—but that hope's runnin' thin." He made for the door. "Thank you for everything. My condolences on your loss."

"Mine to yours, *mijo*—for Vanda. You mustn't think that way about the other girl, 'til she's found. I'll pray for her safety." She kissed a gold crucifix, dangling around her neck. "Vanda and Erma only wanted to live life on their terms. I can see that now. Still, someone took that away." She untied her apron and approached, arms out.

He hugged her, remembering the softness of an elderly

squeeze. He thought of Ma.

Cecilia patted him on the back, whispering, "Sooner or later, someone will find the *cochinos* responsible, and they will pay. Lord knows it won't be the poleese—God has his own vengeful ways."

The radio was tuned to a.m. stations for the ride home. Alvi was trying to catch the hours' top news stories, hoping for answers. A broke down school bus had gridlocked the 405, clogging airwaves. He reached to flip the dial; hand trembled, stomach did the Twist. He managed to pop in a Kill Dads cassette. The Benz floated over the 6th Street Bridge into downtown. Three coffins helped calm busted nerves. Had to chew them though. Mouth was dry as the concrete river below.

He detoured up Sunset, cruising by the Paradise, scoping for Chester's Rambler in the lot. *Nope—must be workin'*. Liquor Royale waved up ahead, its King Cobra sign winking through barred windows. *We meet again, old friend.*

Grabbed a *Times* at the counter, checking the front page before noticing the date. He smirked, shaking his head. This was a first. Was usually everyone else's birthday he forgot. *Thirty-fuckin'-eight*. He grabbed the clanking paper sack, pocketing fresh smokes, thinking, *Light upstairs is dwindlin', old boy.*

A child approached the counter, grimy hands ransacking a licorice jar. Mom was having trouble holding twin boxes of Merlot.

"Get yer hands outta dere, Jake! Come help."

"Ah, just a couple?"

"I said, no!" She set a box down to smack his skull.

Alvi got goose bumps: familiar pains of youth. The cashier sprinkled change. He left it on the counter, nodding towards the boy. "G'head, kid. Grab all you can for eighty cents."

"Thanks buddy!"

A grin washed over Alvi as the kid clawed the jar with filthy black nails. One of those things he'd wished would've happened, back then.

Mother sent Alvi scornful eyes, floating crunched dollars for her supply.

"Sorry, lady—struck a chord. Your boy reminds me of someone I knew."

She prissed.

He winked at the kid, whispering, "Don't worry, Jake. I turned out all right."

Out the parking lot, Alvi's need for the bottle nearly had him crash into a walking man, shirtless and leathered. He sighed, cursing stupidity before soldiering on. Had been a while since he drove this stretch in daylight. Signage for a foot doctor spun up ahead; a sad foot with arms and legs wobbled on crutches. Tried to remember the last time he was welcomed by the happy healthy foot, on its flipside.

The short dog cracked at a red on Sanborn. He hunched over for mouth numbing nips; friendly drips burned the esophagus. Surrounding sidewalks were alive and hip. Slender bodies rotted in magnificent sun. Sunset Junction had newfangled charm but Alvi missed those pre-gentrified days. He fixated on a flamboyant stud, weaving through idle commuters, waving a baby chainsaw, screaming, "Five-bucks, people! Who wants it?" This peddler had been around for years, living in a gypsy commune behind the Jiffy Lube. Usually carried a rainbow flag, wearing only cut-offs, always slanging something odd for survival. By the flabbergasted looks towards today's appendage slicer, the bargain seemed a no go. The peddler couldn't care less, swinging his sharp toothed apparatus like Townsend at Leeds. Was nice to see something remained wild on the beat.

The pill-booze punch began to swell. His stomach felt right again, hands could build model airplanes. Rest of the ride home became a slow blur of ruby taillights. Alvi licked his lips and scratched a welcomed tickle on the nose, thinking, *Back on top, baby.*

* * *

Night re-cloaked the city, returning comfort. Alvi was overly productive in his party zone. Just finished scrubbing the bathroom and was gently packaging each of the skate decks for shipment when three knocks came at the door. He snuffed a Parliament into a crumpled tallboy before answering. *Please don't be Faye.* Through the peephole, Doreen stood sketchy, arms crossed, chomping violently on a pink wad of gum. He flung open the door, wafting in cotton candy Bubblicious.

"Alvi! Come on, we gotta go! Mongo needs our help—down in the Zimba."

"Wait—what's up?"

"Alls I know is that it's urgent. I think Mongo's in big trouble or somethin'."

"Shit—okay, one sec." He grabbed a flannel off the floor, slid into kicks and rushed out past her.

19.

Freddie was silent the whole drive down, still napping as the rancheros loaded fifty boxes in back. Rocco locked the load after verifying bricks. The cab door's *slam* jarred Freddie back to life.

"The fuck, ay? Mess up my beauty sleep."

Rocco sneered.

"Lemme drive, fool."

Rocco had no complaint, eyes burning—scratchy. Sun would be up in a few hours. He yawned while exiting, heading around the rig. Freddie slid over and sparked the beast to life, punching it towards the freeway.

"Slow the fuck down," said Rocco.

"Shuddup—don't trip."

Rocco slapped himself awake. "Pull over."

"Nah."

"Ain't asking, *pendejo*."

Freddie's gold tooth glinted, bum eye milky with discharge.

"Can you even see that road, man? Pull the fuck over…now!" Rocco deked a fist.

Freddie flinched, laughing as he pulled a Glock from out his jacket and leveled it back. "Thought *I* was da pussy, ay? Should see your fuckin' face right now."

Rocco's palms shot out. "Just playin', damn."

"Me too, homie—this' how *I* play doh. Same as Ray play.

Just 'cause you his blood don't make you shit, son." He took quick glances back at the road, careful not to leave Rocco to his thoughts. Roadside lamps flickered inside the cab. "Just 'cause shit falls into your lap don't mean you get respec'. I earn my shit. Ray tells us to respec' you—but we don't. You a weak punchline, dog—a wet *pedo*. So, you dump a few bodies—big fuckin' deal. Why should we respec' you? You don't respec' Ray—or us—the operation—bein' all scandalous with that *puta* you be fuckin' wit. Ray tol' me today. Her *amiga's* the one tried to fuck us, and you ain't even trippin'! Tell you what, I ain't even trippin' too, dog—that shit'll get straight soon as we get back. No respec'? Then we gotta teach you, fool."

"Damn, that sounded pretty hard—*big* man."

Freddie stewed.

"Most wetbacks butcher the English language—not you, Freddie. That delivery—cadence...I dig it—could almost get what the fuck you're talkin' about?"

"Talkin' 'bout you, stoopid. Things are 'bout to change, ay. That *puta* ain't gonna bring no prolems no more."

Rocco chuckled, "Bullshit. Maybe you ain't half as dumb as them girls say you are."

Freddie puffed up. "Keep talkin' that shit! Bitch Vanda got it easy, homie. You'll see."

"Yeah—yeah." Rocco's hands slid behind his head to nap. The mind raced, contemplating what lie in store upon their return and better yet, what to do in the meantime.

Nearly an hour had passed. Rocco came to, sneaking peaks at Freddie, hauling away; gun still in hand but resting on a knee. He gave a few more snores, peeping the peripheral. The Inland Empire was a landfill. Freeway was damn near dead, cars every few minutes. Rocco waited for oncoming headlights to pass. Freddie yawned. He attacked.

Freddie's grip tightened soon as Rocco grabbed the gun

handle. A shot blasted the windshield, spraying a glass web. Grunting and snarling, they struggled in deadlock; a second report punctured the roof. The truck swerved from lane to lane. Rocco gained upper hand, the barrel staring at Freddie. Rocco twisted with all he had. Freddie winced, abandoning the wheel so his other hand could help. Rocco glanced at the road as another round fired. Before he could grab the wheel, the rig tipped down an embankment.

In quiet and grace, he could almost hear angels.

The force crunched him against Freddie. Blackness overcame. He awoke covered in glass, the side of his face wet, body aching. Slowly, he propped himself, grasping the steering wheel. Freddie was frozen, neck limp with a gunshot through his good eye. A ruby cascade pooled below. Rocco checked his limbs and torso before finding the Glock, climbing out the windshield and collapsing on damp soil.

Wailing sirens hit him with a bolt of adrenaline. The neck pain was horrendous, rocketing up his skull, down the spine. He used both hands to brace, walking from the first off-ramp into a residential neighborhood, searching for a hose. Cold water on his face proved the blood wasn't his. Just some shards in a palm. Jacket was soaked but his shirt, pants and shoes barely had speckles. Luck never got old. He pilfered each pocket before tossing the coat into a curbside trash bin. The Gucci sunglasses were toast but his geek specs only lost a limb. He propped them on, dialing a cab on his cell.

The hack first stopped at a twenty-four-hour Rite Aid, meter running. Roc sprang for bandages and a neckbrace. Clerk gave him a *Rough night, buddy*, look. He smiled, glasses dangling on his scraped nose.

"Will that be all, sir?"

"Got any Chivas back there?"

"As a matter of fact we do, sir, but we're not allowed to sell alcohol for another hour."

Rocco tossed a hundo on the counter.

The clerk grabbed the hooch and slid it into a paper bag.

It was another one of those dreams where she was headlining the Palladium when a coarse hand over Gabby's mouth woke her from backstage debauchery. She began a muffled scream before noticing it was Rocco, roughed up with a finger to his lips.

"Shhh." He removed his hand.

She touched the neckbrace and giggled.

He gazed back puzzled before handing her a coat. JaTonya snored naked from the bottom bunk. Didn't have to go in close for a whiff—whole room reeked of low tide. They exited quietly, heading for the roof.

Dawn streaked the sky into shades of sherbet; clouds had eyelashes. They embraced.

Gabby looked him over and worked up a sob. "This' all my fault."

Rocco grabbed her by the shoulders. "No it's not—now listen, we're in a lot of danger right now—I have a plan to get us out of here, okay?"

"What happened to you?"

"Right now, that's not important. We don't have the time but I'm okay—okay?"

Her lip quivered.

"Before we go any further you need to level with me."

She nodded.

"Do you love me?"

She choked words. "Completely—I do. Never felt so alive."

He squeezed her, "Me too," planting a kiss. "I need you to be honest with me, baby. I know you know more about this shit with your friend Vanda than you're letting on. She threatened to go to the cops about something—but what? Tell me what you know—everything."

"I don't want to drag you into this."

"Look at me, Gabby! I'm already buried, soon as we run. We're a team, remember. France, beaches—all that stuff."

"Okay, honey," She rested her head on his shoulder, collecting herself. "Vanda said it was just an idea—didn't think she'd do it. Then everything shot straight to hell…"

THREE

The Underground Web

Second Sidebust...

Albuquerque, New Mexico—A Sunday, 9:33 a.m.

The Hawaiian Punch ring 'round Shasta's mouth was the least of Colt's worries. Her best church dress was now soaked bright red. Lottie Mae snickered as Shasta licked clown lips, squeezing her favorite stuffed elephant, powder blue, maimed with only three legs. Being Daddy sucked balls today. A voice came over his shoulder. Colton, what have I done told you about feeding these dolls that garbage. A rotund woman swiped three donut holes from Lottie Mae's hand and kissed her on the cheek. Grandma, give 'em back! The lady stuck out her gray tongue and deposited each, barely chewing twice. Ma, think this stain'll lift? She hunched over for a closer look. Might be able to pull a number on it. Heck, I just bought her that last Christmas! Colt stood, bleeding napkins in hand, exhaling, trying to regroup. Stay calm. Preacher Evans waved at him from the coffee cakes. Colt forced a smile. Nothing like kid chaos after Mass. He thought about how life was beforehand. The wife in her pre-delusional days. Could taste the love when his phone began to blast Pantera out his Dockers. Was either Tommy or Cal. Shit. Ma, keep an eye on the girls a sec. She gave uninterested eyes. It's fuckin' work, Momma! Don't swear near the Lord's house! He rushed out to the parking lot, leaning against his 'Stang, flipping the cell. Fuck's wrong now? Cal: Usual boss, gotta use the Cat to prop up the whole lot over here. Lobos lost their ass, and they gon' done it again. Colt pulled the phone from his ear, giving a swift kick to his Nitto race tire. Tell Tommy to sit fuckin' tight, okay—no drinkin'. I'm on my way.

The sight was sickening, smell even worse. Colt pulled into the construction site, Cat on a trailer behind. Those bastards had to tip over all twenty port-o-johns? Cal and Tommy were on chairs in the back of the company's busted Silverado, sippin' Schlitz. Colt approached, snatching a brew flung at him, mid-air. Thanks for stayin' dry, fellas. Tommy flashed tobacco teeth. Cal peered inside the 'Stang. Girls ain't witchoo? Naw, at Momma's. You guys seen who done all this? Tommy said he thought it was them boys from Louie's Bar, but he ain't sure. Tommy shrugged, Lobos lost by a field goal—heartbreaker. Colt popped the brew. Good lookin' out, boys.

They unloaded the Cat, agreeing afterward for the mess to be cleaned by rookies, coming on shift in an hour. Eighteen crumpled beer cans littered the dirt. Colt knew he should be heading on but this was the closest to Happy Hour he'd been in some time. He grabbed five cans and fixed them on a fence post in the distance. No one lived 'round for blocks, figured he'd have some fun, heading for the glovebox. Tommy and Cal were arguing over Mannings when the first shot shut them up. Colt fired another, this time killing the far left can. Two more squeezes and two more kills. Cal shouted, Hell, Colt, ain't never seen you hit four in a row since weez in high school. What's the trick now, only a deadshot when yer soused? Colt relaxed the piece and waved for another beer. I just pretend it's the wife's face and let 'em fly. Shit hasn't failed in almost two years. Tommy asked, She still ain't back, man? He shook his head, thinking, Prolly fucked the whole damn world by now. That day he caught her blipped back in the brain, guilt dripping down her thigh. Cal's words snapped him back. Sorry to hear that, big guy. No worries, buddy boy. She best stay gone, 'less she wants some-a-dis. Another blamm sent the final can flipping like Mary Lou Retton.

20.

Alvi sped down stairs, barely grasping the rail, leaping every fourth step. The Lafayette was eerily quiet for a Tuesday night. His mind thought the worst, naturally. If Mongo was hurt or in trouble—*fuck*. He was prepared for horror, flying outside, dodging a stained mattress, gripping the Zimba's front door and slamming it open.

The sight had him startled. A jumbled sea of familiar faces, all crammed around Mongo holding a blue frosted cake.

"SURPRISE!"

The hum of a harmonica broke everyone into song.

Alvi's face went lax, expelling a deep sigh. He buttoned his shirt as the ditty belted. Ronnie patted him on the back as Maribel led the chorus, baritone. Noodles and Vargas clapped around a fresh keg. His head did a number, the walls spun. Everyone was there: Bootsie, Dita, Faye, Elvira—Lexi with her eggplant eyes. Even a few folks he hadn't seen in ages, old neighbors at the Lafayette. He tried not to blush while blowing candles. Almost forgot to make a wish. He smiled at the warm inscription and rainbow sprinkles, basking in the love that drenched the room. Mongo put down the cake and delivered a monster hug as the party kicked into full swing.

***

"So that's when the fucker slashed me."

"For using your teeth?"

"Can you believe that? Here I go, thirty fuckin' years on the street, thinking I'm the blowjob queen a Hollywood, and this bastard cuts me for giving him the same suck Blackie Lawless got!"

Alvi busted. Hadn't seen Durty Jerzy in over a year. The woman was a riot, fashionably disheveled with a tat reading *Lick Me Wet* above her left tit. Hard lines added fifteen years to her face. Used to slum down the hall from him, always bumming smokes. He grabbed her chin, analyzing the scar down her neck.

"Ah, ain't so bad."

"That's what the Handsome Man says." She poked the ribs of an elderly black man beside her, perma-grinned, sporting two walking casts and a gold cane. "To hell with both you fuckers. Momma needs some milk." She grabbed her man's hand, ushering him towards the keg.

Alvi turned into a bear hug.

"Look at you, baby boy! All grown up and shit."

Bootsie.

"Ha! I knew I smelled somethin'."

"Oh, fuck you, bro. Tell you what was smelly though." He hoisted three fingers. "Dude, this Portugese chick stayed at the hostel last night and—"

Someone tapped Alvi's shoulder. He turned to see Faye, holding a present. "What's this?"

"You get gifts on this day, right?" Her cheeks dimpled.

"Guess so."

"Well...open it already."

He tore at the flat rectangle, wrapped in today's funnies. A book: *Los Angeles Neon*. He lit up and flipped through, ignoring library stamps on the first page. "This is fuckin' amazin', Faye!"

"Thought you'd dig it."

Their eyes met.

"I really appreciate this—means a lot. Thanks."

She leaned in and pecked his cheek, whispering, "Happy Birthday, Alvi," before heading back to Lexi and Elvira, giddy in the distance.

Alvi watched her hips bounce through the crowd before returning to the cover, finding the author, pretending it was Angelica Drake. He smiled, approaching the keg for another pint. Noodles and Vargas chugged Robitussin as Ronnie riddled them jokes.

"So these two lawyers are walking along the beach right."

Noodles eyes were beyond bloodshot. "What beach?"

"Doesn't matter—any beach. So they're walking along and notice this woman, fully nude, sunbathing all by herself."

Vargas interrupted. "Wait—this supposed to be in Cali or like some foreign land or what?"

Ronnie sighed. "Just shut the fuck up and listen to the joke, okay?"

The boys smirked, trying to get serious.

"So this bitch is nude right, spread eagle on the beach. One of the lawyers turns to the other and says, 'We oughta go fuck that chick.' The other lawyer turns to him and says, 'Yeah, but *outta* what?'"

Yuks out Ronnie and Alvi were met by blank stares from the boys.

"That's a killer! Right, Alvi?"

"Pretty good." He spun, trying to find Mongo. She was grating pills at the bar. As he approached, another blast from the past cut him off.

"Happy Birthday, kid!"

"Shit—long time, Charlie. How goes it?"

They traded skins, Alvi patting Charlie's cracked leather blazer.

"Been good, you know? Got me a jobbie job, bussin' tables at Miceli's."

"That's rad, man—good for you. Still writin' music, or what?"

"Nah, got a honey with a boy on the way. You know how that goes?"

Alvi paused, frozen smile.

"Where's your girl, man—whatsherface—punker chick?"

"Gabby."

"Yeah, you still with her? Man, I remember the first time I saw that chick—"

"Broke up awhile back."

"Damn, kid. I'm sorry—didn't mean to hash shit up. Just figured..."

Alvi contemplated laying out current events but the mood was too jovial, first time in a long time. "Yeah, me too, man. Sometimes things just go south."

"Because a her job, right?"

"That stuff never really bothered me. Just...some messed up shit went down, you know?"

"Heard that. If my honey ever stripped at Cheetahs, I'd prolly drop her ass too—that afterhours club they got is fuckin' nuts, man."

Alvi was puzzled; figured Charlie was talking about Gabby on the boulevard. "Cheetahs?"

"Oh shit, you didn't know? I thought you knew, buddy. Fuck, I—I'm just gonna go over there and shove this foot in my mouth. Sorry—nice seeing you though." He turned.

Alvi spun him back. "When she work there?"

"Who cares, you're broken up now—sorry I brought it up, okay?"

Alvi dropped the book and grabbed Charlie by the lapels. "Just fuckin' tell me, man."

Charlie paused, flabbergasted. "Alright—alright, saw her there 'bout a year ago, went in with the guys after a gig. Got a dance, she invited me to this afterhours party—some V.I.P. bullshit, needed to be with a Cheetahs girl to get in. Shit was crazy—blow, box, gambling—you name it. Like I said, if my honey worked there—"

"Where's this place?"

"Fuck, I couldn't even begin to tell you. She took me there, walked a few blocks from the joint. I was high as fuck, kid."

Mongo stood between them. Alvi let Charlie go.

"Everythin' okay here?"

Alvi picked the book off the floor. "We're good, Mong. Listen, thanks for everythin'."

"Ugh-uh—you ain't leavin' awready?"

"Be back in a bit. Just hang tight, alright?"

Alvi pierced the crowd and rushed out the front door. Maybe that birthday wish would come true.

Faye watched with curiosity.

Mongo turned to Charlie. "Fuck was dat all 'bout?"

"Nothin', just some drama about his ex. You got any yay up in here?"

Mongo shook her head in disgust. "Baby, I'm sure somebody do."

Blood trickled down Chester's arm, sweet to the lips. He sucked the drip, loving every drop; same as yesterday, same as the day before. Eyes rolled, nude body stiffening into that comfort zone, falling back to the bed, lungs gripped by conquering bliss. The pretty gal lying next to him tapped a knife to his wiry chest. Was clad in Latex, except for the naughty bits; makeup like six-layer dip. She slapped his face, over and over, bringing him back to their wicked world. He exhaled a pungent burst before smiling.

"Jus' tell me when, daddy. I owe you another turn."

"Give me a minute...princess."

The girl went and sat at the table, swiping a pair of hundreds into her purse before pulling out a glass rose and torch.

"Priscilla."

The rose clanked her teeth. "What."

"How long we been...meetin'...like this."

"Uh, I dunno. Three years?"

"Ever tell ya, you're the only girl...hasn't asked me what it's...all 'bout?"

"What what's all about, daddy?"

"This...the role play...everythin'."

"None a my beeswax."

"Must...wonder though."

"Not really but lemme guess—you're gonna tell me, right?" She lit the torch and cooked.

"I had a daughter...Letty. Met her mom at one of those...hotel conventions...near LAX—one for television repair. Was just a one-night fling but then...then came Letty...my sweet girl."

Priscilla exhaled a clear plume. "You keep in contact? Alls I had was a stepdad—he kicked the can years ago though."

"Never got to see her in person. Just a letter in the mail...with a photo, relieving me of fatherly duties. She took the baby back home to raise alone...hey, that's shitty about your stepdad. I'm sorry."

"Don't be. Fuckin' prick. So wait—you never got to see her in real life?"

His eyes shut. "Huh?"

"Letty."

"Oh...no. Didn't know where to look."

"Seriously? Most dads would've gone to China an' back."

"True...true...not this one."

Her eyes squinted, bewildered for a beat before remembering she was to the moon and so was he.

"And here we are." He waved her over.

She picked up the knife and knelt on the bed, three rings dangling from her clit.

He stroked her thigh, nodding *now*.

She took the blade and pressed it to his jugular. "Daddy, you've been a bad daddy."

"I know princess, I know." His teeth gnashed. "But, I...never...meant to be."

"Be good, daddy. Be good!"

"I can't, sweetie pie. I...just can't."

"Here daddy, let me show you."

Her free hand cupped his cock before squeezing an iron grip, tugging and twisting like a balloon contortionist. With each aching grunt, she applied pressure to the blade, berating him for his misdeeds, spitting on his face. "Shut the fuck up, daddy. Be a *man*, daddy!"

He began to weep when a loud *bang* came at the door. Priscilla shot up and lunged for her purse. Chester wiped his face, giving her a *be quiet* palm, "Who—who is it?"

"Alvi, man! Open the fuck up!"

Chester nodded, letting her know everything was square. "Hold up a minute!"

"Nah, never said nothin' to me 'bout Cheetahs."

Alvi leaned against the TV, thinking, eyes on the fleshy girl cracklin' rock like candy. "She ever tell you where she was from?"

"Not exactly, said she grew up on a ranch somewheres. Moved out here to—well, you know. Was pretty closed up when it came to personal stuff, but she was startin' to open up to me—was a lot more to her than just that pipe dream."

Alvi smirked.

"Seriously, she had a really sweet heart. Envisioned a future with cute kids and a dog named—"

"Georgie."

Chester grimaced.

"Girl couldn't play a fuckin' chord but she sure could strum those heartstrings—when she wanted somethin'."

Priscilla asked, "Who the fuck we talkin' about?"

Alvi packed fresh smokes. "Honey, *we* ain't talkin' at all. Chester and I are having a little powwow—got it?"

She stuck out her tongue, re-loading the rose. "You should do something about that nose bleed."

Alvi sniffled before drops hit his shirt. "Fuck." He went in the bathroom and jammed coarse tissue.

Chester ran a hand through his hair. "So, what's with this

Cheetahs business?"

Alvi brought him up to speed, pulling out the newspaper clippings. Went through them one at a time, summarizing each on the two dead girls, his amateur investigation so far and how Cheetahs linked all three girls together.

Chester scanned the small print, first Erma's then Vanda's. "Think they're related, huh?"

"Seems a bit odd that each of 'em knew one another and stripped at the same joint before going missing—then two of 'em turn up *dead*. I'm not sayin' that Gabby's dead or that Cheetahs had anythin' to do with it—just that it's a startin' point. Somethin' fucked is going down and this' the only hand I got to play with."

Chester bobbed his head. "What you wanna do? Go down there and ding some skulls."

"Guy I know says they have some underground afterhours club—anything goes type-a-deal. Say we head down, grab us a few girls and see what's doin'."

Chester rose off the bed to grab his steel toes.

Priscilla blurted, "Randi works there most nights."

That had their attention.

Chester turned. "What's that?"

"My friend…Randi."

"She a broad?"

The girl giggled, eraser nips at full salute. "Duh!"

Chester turned to Alvi, swapping thoughts via facial tics before asking, "Think she wants to party?"

"Hell yes!" Black toes wiggled as she scrolled through her cell.

Alvi tilted his head back, waiting for the leak to stop, pondering all the knife marks on the ceiling.

21.

Ray whispered into Dominic's ear that tennis with the D.A. had to be rescheduled. He commenced brooding at the dining table, clad in silk pajamas, trying not to yawn. Holt was there, barking into a cell, smearing footprints on the cream carpet with erratic pacing. Dom slid Ray some coffee.

Holt's 'stache swished like a street sweeper as he held out the phone and yelled, "Then fucking *make* it happen," before smashing it through the Wurlitzer.

Ray blew on the mug and took a sip. He cringed.

Holt took notice. "Too hot for you, huh—can't handle it, just like everything else!"

Ray sat silent.

"The accident happened outside county lines. Everything's fucked so far. If it'd gone down ten miles later, this wouldn't be an issue." He orbited the table. "Needless to say, the Mayor's furious."

"So am I."

Holt smiled. "That's good, Ray—I'm glad." He pinched his septum. "Listen, the load is being hauled to the Ontario station. Just so happens, our ties are strained at the moment."

"How so?"

"Let's just say the Mayor's personal life has displeased some San Berdoo councilmen—their whore wives. It's gonna take some cash to make sure we get the shipment back quietly—can't get the Feds involved. As of right now, Ray, you're in debt. Your boy blew a simple run, and it's gonna cost you."

"Was an accident."

"You mean Freddie *accidently* got shot in the face and crashed the rig? Look, I don't know who might be after you or whose toes you've been stomping or how clean your nose is— none of that's my fucking concern. The millions in uncut tar *not* in the warehouse, that's what I care about. As we speak, some snot-nosed flatfoots have their hands all over it—be lucky to get it all back intact." He rubbed his eyes. "Why the hell would you only send *one* man to pick-up the whole load?"

"Didn't think—"

"That's what I thought. Let's just hope everything pans out, okay—for your sake...the casitas, this whole fucking deal, 'cause as it stands, you're more of an embarrassment to this city than Frank fuckin' McCourt." He fished the cell from the juke's shattered glass and headed for the door. "Be in touch, Ray."

Ray blew on the mug. Dom rushed back in the room.

"Anything yet?"

"Still no word."

Ray sipped cautiously. "Gotta go get him then, see what went down." He leered. "Our asses are on the line for this— everythin's up in the air. Go find Roc—don't come back without him."

Rocco took a seat on the roof, Gabby's words burning his brain. The scheme involved Erma—*that Erma*. The past flashed behind his eyes, newspaper headlines twirling. Satin's quick work of Vanda was troubling. Gabby's ignorance had kept her alive, so far. What the hell went down that night with his dad?

Gabby looked on, awaiting a response.

"That girl was murdered beside my father."

Gabby recoiled. "What?"

"She was my pop's girlfriend. They disappeared together—same night."

Gabby stood quietly, contemplating. *Of course!* Rocco's dad was Ray's brother—his *uncle*. Why hadn't she connected it before? *So stupid.* This put her in overdrive. She hadn't disclosed the full truth of the matter to anyone, including Rocco; didn't want to end up like Vanda. Now the stakes had shifted in her favor. Rocco was under her thumb. She had a bombshell on deck. Knew they would come in handy sooner or later.

Rocco was spacing out, popping knuckles like packing bubbles.

She rubbed the back of his head. "I had no idea, honey...I—I haven't told you everything."

Hungry eyes met hers.

"Vanda wasn't stringing Satin along with her blackmail. There's proof—a text message photo. It's a hunerd percent real, and I have it."

He shot up. "Show me."

Gabby gnawed her tongue, digging an arm deep through a slit in her mattress. Rocco stood guard at the door. She pulled out some folded papers.

"Got it."

They scurried back to the roof.

Gabby said Vanda forwarded the text to an e-mail and printed out two copies because her service was being disconnected. The image was as clear as any two-bit cell could muster. A puckering snapshot of Erma, dolled up, eyes far gone. The two men over her shoulder, in the back seat of the car, had Rocco stiff.

Holt.

Satin.

Things were falling together. The time on the text rang true.

These were the final moments before his life derailed. Before his father evaporated from the world—he and Erma, incinerated to dust.

Gabby slung arms around his waist.

Rocco's jaw locked. He pocketed one of the pictures, giving the other back to her. Those words from that shit cop thumped the temples.

'*Know if we gotta burn this one?*'

—*BURN!*

—*THIS ONE!*

Gabby squeezed. "What we gonna do now, baby?"

Rocco ransacked the upstairs lair. Club was empty, except for a single janitor mopping the floor, belting a *norteño* number at the top of his lungs. Satin's desk usually housed the previous night's take; had to count it personally before depositing it in the safe. No time. Rocco's bankroll would only last them so long. This was their one shot to glom a large sum before hitting the road.

Drawer after drawer delivered bubkis. Plenty of B-girl files with background checks, photos, addresses. Satin must have settled things late night. Rocco sat, brainstorming. He rifled through the G files. No Gabby. No Gretsch?

To the safe!

Locked shut. He took one final scan of the lair before bolting back down the stairs, towards the *pollería*.

The lights were dim as the store was closed. Ever since the Cockfighting Task Force and dope hoarding, Satin locked up shop most weekdays. Rocco knew where to hit paydirt. Just as he thought, one canister remained. He cranked the lid amongst animal cries. Ten bricks. Knew the crash had halted any new supply; whatever he took would be missed. His brow beaded, bombed. No time to figure how to unload it. He grabbed two and rushed out.

* * *

Back in the girls' room, JaTonya was still snoozin'. Rocco stuffed the bricks deep into Gabby's mattress. Bedbugs.

"Gotta figure out who'll buy this and quick."

Gabby said, "I might know a guy."

"Who?"

"Friend of mine, a user but he can move it for sure. Might not get street value but we haven't the time, baby. There wasn't any cash in the whole damn joint?"

"Not where it should be."

"The registers?"

"His desk—was only filled with files of the girls."

"Wait—what?"

"Background stuff on all you guys. Tried to grab yours but it wasn't in the G's." He glared back.

Gabby pulled the binky from her pocket and rubbed, weighing options. No file, no harm...for now. Ray could keep copies but doubtful. She sniffed that warm powder scent. Rocco would read it once he got it; secrets unveiled. She took another whiff. *Was worth the risk.*

"You gotta go back and grab that before we bail, baby. He'll use it to hunt us down."

"Where would it be then?"

"Check under Wang."

"*Wang?*"

"I'll explain later—on our plane ride to forever."

Rocco re-rifled. Weintraub, Bethany—Whitley, Monique Z. Fresh paper cuts throbbed. Wasserman, Kimmie. Wagner, Coco K. Where the fuck was it? He scanned profile pics instead; Blacks and Latinas sprinkled amongst white trash. Three more to go.

The Mohawk threw him at first. File was a quarter inch deep. He scoped for the name. Gabriella Wang—

The door flung open.
Dominic: "There he is!"
Primo: "Whatcha doin', mang?"
Rocco set the file on the desk, closing the drawer.
Primo: "You look guilty as a muthafucka!"
Dom: "What happened to you—Ray's been shittin' bricks."
He thought quick and rubbed his head. "I—I don't remember."
Primo: "Don't know how you got that neckbrace, huh?"
He touched the foam. "Nah."
Dom: "Prolly too much bobbin' knob."
They chuckled.
"Fuck you guys—I'm hurt."
Dom flashed a chrome piece in his waistband, eyes rolling. "Ray needs a word—for real."
Rocco contemplated the Glock wedged at his lower back. No time.
Primo strong-armed. "Come on!"

22.

A platinum blonde wormed up the pole, straining for a sec before hitching a bony thigh to snail-trail back down. Alvi got a load of the *Integrity* scribed on her forearm, reflecting off walls of smudged mirrors. He and Chester huddled in a corner booth by the stage. Shit music blared. Priscilla fumbled quarters into a vending machine by the bar. Tonight Jumbo's harbored a questionable turnout: Goths sipping Shiraz, Hipsters howling at burlesque Barbies. Priscilla approached with a bag of Flamin' Hots, pointing a red powdered finger to the stage. "That's her!"

Outside, they loitered at the Rambler. Priscilla mellowed, puffing a spliff. The girl came out, bikini covered by fake black fur; piggies crunched into pink Lucite platforms. They sped towards each other, screaming, arms flailing, the way girlie girls know how. Priscilla brought her over.

"Randi, this' Chester and he's Alvi."

The girl stuck out French tips, tongue turtled. "Randi— pleasure."

Chester spoke, stammering. Alvi butted in.

"Need a Cheetahs girl to get us in their afterhours club. Your gal pal here says you work there."

"Some nights—pick up shifts whenever, you know?"

"You get us in, or what?"

"Sure, how much?"

Chester: "Same as Priscilla."
Randi swayed, lips puckered.
Priscilla handed her the roach. Chester unlocked the doors.
Alvi said, "What's the name of this place anyways?"
Randi exhaled, coughing wet.
He waited for her recovery.
She wiped tears and said, "Fitzie's."

Cheetahs wasn't far. Its color and shape mimicked a giant caramel chew. The cheapo marquee said it all: full bar, bare jugs, faux class. Priscilla and Randi waltzed in. The guys hung back, eyefucked by a hulking Armenian.

"Ten cover, two dlink minimum."

Randi's head shot back in the door frame, winking. "These two are good, sugar."

The bouncer panned back to Sunset. She curled a finger before disappearing inside.

The guts were your typical flesh market façade: dim lights, dark corners—anything to overshadow ass zits for gents. An underlying scent of strawberry lube wafted about. Alvi and Chester sipped MacGregor's and milk.

"Not bad, man."

"Told ya."

Priscilla spent time catching up with hatchet-faced friends. Randi was on shift, lost in dim booths, riding white collars for fins. Fitzie's wouldn't open for another hour. Chester sat at the catwalk as Alvi hit the head, crushing coffin rails atop the toilet, evening out.

At two, they walked south through the neighborhood, hand in hand: Chester/Priscilla, Alvi/Randi. Ancient branches cast each block in dark shadows. A fire engine wailed to life in the distance. Alvi peered over a shoulder.

Randi squeezed the web between his thumb and index. "Sounds like someone had too much fun."

Single-family homes dissipated into rows of clumsy apartments. Nighthawks lurked. Brake lights begged company; a pack of prosties stomped cigarettes, hooting under dim streetlamps. Randi guided them into a trash lined alley. A purple curtain shimmered behind a brick complex. Chester shot Alvi a weird look.

Randi forged ahead. "Boys, if anyone asks, gotta say you're with *Randi Roxx*—okay?"

They pierced the veil. Two men with afros were stationed to frisk, guns holstered in armpits. One scoured the girls' purses while the other manhandled the men. A thumb directed them, once clean.

They descended stairs to a basement. The corridor reeked of mildew—leaky pipes. Another velvet veil and they hit bliss: slot machines, booze, coke splashed across glass tables. Six dudes scattered the room, all random, all wasted. Cheetahs' girls lounged on suede couches, touchy-feely. No dance floor. No music. This place was just for kicks. They posted at the bar.

Alvi saw Chester's glowing face. "Hey, man. 'Member why we're here."

Chester tightened up.

They each played the part, trolling the club, their girls in tow, partaking in this, dabbling in that. Bartenders and dealers shook hands and smiled. Alvi told Randi to point out Fitzie. They gambled on as patrons came and went. Sex sounds resonated from the rear. Hepcats preached, 'That guy who played *Scarface* shot pool here, night before.'

Was nearly four when Randi clawed his shoulder, huddled with Chester at Blackjack.

"That's her."

Her?

Alvi watched as a gal with a pompadour made the rounds, greeting clientele, hugging the help. Chester sat stupefied. This sweet old woman, flanked by knockouts, was the club's number-one boy? She approached their table, embracing Randi with a peck on the lips before sending out a hand. Alvi gripped warm. Fitzie waded past, her bimbos leading towards a far party room.

Alvi whispered to Randi, "Get us in there."

Her name was Nikki Fitz, quite personable from the get go; not all Big Time like most crooks. When it came to storytelling, she was the everyman: longwinded, stammering—get to the fucking point already. Chaining Newports, she rattled tall tales for hours. Felt like days.

"So the guy finally says to me, 'Fitzie, what you mean', right? So, I—what you call it—flip 'em the bird, tellim ta sit on it and say, *Muthafucker—I quit!*"

Alvi and Chester charmed, sipping Moet on a loveseat across, buttocks numb as their brains.

"So, ya know, that's when I went ta binness for m'self—ain't doin' too bad neither."

"From Denny's to Fitzie's," Alvi said. "Pretty good run."

She inhaled her success, all but refraining from the rich man belly slap.

The girls sat huddled in the corner around a plate of powder. Fitzie's knockouts were playing nice with Randi and Priscilla. Alvi could tell it was getting Fitzie going, unbuttoning her collar, laxing the Windsor.

"So, how long you two know Randi ovadere?"

Chester chimed. "Not too long. Sweet gal, though. Met her through Priscilla."

Fitzie leaned forward. "You tellin' me neither you two fucked that yet?"

They shrugged.

She busted. "Well, when ya do, she's got this—what you call it—trick or somethin'. Holy shit, gal turned me into a sprinkla. Man, oh man! Sure it'll work on peckers too."

Alvi said, "Good to know, honey—but I squirt every time."

They chuckled. A server brought more champagne. Chester

hit the pisser. Alvi shifted gears.

"You must have a pretty mean list goin', considerin' all the gals you got runnin' through here."

"I do okay. Don't hurt bein' da boss neither."

"Don't see too many Mexicans 'round, just about everythin' else though. I remember this one chick, danced at Cheetahs—God, her name started with a V...I can't fuckin' remember—Vanda maybe?"

"Yeah, that's her. Nah, she hit the bricks 'while back."

"Some piece—her friend too...ugh—Gabby!"

Fitzie smiled, champagne bubbles tickling her nose.

"Where they run to?"

"Both bounced to a rival club—some piece a shit off Virgil and Beverly. Hey, forget 'em!" Her finger swirled. "Look 'round, big boy—L.A.'s primo pussy is only here at *Fitzie's*."

He grinned. "Then why'd they leave? These new pretty girls scare 'em off?"

"Didn't ask—don't care. Every day I get some new bumpkins off the bus, beggin' for jobs—fuckin' starlets, right?"

"You lose a lotta girls to this club?"

"Why you give a shit?"

His hands went up. "Just making conversation, that's all."

She nodded, softening her tone at his surrender. "Number one competitor—pay's better but the business is *waaay* shadier."

"What's the name of it—case I wanna go see 'em."

"Ain't gotta name but believe me—*you* ain't gettin' in to see those dancin' cockroaches. Used to send buddies there to try and scope what was going on inside—only one was successful, brought a girl to give 'em—for work." She mimed sucking cock. "Even then, guy could only stay for a few hours—said *our* place was lightyears better, by the way. I was you, just leave it alone. Both them broads ain't worth the grief—guy who runs it now's a fuckin' psycho anyway."

"Who?"

"Some sleaze named Ray Satin—big time, silver Bentley, all

that jazz. Took over after his brother got taken out. Streets say he authorized the hit too. Like I said—*psycho*. Hates my fuckin' guts! Like there ain't enough pussy for all us? That's a whole nudder world that I try to keep outta. Like I said, look in every direction down here—"

"Yeah, primo tail—I ain't disagreein' with you, Fitzie. Just curious about some old friends…but fuck 'em. Sounds like they made a bad choice."

One of the girls came over and sat on Fitzie's lap—white ringed nostrils like she tried jamming a powdered donut in her head. They cuddled as Alvi's brain mashed.

Erma, Vanda, Gabby: Cheetahs girls.

New Links: Vanda worked Fitzie's—along with Gabby. They left for this other club run by Ray Satin—supposed psycho.

Cecilia Rios: "Real flashy car—silver, one of those you see in the movies."

Satin: Drives a silver Bentley. Is he responsible for the murders of Vanda and fam?

Erma: Worked Cheetahs, means she worked Fitzie's too. Died months before Vanda and Gabby left to work for Ray. Was she the first to leave Fitzie's for this other club? Did Ray have something to do with her demise too?

Why would Vanda and Gabby go work for a psycho? Money as a motivator? Not if they thought he could've killed their friend. Something more. Something missing.

He drifted till—

A thunderous crash came at the front of the club. Fitzie jumped, flying out the room. Heard screams, smashing, mass pandemonium. Cops—a baker's dozen in riot gear, busting up the joint. Alvi tossed his remaining coffins under the table. Randi and Priscilla sat shaking with the bimbos. Dealers and johns were being hoarded out: booze busted, carpet soaked, girls tossed aflutter. Fitzie resisted and took a blow to the face. Tough cookie, raised hell. Two more dropped her to the floor.

Before Alvi could think, a piglet shoved a baton into his kidney.

"Move it, asshole!"

His palms shot up.

Chester strolled back from the pisser, coming up behind. "Hey, what the fuck's goin' on?"

The piglet jumped, swinging the baton in fear. The stick cracked Chester on the cheek, knocking him senseless. Alvi shot back.

"The fuck, man!"

An older officer ran over, tackling him to the floor. Rum-soaked carpet fibers clung to his lip, wrists shackled.

The piglet explained. "I was calmly escorting this one out when this fella snuck up behind me—didn't know if he was gonna make a play for my firearm, sir."

Alvi cried, "That's bullshit, officer!"

The vet didn't care, quiet as he ripped Alvi up off the ground. Chester shook cobwebs as he was propped by the youngster and cuffed. They stepped over Fitzie at the doorway, stiff as beef jerky.

Berries twirled outside, sparking an alleyway rave. Johns, dealers and girls were chest down on squad hoods. More cops blocked off the street. Alvi noticed some random in a blue suit, moustache like a shoe buff—no pig stigma, more class. He stared hard as he passed. The 'stache noticed.

"Fuck you looking at, Freak Show?"

Alvi smiled as the vet slammed him on a hood and said, "Sorry, Mr. Holt." Alvi winced and watched the guy's wingtips approach.

"Process these bastards and hold them overnight. If they got outstandings, you know what to do." The tips shifted. "Ladies and gentlemen, the days of underground casitas are over! The city has now closed the doors on each and every one! Take your sins to the Orange Curtain or San Berdoo from now on—L.A. doesn't love you anymore!"

Alvi pressed his cheek against the warm steel and watched

the wingtips click towards a Town Car. He shut his eyes and sighed. *Mother Fuck!*

23.

Something was taking too long. Gabby got that warm feeling in her gut, worms in mud. She stared out the window; a stickerless ice cream truck slugged down the alley droning "Three Blind Mice." Once passed, she noticed a second car in the lot, beside Rocco's. As panic set, she witnessed him flying out the club. Primo continued shoving as Dominic opened car doors. Her hands touched the glass, as if she could grab him. In a blink, her man was gone.

JaTonya was on the can, gearing up for a shower. Gabby awaited waterworks before grabbing her duffel of clothes and pulling the bricks from out the mattress. She tossed the innards onto the bed, deposited the drugs and text photo, packing garb on top. She stashed it in the closet and brainstormed. Was locked in here till her shift started—few hours. Best shot was to work it and run afterwards, trains hauled in the morning. There was no way they'd escort her to the club holding the bag either; might as well hand them a note saying, *Later Guys*. Had to find a place outside to stash it. She cracked open the window and peered down. No fire ladders, just freefall till shattered legs. Nowhere to toss the bag and remain hidden, probably would bust the bricks on impact too. She pulled out the binky, its scent calming her heart. How was this gonna happen? *Had to be a way.*

The bathroom door opened. JaTonya was nude, droplets bombing from her nips, hips and lips.

"Can I use ya towel?"

It hit; could be easier than she thought. Gabby smiled. "Sure, babydoll—hey, what say you do me a favor?"

They were taking him to the Glendale warehouse. Dominic drove while Primo sat beside Rocco in the back seat. Jazz thumped out speakers. Primo twitched.

"Why you listen to this crap? Flip that shit!"

"Fuck you, mang."

Dom sneered. Rocco followed suit as they glided into the warehouse.

Primo turned to him. "Fuck you laughin' at, Poncho?"

Rocco pulled the Glock from out his back. Primo's eyes bugged. He unloaded twice, chewing Primo's face into burger. The interior was blanketed in tiny brain bits. His ears rang. Before Dom could go for his gun, Rocco's was already at his temple, dripping Primo juice on his shoulder. "Hand it over—kill the car."

Heavy duty zip-ties strapped Dom to a metal chair. A chamois helped wash the blood from Rocco's face and hands, doubling as a gag for Dom when he was through. Clothes were done though. A back locker room harbored some soiled Carhartt coveralls; murder stains traded for grease ones. He folded out the text image and approached his hostage.

Rocco softened Dom up with a tire iron before asking any questions. His father's rage felt right.

Dom spat teeth, pleading ignorance at first. A bullet through the shoulder cleared his memory. Rocco put the Glock on the hood and approached with a long black zip-tie, cinching it around Dom's neck like an electric dog collar. Dom squirmed. Rocco pulled up another seat and held the picture out one more time.

"Already know *what* happened—just gotta tell me the *whys*?"

Dom eyed the far wall.

Rocco cinched two more of the zip's teeth. Dom's neck turned rosy, breathing heavier. "I know you know, Dom—you're Ray's boy toy. Bodies are piled high because of this picture—that girl Vanda—her whole fuckin' family! Satin doesn't want anyone to know him and Holt were behind *this*—the murder of *my* fuckin' family!" He zipped another tooth, just enough to let him swallow. The tire iron pressed into the gunshot, seeping gross slimy sounds. Dom wailed. Rocco let up. "Why'd they do it?"

He spoke in raspy gurgles. "Holt wanted in on the place—your pops told him to fuck off. Hector wasn't into drug trafficking anymore. Didn't want anything to do with the dope Holt tried to move out the store—figured we were making a shitload already, why bother with a new partner." He coughed.

"Keep going."

"Holt threatened us. Your pops didn't budge. That's when Satin saw an opportunity. Knew it'd be years before he'd even have a chance to take over—couldn't wait. Called up Holt and struck a deal."

Rocco remembered Ray's words: '*Holt approached months ago—guaranteed the po-po would look the other way...*' "Keep heat off the casita and he'd make everything happen?"

Saliva dribbled from his lips. "Yeah."

Rocco sat back. "They killed Hector for the club."

Dom shut his eyes in nod. "Holt wouldn't let us do the hit. Made Satin do it himself—to prove the deal was for real. Wanted to watch it too."

"How does he figure in with the Mayor—he a cop or somethin'?"

"Nah, Ray said he was a runner back in the day—one of the bigger cartels. Hector used to buy from him when he pushed goods out the joint. Got busted in town with the largest score ever to make it in the city. You didn't read about it though—

Reynaga kept it under wraps. Tallied the potential revenue and brought Holt in as an assistant—struck a deal—like with Ray." He paused, gurgling. "Holt is Reynaga's main front to filter dope into the city—collect a fat check. Ray see's Holt on top and wants to be just like him. I tell him to be careful, but you know your uncle."

Rocco fumed. Ray and Holt now had X's for eyes.

Dominic wheezed. "Hey, man—cut this strap off me. Can hardly breathe."

"Sure thing."

Rocco got behind and grabbed the zip with both hands. He propped a foot to the back of the chair and pulled as if starting a mower. Zip cinched tighter than he thought possible, turning Dom's head into a boiling ball, eyes bulging. Rocco watched him thrash, all the while thinking, *Lucky prick—Ray and Holt won't get it this easy.*

Kang launched into the club, eerily quiet, hollering for Dom and Primo until it was obvious—they weren't there. Had only been a few hours since Ray lost touch with the two, neither answering cells; something was off.

Kang used the lair phone to notify.

"Yeah, just Roc's car in the lot."

Satin's end grumbled engine revs and car horns. "Stay put, make sure the girls are getting ready. I'll be there shortly."

The Bentley threaded commuter constipation on the I-5 until screeching off at Colorado. Primo and Dom were supposed to call when they had Rocco at the warehouse. Then he'd come and get to the bottom of this mess—nice as possible. *Easy enough, right?* Not for *his* men. Unless there was a righteous excuse of divine intervention, nice was now off the table for all of them. First, he had to see if they even made it there.

* * *

A knock came at the door before a jangling of keys. Gabby rushed bedside, pointing JaTonya towards the bathroom. Kang walked in and Gabby greeted with sugar. The shower faucet turned off. He pointed towards the sound.

"Why ain't she ready?"

Gabby shrugged, arms behind her back, smiling. The bathroom door flung open. JaTonya dripped all over, fingers strumming chocolate curves as she puddled up the floor.

"Kang, baby—we outta towels. Can ya help me? M'all wet."

His face cracked as she sucked her lip. A finger curled him over.

Soon as he grabbed handfuls, Gabby inched towards the door. His belt unclanked; she made for the stairwell.

Carefully ascending, she exited to the courtyard. Figured it was the closest prime spot; after shift she could make like heading to her room, grab the stash, then bolt. An early morning escape would give her more time before anyone noticed.

She made sure no one was watching before selecting a perfect spot. A few cracked pots and weathered lawn furniture did nothing. *The dumpster!* She ran and slid the duffel under the large, rusted bin. Could hear something coming up the alley. Her nerves tingled. Didn't wait to see what it was, rushing for the stairs.

By the time she launched back into the room, primal screams were subsiding. The shower started back up as Kang emerged flush, pointing at her.

"I'll have you later."

She blew a kiss.

"JaTonya's cleanin' up. Be back for you two in a few." He bolted the door behind him.

Gabby punched her pillow in relief. JaTonya squatted on the toilet, less than amused. Gabby gazed somberly at her.

"Bitch, you owe me *big*."

24.

Out the car's side view mirror, Alvi gazed at snowcapped peaks falling further in the distance. Sharp and white, he wanted to stick a hand through the mirror and snatch a fistful for Chester's busted face. He felt like a punished toddler in the backseat of his Benz. Mongo got his one phone call; took some coaxing to calm her, still fuming about his party ditch. Faye helped out, reasoning her down, coming with her to pick them up once released. All was quiet now. Chester poked his face, grimacing, cold sweat beading for the needle. His moans kept Alvi up all night. Mongo drove with caution, haggard as hell, Faye beside her.

Faye asked, "So what hap—"

"*Shhh*," said Mongo, "We don't give a fuck, 'member?"

Alvi rolled his eyes, attention back to those icy peaks, thinking about Gabby and that club and how he was going to find it and get inside.

They dropped Chester at the Paradise. He fumbled keys, catching a retch before waving back and entering another long day of bliss. His overnight phoner went to Swami's, calling in "sick." Alvi agreed to keep him in the loop about further plans but after witnessing the codger get bludgeoned, was best to nix him from what lie ahead. Alvi slid over between the girls.

"So here's what went down…"

Laundromat daze.

Mongo pushed quarters into a dryer before loading a family sized washer with rainbow garments. Alvi sat at the folding counter, scanning *Times* editions left in a stack from the past few days. Today's headlines had nothing on last night's raid of Fitzie's, understandable considering the hour it went down. Nothing else drew alarm; he tossed the pages back.

Faye handed him yesterday's front page. She watched his brow squirm, wondering what could peek his interest more than the companionship of a perky teen redhead. If she tossed her shirt right now, he would've kept on reading. She sighed, helping Mongo fold frayed lingerie.

Alvi scanned.

**HUNDREDS SICKENED AT
PLAYBOY MANSION PARTY**

**BEVERLY HILLS MOVIE PRODUCER
PLEADS GUILTY TO MOLESTATION**

**ONE FATALITY IN OVERTURNED
JUMEX TRUCK OFF 60 FREEWAY**

Then.

**FEMALE BODY FOUND IN
GRIFFITH PARK RESERVIOR**

He bugged.

…Female between the ages of 25 and 40…filed as
Jane Doe…no apparent signs of foul play…drug

paraphernalia confiscated at scene...Further tests
pending...

He tore out the article and passed it to Mongo. She poo-pooed
it.
"No way it's her. Gabby don't be fuckin' with no dope."
Faye grabbed it.
"Never know," said Alvi. "Think how easy it could be to just
dump a body in the park and scatter a buncha rigs 'round it?"
A geezer pushed a cart of whites by them, hawking an evil
eye. The girls smiled.
Alvi took the article from Faye and pocketed it. "You really
think the pigs give a fuck about another dead junkie? To them
that's *case closed*."
Faye asked, "You guys think this' your friend, Gabby?"
Mongo shrugged, taking a warm basket out to the car.
Alvi picked the paper back up and folded over the front
page. Didn't think much of the headline—

MAYOR HONORS COCKFIGHTING TASK FORCE

Then the photo burned a whole through his skull: a group of
men huddled around a podium. Guy behind the Mayor, nearly
cropped out the picture—bushy moustache. Was at the Fitzie's
bust: "Fuck you looking at, Freak Show?" Alvi skimmed the
caption. No name for the moustache but something far better.
*King Carne...121 N. Virgil Avenue...Raymond Satin...Mayor
Vicente Reynaga.* The two men were shaking hands—chummy
chummy. Satin's canines brought chills.
Alvi shot up. "The hell is going on?"

Alvi tacked new articles on the wall beside Angie and Gabby,
taking a step back. Their chronological placement had connected
a few more dots. He began to scribble revelations on scratch,

trying to piece the puzzle together.

Ray Satin had sounded familiar out Fitzie's mouth because he was mentioned in an Erma abduction article. Alvi perused the wall and re-read the exact clipping. Her body was found beside an older male, Hector Felix—article linked him as Satin's stepbrother, touching upon their checkered past, blah, blah, blah. Fitzie's voice sang in his head—*'Streets said Satin authorized the hit.'* He took a step back, lit a cig and contemplated.

Erma: wrong place, right time?

Satin: Killer. Body count piling: Erma and Hector plus Vanda and family.

He gazed at the wall, conjuring horrors. Smoke danced between images of the dead, Satin's sharp teeth beaming amongst.

Mayor: Satin's buddy? Partners?

Moustache guy: at Fitzie's raid—also in C.F. Task Force picture. Vet cop: 'Sorry, Mr. Holt.' Said L.A. casitas were all busted.

Satin runs one of the best. Why the smile? Still operating? Cockfighting Task Force?

His brain fried. Too many question marks. He cracked a King Cobra and contemplated the next move. Fitzie said the rival club was off Virgil and Beverly. Not far from the Lafayette. He found the address of King Carne: 121 N. Virgil. Club had to be in its vicinity.

He wasn't going to tell Mongo till he was absolutely sure, cruising out solo. He pulled into a church parking lot next to King Carne, article in hand; same giant rooster loomed above. He sat and peeped. Two other cars in the lot but the store was closed— could hear air conditioners blasting out the rear. Strange. He got out and approached with caution.

An empty chicken cage helped prop him to a window. The tint was beyond limo, filthy. He squinted, face to glass. Place was deserted, could see a dance floor, bar, booths—typical backdoor dive. *A meat market front.* Buckets of fresh ice were lined at the rear door. Light cast inside the joint. Alvi ducked, careful not to make any noise. One eye peered through the window's corner. A tiny man with a broom began to sweep behind the bar. Alvi watched for minutes as the guy carefully dusted bottles, singing in Spanish while packing beers with more ice. *Guess the city closed every casita but this one.* He was careful getting down, noiseless, scanning the perimeter for anyone watching.

Back at the car, he gazed at the Satin-Reynaga photo, panning from it to the store. Something ugly was afoot, but that wasn't his main concern. He re-focused on Gabby. *She* had brought him here. All else was on the back burner. Figured the party kicked-off late night, like Fitzie's. He started the car, thinking, *Gotta get ready—talk Mongo into doing one more solid.*

By the time Alvi returned, a few rain clouds had rolled in. Streetlamps wept outside Mongo's window as she stood silent, shaking her silver wig, duded to the nines in boulevard garb. Alvi sat patient on her bed, awaiting a response to his proposal. Mongo sighed.

"Alvi, why go an' do this to yourself, huh? I tell you 'bout the bitch leavin' and what you say?"

He rolled his eyes.

"Oh yeah, 'Forget her, Mongo. That's just Gabby pullin' a *Gabby.*' So, I do. Forgot the cunt walked dis Earf. Now look at *you*, sittin' dere, askin' me what you be askin'. Sheeit, son! Why can't you just leave it alone? Don't 'member us pickin' you up today from muthafuckin' *jail?*"

He rose. "I got a Ma back home to give me shit, okay—you gonna help or not?"

"I shouldn't—new *Xpress* hits the streets tonight. 'Memba, me on the fuckin' cover? Should be out celebratin', showin' off this purdy face!" She bit a nail. "Imma help you, Alvi, but I want some conditions made."

"Shoot."

"Firs' off, you gonna spot my pills next time with the connect."

"What else?"

"Drive me 'round tomorrow, all the newsstands. I'm gonna strut this covagirl ass!"

"That all?"

"No! Why you goin' through all this just to find her, baby? Be honest!"

Alvi rolled his eyes. "Mongo—"

"No, don't fuckin' *Mongo* me—take a look at what you already got, boy! Look at all the folks who love you—showed up to the party—for *you* and only *you*. Why ain't you reconize dat, 'stead a chasin' some girl who won't love you back?"

"Dammit—you *know* why!"

A hand shot to her hip. "Alvi, I told you what she said—"

"But why would she—"

Her acrylics cupped into a megaphone. "THERE...WAS...NO...BABY!"

"Yeah—well, I want *her* to tell me."

"Come on, hun. Stop. Don't believe me?"

"I want an explanation. How could she just rule me out— toss me aside like some fuckin' bum?"

"All the time she was here, before all this—you didn't need no fuckin' *explanation*."

"Was hurtin', Mong. Figured I had time to confront her— then she disappears. I didn't think—"

Mongo tossed the wig across the room. "Ya ain't thinkin'! Dat's ya prolem! Jus' thrillseekin', like ya boy Blisko say: 'Can't *SAVE* everybody, Alvi!' Some bitches just perma-fucked!"

He stewed in silence.

"Listen, imma go witchu—but after tonight, I need a break from bein' yo friend. Shit's exhaustin'—bad for my complexion."

Alvi rose off the bed. "There's one more thing."

"What."

"We need a girl—to work for them. It's the only shot we got

of gettin' in."

"So, why ain't you tell me 'fore I start undressin'?"

"Well, we need a…um."

"*Real* woman, huh? It's okay—you ain't gotta say it."

"Think Doreen would come with us?"

"She awready gone for the night."

A third voice resonated.

"You guys need a girl for something?"

Faye stood, leaning in the doorway.

Alvi and Mongo met eye to eye.

Faye grinned at Alvi. "What we doing?"

25.

Kang was in a thinkers' crouch at the couch as Satin popped a fresh bottle of Grey Goose, hands stained by the crusted blood of his boys. He sat at his desk, nipping slug after slug, thinking, *Why Rocco?* Like he didn't already know, peering out the window at the club below. The reason tended bar, sliding pints to degenerates—he knew it, thumping the misplaced Gabby Wang folder on his desk. *Rocco you stupid fuck.*

Kang asked, "What's our move?"

Ray fiddled with his favorite screwdriver, cleaning blood from under his nails. "Need more men. Holt could provide some of his crew but how would that make us look, huh? Supposed to be takin' care a binness—not like this."

"Could call my brother? Supposed to be in town."

Ray hated the thought but what other options did he have? He nodded and took a slow pull. The vodka cleansed his nostrils of that warehouse stank. *His boys.* Dead boys. Eyes got heavy— poor Dom. He snapped back. "In the meantime, we wait for Roc."

"You think he's gonna show his face 'round here?"

"He'll be back for *her*," tapping the folder, "else it was all for nothin'."

***

A taxi dropped Rocco at the Bunker Hill Towers and waited. Grimy coveralls and the neck brace raised attention. Random execs waiting on valets sent the awkward eye. He powered through for the elevator with only one thing in mind.

The apartment was empty, shattered glass from the juke sparkled the carpet; most likely a Satin tantrum. He went into his bedroom and tossed the gun on the sheets, catching a glimpse in the mirror. *What a mess.* He stripped and turned on the shower.

Satin's medicine cabinet had enough painkillers to soothe a stunt man. He settled for a double dose of Aleve, not sure which pill could put him out. The purple sharkskin he'd worn to the Ritz still hung behind his door. Might as well kill them with class.

He rummaged through a sock drawer for his family. A creased Polaroid was all he had left; fit snug in his breast pocket, along with the text photo. He pulled out his cell and dialed. One ring.

"What it do, nephew! Been lookin' for your ass. Everythin' okay?"

"Nah, Ray. I'm pretty busted up."

"Figured that. You in the hospital or what?"

"On my way to the club, actually. Gonna be there?"

"You know it. Hurry'n get over here. Wanna get a look atchu—hear all about what happened. Haven't seen Primo and Kang by any chance?"

"Nah."

"Huh, dunno where they went. Musta got tied up.

"Must've."

Satin paused. "See you in a few, nephew."

"Sure thing, *tio.*"

Inside the *pollería*, Satin clicked the call, grinning at Kang. "What I tell you?"

"Who your nephew think he's dealin' with, huh?"

"He's like Hector. No respect—or brains."

They stood over the final dope canister, noticeably low.

"Holt's gonna hate us even more now."

Kang asked, "Got any ideas who might've skimmed the bricks?"

Satin shrugged. Instinct pointed to Rocco but he wasn't convinced. "One thing I do know—this canister's only been cut once. Whoever slams' goin' straight to the grave."

Kang's cell buzzed. "What? Right now?" He turned to Satin, resealing the canister lid with punches in bunches. "They're in the parking lot."

"Bring 'em upstairs."

A fresh suit had Satin relaxed. He surfed the tube, swilling vodka when he heard Kang climbing the stairway. The sight of his guests brought him to his feet. Three guys—Kang's brother Marky, some albino and an Indian. Each was sporting dreads and giant pants; fluorescent beads draped off every appendage.

Marky took the glowing pacifier out his mouth. "Long time, Ray."

Ray didn't respond, pulling Kang close. "Fuck's this shit, huh? They hittin' a Care Bear convention or somethin'?"

Marky approached. "We're up for a rave—Cuddle Fest at the Coliseum. Don't be trippin', we ain't rollin'...yet." He chuckled, flashing a bag of purple pills.

Kang grabbed it. Each had a crucifix imprint. "What I tell you 'bout this?"

"What?"

Kang's nostrils flared. "Don't act stupid."

Ray stood speechless, panning from Kang to the three, cursing how it all went wrong. He sat back down.

Kang asked, "You still want these fools, Ray?"

Satin's fingers washed his face, deliberating sanity. *Fuckin' Rocco!* He knew Marky could keep his mouth shut, and these were his buds. *Desperate times.* "Yeah alright, but they gotta change outta that Fruity Pebbles gear. Should be some stuff in the closet" He pointed behind the far couch. "See what fits then get 'em on the floor." He approached the three. "You kids are on my dime now—act professional—don't fuck with the girls unless I say so. Kang'll brief you on the rest."

Marky asked, "Don't you wanna know who these guys are?"

Ray twitched, nonchalantly.

"This here's my boy Roach and our homie Sweetbreads."

"Christ."

Kang rushed them out the door, mumbling at Marky.

"What? What I say?"

Ray dove back into the bottle, launching it across the room before biting a knuckle.

Rocco had the cab stop at Gabby's apartment. An extra hundo had the gypsy forget his fare. With the girls at work, the complex cast echoes. He felt like a sausage, climbing the stairs in his tapered suit, neck brace clamping hard. Once inside her unit, he noticed the bricks were gone. Closet was empty too. No clothes. No shoes. *No way.* He wouldn't believe it, rushing back down the stairs and out towards the club.

A line formed at the door as bouncers patted down patrons in Polyester suits and leather pants. Rain was now at a light drizzle. Rocco bumped past a councilman dressed like Johnny Wadd. *Disco Night?*

The club pulsed as girls scampered about in tube tops and glitter. Flatscreens blasted Annie Sprinkle, squirming, holes drilled, hairy balls bouncing. He worked through the distractions, scanning closely. *Bingo.* Behind the bar with big hair, her presence washed relief. Knew she would never, but now it was in stone.

***

Gabby caught him lasering from across the dance floor. Her body popped in excitement seeing him in the flesh. She adjusted her mesh halter. Their escape was back on track. He shimmered purple, approaching the bar. That brace still had her giggling inside. She rushed over.

"Act cool, baby—relax."

She poured him a double and began wiping up dregs.

"How you doing? Everything okay?"

Rocco gulped the glass. "'Bout to be better. Where's the stuff?"

"I stashed it in the courtyard. Didn't know if you were gone for good." She began to work herself up.

Rocco smirked. *Managed to get out but didn't run without him.* He touched her hand. "Listen, I have to go meet with Ray. Things might get crazy—next time you see me, be ready to bail."

"Wait."

"What is it?"

"He's got some new men in here."

Rocco swiveled, scoping. Knew Ray would replace the boys once he was sure they had been scratched.

So, he knew.

Rocco got up to leave when Gabby grabbed his arm and pulled him close, whispering, "Be careful, baby—love you." He met her eyes, aching for one forbidden kiss before wading back through the carnival.

Kang was adjusting Marky's tie when he took notice.

"Ray—he's here!"

"Where?"

"At the bar—in a neck brace."

Ray dashed to see. Rocco was making his way to the stairs. He thought fast. Didn't want to intimidate just yet. Sweetbreads and Roach were still searching for clothes that fit. "Quick— everyone in the closet!"

Kang and Marky rushed over.

Ray said, "Keep it open a sliver—I'll nod when to grab him. Want him all to myself."

Rocco knocked before entering. Ray played like he was lost in drunken stupor on the couch—solo. Rocco shut the door.

"Rocco Felix!" Ray rose with enthusiasm. "You look like shit, nephew."

Rocco adjusted his collar. "Feel like it, too."

"What's with those glasses?"

"Sorry—other ones broke."

"Siddown, siddown! Tell me what the fuck happened out there?"

He grabbed a seat while Ray got a refill.

"What you drinkin'?"

"Chivas."

Rocco watched as Ray retrieved the screwdriver from his desk to chip some ice. Gabby's file was still resting where he left it, open. He stood back up, nerves prickling his skull. Had to grab it after the deed.

Ray turned with the drinks. "Siddown already!"

"I'm good—back's too sore. Hey—don't you think these themed nights are getting a bit outta hand? I mean, fuck—what happened to discretion?"

Ray passed the glass, screwdriver tucked down the front of his pants. "Tonight's all Reynaga's doin'. Some buddy of his wanted a Plato's Retreat birthday bash. Quit sweatin' the small shit. We're in good hands, a'ight?

Rocco played dumb. "Where's everybody?"

"Oh, on a drop." He slunk to the couch. "Had to make another since yours got fucked. Holt's been up my ass, kid—fuckin' hemorrhoids. Freddie's dead—but you prolly knew that."

Silence.

Rocco turned his back and looked down at the crowd, still

not noticing any of these new characters Gabby had warned of. He fingered the Glock. "Hey, Ray."

"Yeah?" He nodded to the closet door.

"Got a new lead on Hector—been thinkin' about that *tenfold* promise."

Rocco pulled the gun and spun. Before his finger squeezed, he was tackled to the floor. Pain surged in his neck as bodies piled upon him. His heart raced; a zebra devoured by lions. Wild hands ripped his jacket in two.

Ray watched as the guys held down Rocco's arms and legs. The Indian's strength was impressive. Rage boiled in Rocco's face. Kang grabbed the gun off the floor and looked back for command. Satin gave the go ahead. Kang drove the butt of the piece down hard through Rocco's septum, crunching his geek specs in two.

26.

They waited in line with the rest of the heathens. Mongo held a clear vinyl umbrella over Faye, leaving Alvi to absorb scattered droplets. They took in perv costumes aplenty, perplexed by faux afros and chest hair. Alvi never would have guessed the casita had thematic parties, then again he didn't know what to expect. *Their* style changes were simple ploys to look more questionable, less conspicuous—snug for the scene. Thought they did a decent job of it too. Instead, their new clothes blared *outsiders*.

Mongo was overtly flustered by the customers' digs. If she'd known there was a seventies' club theme, would've worn something fabulous under Gabby's frayed denim jacket; only thing mannish she approved of since Alvi's clothes tented her slender frame. Alvi couldn't care less about the festivities, focused on his entrance scheme, distracted by the silver Bentley in the parking lot.

"Faye honey, you got a compact on ya?"

Alvi smirked at Mongo's fake throaty voice.

Faye shivered in a pleather halter and blue mini, handing over the pastel disc.

Mongo gave the umbrella to Faye, took a black pencil from out her pocket and began sketching a thin handlebar moustache. Her nails were chipped and brittle with remnants of press-on glue. She caught their awkward stares. "It's a costume party, y'all. Ain't one to dampen no atmosphere."

The line inched forward.

Alvi admired the white cowboy boots Ronnie had lent him. They shone like pearls under black jeans and a moto jacket (all Ronnie's too). He stepped aside and noticed the entryway unguarded. "Wait here."

Once he got close, a wall in a black blazer shot up from patting down a patron and blocked the door. "Sir, I'm going to need you to get back in line."

"Oh, I'm not here for the party, man. Got some business to discuss with *Mr. Satin*." His hands cupped air breasts before pointing out Faye in the distance.

"He expecting you?"

"Of course—she's the first of Fitzie's girls I'll be bringin' him—names' Rat. I'm sure you heard 'bout last night's raid— shit left me with a gang a gals, just like this one—all outta work and itchin' hustle."

The wall pressed his earpiece and snarled. "I have a guy here who's brought a girl for some work." He scoped Alvi up and down, squinting. "I know that sir but he says she's one of *Fitzie's*...Yes—*Fitzie's*, sir. Considering the circumstances, I thought you'd like to know. Should I send him away? Okay...Yes sir, I will...Not a problem."

Alvi popped a cig from out the pack, catching it with his lips.

"Sir, bring the woman over here. I need to frisk you, her and your associate. Someone will be here shortly for further assistance."

Alvi waved them over and sparked a match.

Within minutes, a strange looking Asian peered out the door, scanning Faye with x-ray eyes before approaching. He spoke in a low tone to Alvi. "Fitzie's, huh?"

Alvi nodded. "I used to book the *talent*." He grabbed Faye's hand and spun her like a ballerina. "She's the first a many I got for you guys—now that Fitzie's is no more."

Kang spat. *Ray'll like the sound of that.*

Alvi stuck out a hand. "Rat—pleasure."
Their grips met.
"Kang—follow me."

They barely made it through the entrance unscathed. A party mob had the room throbbing wall to wall; jovial screams and shattered glass became drowned out by speakers blaring "Heart of Glass." Flamboyant banners, balloons and streamers juxtaposed old white men blanketing nubile felines—faces hardened beyond their years. The scene washed across Mongo and Faye differently: jubilation/trepidation. Alvi scoped for Gabby but it was no use; clusterfuck, too tame a word. Kang used a forearm and flashlight to pierce them towards a staircase. Before climbing, his hand shot out in yield.

Attention was set on the upstairs office. Three dreadlocked dudes in ill-fitting suits hoisted a limp body above their heads, ascending in clamor like Laurel and Hardy with that damn piano. Kang screamed to abolish the amateur effort, only making matters worse. At the last step, they fumbled. The cargo crashed onto Kang's torso. Dead weight forced him back into Alvi, sending them both pretzeled to the floor. Writhing, they struggled for freedom until the suits re-propped their wet noodle. Randoms in the crowd took notice, pointing—some laughing. Kang boiled.

"I told you shitheads to get him in the store on the sly. The fuck is this?"

Marky: "Listen—this joint ain't exactly open ocean, yo. Figured we'd surf the fucker overhead instead, alright?"

Kang grunted, leaning to whisper in Marky's ear.

Alvi tried wiping blood specs off the boots, only making matters worse.

Marky gawked at Faye before re-positioning a lax limb on his shoulder. "Yeah okay—I'll tellim."

Mongo and Faye watched the body moan, face to pulp over a pink stained neck brace. Poor guy was whisked above the crowd through falling confetti like a float of the Madonna. Kang beckoned them up to the office, smoothing the situation, claiming the bum to be just another drunkard.

"I've sent one of my crew to notify Mr. Satin."

Alvi asked if there was a towel in the office.

Kang approached the wet bar and threw one over. "Anyone like a drink?"

Mongo eyed the Grey Goose. "Take a vodka-tonic."

Kang pointed to Faye.

"I'm good, thanks."

Alvi tossed the blotted towel back. "Rye if you got it."

Kang scooped a few remaining ice bits, accommodating the guests. After pouring Goose, he fumbled through the slender shelves, searching. "Looks like we're outta tonic."

"Straight's fine."

"I'll have some sent up. Only be a sec." He passed Alvi three fingers before swiping the desk phone.

Faye whispered to Mong, "Drinkin' it straight'll turn ya straight."

Mongo giggled in puffs, catching herself before any snorting.

Alvi stepped on a torn sharkskin jacket—purple. By the looks of it, belonged to the poor bastard that was just dragged out. He tossed it on a couch and peered out the windows. The view below conjured thoughts of fresh maggots. His eyes panned the bar, swishing cheeks with rye. Guy at the counter looked like that cowboy in those car commercials. Beyond his Stetson, a girl answered a wall phone. The sight struck him cold, nearly spitting the mouthful across the window. He forced a gulp. Had never been so certain of anything in his whole wretched life.

Kang addressed the phone: "Couple bottles of tonic and a lemon. Thanks."

Alvi watched Gabby mouth, "You got it," then heard Kang click the phone dead.

Kang slouched on the desk, snapping a Tecate.

Like crosshairs on a quail, Alvi darted her every move. She grabbed a set of keys above the register before handing tonic to a bouncer by the DJ stand, directing him upstairs. Jumping in place, she attempted to see over the sizzling crowd. Seemed distraught. Alvi noticed a far door in her field of vision. Soon as he panned back to the bar, she was gone.

Kang mused. "How long your girl here work for Fitzie?"

Alvi spun and put the drink down, grabbing his guts. "Oh, man."

"What's the matter?"

"Rye ain't agreein' with me. Where's the can?"

"Bottom of the stairs—hurry back."

Alvi jetted past the girls' eager stares and out the door.

The dance floor bucked and wailed as he elbowed through. Glimpses of raven hair blipped between grinning heads every few feet. Could see her approach that far door, punch a key and vanish. Just as he slid past the party zone, a hand grabbed his shoulder and spun him.

Marky: "Don't be rushin' through here like some asshole, yo! I fuckin' kick ya ass *right* out."

"Sorry, I—it won't happen again."

Dreadlocks gave a pom-pom tilt. "You da fool with da girl, huh?"

He nodded.

"Awe fuck—"

Alvi watched the goon rush that same door, insert a key and knock, before charging inside.

27.

A shoulder was on fire. Rocco gazed at the clear green handle jutting from it, arms restrained to a fold-out chair. Satin left it in, retrieving another screwdriver. A stained butcher's block told Rocco he was in the store's kitchen. Couldn't remember how he got there. Jacket and shirt had been removed. Additional agony gripped his face and neck. Endorphins bubbled in a dream state. *Was he a voodoo pincushion?* Telekinesis couldn't budge the shank as Ray approached, humming, cherry speckled sleeves rolled high.

"This' prolly how Dom felt, huh? Before *you* did it."

Rocco drooled. "Fuh...fuck you talkin' 'bout?"

Ray opened a chair, straddling it backwards, tapping the tool to his cheek. "That's good...that's good. You dunno, right? Freddie...Primo...Dom—they was all coincidence? New Night Stalker or some shit?" He got up and circled, pausing behind him. "Betchu dunno 'bout the missing horse either, huh?"

"Wha—"

"That's okay, nephew. No worries." His arms shot up. "I forgive you! Family means putting up with crazy shit from time to time." He placed the spike at Rocco's neck. "Here's a tip though. If you did take my dope—cut it some more before you dole it out—'less you wanna be pilin' *more* bodies." He laughed. "Keep the bricks if you got 'em—make some money. Holt'll be pissed but it'll pass. Just money. Don't mean shit to me. Fuckin' Kang's still breathin'—kill that fucker too. No big deal—fools like him get outta lock-up every day. Ain't no thang, we big dogs now. The help'll come to us." He leaned down to Rocco's ear. "We're blood, boy. You pullin' all this, I can understand. Got the same evil inside. Can't help ourselves. *Why* you pullin' it, now that's a whole 'nother deal.

"You ask me, I act out in my own best interest—got something to gain from it. Money—Power—Fear. Why the fuck you doin' it?"

Rocco wanted to moan, pain numbing to a seared burn.

"Ain't gonna tell me? 'Kay…We'll get back to it." He tossed the tool from hand to hand. "I ever tell you why I use the screwdriver…? No?"

A knock came at the club door. Marky entered.

"The fuck you doin'—get back on the floor." He pointed towards Rocco. "Fuckin' busy!"

"Yeah, I know but I forgot to tell you—Kang says you got some business waiting in the office. Some dude's got this fly bitch, ready to work—fat ass ho! Said to tell you she's from *Fitzie's*? Girl looks like she could suck a football through a garden hose. Whatchu want me tellim?"

Fitzie's girls were already making their way over? Was bound to happen. "I'll be up in a few."

"Aiiight." Marky pointed at Rocco and cackled before re-entering the club.

"See that Roc. 'Cause a you, I gotta train this crop a dumb-shits. Where were we?"

Rocco slowly raised his head.

Malnourished ducks gave panicked quacks.

"The screwdriver! You're gonna dig this, Roc. So, me and your pops had ta go school this fool, right? Some *pendejo*, owed us a bunch—back when Hector slanged. We had him all tied up—just like you, only we strapped him to a bench. Hector did his thang, you know, poppin' him a few times, trash talk—still no money. He turns to me and nods, right? That's my cue. So, I reach for my piece, but it ain't there—left it back in the Caddy. Problem's the car's circling the block with Dom as lookout. Had to think quick, you know? Wanted to impress Hector. We were in the fool's garage, so I grabbed this long Phillips off the wall. Thing looked like a midget's sword. Hector left me to work—was always soft when it came to gettin' the hands dirty. So, I jab this fucker and—well you know what that feels like now. Got him in the gut though. Never felt a shank go in so dense. Felt like I popped the *puto*. Played with it, twistin'…Jabbed a few more but he didn't last long." He grabbed the handle in Roc's shoulder and wiggled.

Rocco grunted.

"Fuckin' hurts, right? Feels damn good to me though. Ever since that first time—screwdriver just feels right, you know?" He smirked. "Your pops never looked at me the same way after that. Knew I was stronger then. First time I embraced the fear."

Rocco dribbled, mumbling.

"What's that, nephew?"

"C-c-coward."

Satin paused, raising the stake high before lunging it through Roc's right pec. Rocco wailed and began to gasp, thrashing on one lung, vision waning in warm white blotches. The caged meat stirred in hysterics.

"Shoot," said Ray, "missed the mark. *Sorry*." He straddled opposite. Rocco struggled to wheeze. "Wanted to bring this back to why you tryin' to play me, but seein' as the state you're in, I'll just tell you what I think. Nod if I'm gettin' warm.

"This bitch Gabby got you by the balls. Pepperin' your mind with fairy tales 'bout true love and all kinds a bullshit, right? Listen, when she first got here—tried floating the same sweet notes into these ears."

Rocco wouldn't have it, all lies. Wanted to strangle the bastard for such slander. Tenfold death would never be enough. His nervous system jolted at capacity. The rage washed into subtle waves of happiness, pictures of her in Paris, a re-enactment of his family photo including their dog—Georgie. Could smell her now; taste the fur on her earlobe. She was worth all the risk. Relief soothed the muscles. With these final moments spent dreaming, he knew she would never forget him. Prayed for her safety, opening his eyes back into torment.

Satin continued, breath like sour shoes. "I admit, pussy's ripe, face and body, great eyes—but I could read the bitch right off the bat. Runnin' a place like this breeds lessons on the female kind; girls like her come 'round every so often—starry eyes, open thighs—straight trouble. Who you think tipped me off 'bout all that blackmail bullshit? Bitch tried snitching her friend to get in my good graces. Don't work that way, nephew. I humored her for the most part, beat the pussy, got the info I needed then put her on lockdown. Rats like that can't be trusted. Girl Vanda was bluffing anyhow, didn't have nothin' on me. 'Cause a your sweetheart, you been dumpin' more bodies than necessary lately— feel me? Now, how warm did I get?"

Rocco grumbled apricot bile, blood.

"Thought so."

He growled some more. Wanted to crucify Ray with every word, for his father, for Gabby, for ruining everything that ever meant something to him: morals, dreams—the future. But there was no strength left. Just a soul in a shell. He dug deep.

Satin leaned in to hear his faint spells.

"Ja...k-k-kit."

"Huh? Speak up!" He came closer.

"My j-jacket...p...p-pocket."

Before Ray could move, Rocco clamped onto his ear like a pit-bull to toddler. Ray clawed himself free and shot up, screaming. The top half of his ear dangled at the corner of Rocco's lips. Poultry flapped with fury, cries almost human. Ray pounced, tearing out both jutting handles from Roc's torso, eyeing the stomach before hoisting both stakes one final time.

* * *

The four-legged sink's white plastic basin caught Satin's dripping ear. He applied pressure with a rank sponge as droplets exploded into a still pool. Could pass for pink lemonade. The mirror screamed nightmares beyond. He rinsed the sponge and grabbed a fresh butcher's coat to mask the blotched button-up. As the second arm went through, a few of the chickens stirred in frenzy. He froze, sensing being under a microscope.

"Marky?"

The clamor quieted as he stood in the middle of the mess, craning back and forth, squinting at dark corners. He spun to make sure Rocco wasn't breathing. A droplet bombed the coat.

"Damn."

He lunged for the sponge, admiring his nephew once more before mumbling in short prayer, hitting the light and heading for the door.

As he stepped foot in the club, a body crashed against him. White boots.

"The fuck outta my way!"

Guy stepped aside. Ray mean mugged. Wasn't a regular. Would've remembered face tats. *Reynaga's debutants*, he thought, making it back to the lair.

28.

So this was Satin?

Alvi didn't need an introduction. Even disheveled with a bloody ear, that matchstick moustache had Raymond Satin pegged before the asshole episode. Alvi watched the bastard bump his way through festivities as he carefully wedged a boot to catch the closing door. He held steady for a beat, checking for onlookers before slinking inside.

Took a few beats for his eyes to sync with the shadows. *A meat market indeed.* He wandered through rusted cages, filthy, sausaged with innocence. Flies were everywhere. Couldn't come close to bottling the scent. A single bulb swung in the distance. He approached with caution, only to smash into something solid, square. Yanking the string of beads, a butcher's block cast golden below. Faint drips gurgled, seeping through the floor. Drainage by his foot, caked in feathers and blood; a thin red stream coursing. The source came from behind. He spun.

The movies had it all wrong. Gore could not be glorified. Flesh torn, bare bones. A bludgeoned face, once newborn. He lunged away from the neck brace, crashing into a tower of bunnies. Before he could gage the situation, foreign footsteps had him moving. He grabbed her at the front door, squeezing as she squirmed, muffling screams with a palm. "Shut the fuck up," came in soft whispers. He stared, astonished; a living ghost. If only the moment allowed ovation. Snot slimed his hand as her glassy eyes fixated on the flesh in that chair, trembling. He let her breathe.

One more glance at Rocco and Gabby clicked back. Her mind moved on, arms squeezing Alvi's ribcage, smashing a quick kiss. "You came for me, lover." Didn't even ask for a reason. Just glad he was there. Glad for a new option. She pulled away. "We gotta go, Alvi—he wants *me* too."

Peril mode. Mongo and Faye were now forgotten. He grabbed her hand. "Let's go."

She led him to the store's front door. He unlatched the lock and nixed the dangling bell. The door gave a few inches before crashing to a halt. A thin chain wrapped the outside handles. "There another way out?"

She bit a nail and shook her head.

They turned back.

The club door roared before devouring them.

Mongo and Faye sat silent, frozen on the TV. If only they were camouflaged to the damn couch. The volume was inaudible. They transfixed on a jovial Tampax commercial, waiting for Alvi's return, pretending that a bleeding man did not just barge in screaming with half an ear.

Satin rifled through Rocco's twisted jacket as Kang secured gauze to his mangled ear. Tucked in the breast pocket, a Polaroid and paper. He tossed Rocco's family in the trash, unfolding the slip. One glance at the image, and he quickly re-creased.

"Get 'em the fuck outta here."

Mongo grabbed Faye by the arm and rose.

Satin peered out the window to the crowd below.

Kang approached. "Should I have 'em come back tomorrow or what?"

"Yeah—yeah."

"Guy that brought 'em's in the can. Wait for him to get back an' take 'em out?"

"Sure." He leaned against the glass, trapped in bad thoughts. *How could this be?* After all he'd done to prove the bluff, incriminating evidence still surfaced. He toyed with the concept that Roc had a hand, but there was no way. The boy was too stupid, like Hector. No, the information was fed to him. That silly little cunt. Just wait, Vanda's out would be a foot massage compared to—

"Holy shit!"

"What now, Kang?"

"That's the fucker right there—rushing out with Gabby."

"*Gabby!*" The paper crushed in his fist.

Mongo and Faye's jaws went slack.

Satin scanned below, catching a white streak of boots out the door. *Mother fucker.* He launched towards the stairs, then paused. "Put the Fitzie bitch on lockdown—bring the brutha with us! Radio Marky to get his idiots an' send the Escalade 'round. Shit's 'bout to get *real*."

"I'm parked down the alley!"

The words fell short as Gabby scrambled for the dumpster, sliding to her knees, retrieving the goody bag. Alvi kept an eye on the door, anxious for what may clobber through. She slid the duffel over a shoulder. Soon as they were fixing to bail, Satin and crew smashed their way outside, forcing them to huddle behind the bin.

Satin darted up the alley, searching: a warden outfoxed. Luckily, the courtyard hid them in shadow. Alvi watched the fear permeate Mongo, strong-armed into an Escalade just pulling up front. Satin gave a last quick scan before hopping in shotty as rubber howled across worn gravel.

"Which way to the car?"

Alvi was taken aback at Gabby's crazed glare, wondering how such a sight could simply bounce right off her. Their good *friend*. He pointed a finger. They rose with caution, gently speeding down the alley towards the Benz.

At a red light, Alvi watched a vagrant sob on the steps of a closed florist; remnants of a funeral wreath doubled as an umbrella. He could hear the man's every moan as Gabby squeezed the duffel like a newborn, eyes on the road as if it could crumble beneath them. He wanted to explode but decided to wait. Her hand slid on his. Within seconds, they pulled into the Lafayette parking lot. Up the fire escape, they crept in without being noticed. Alvi unlocked his door and ushered her inside.

Dead soldiers peppered the floor. Gabby goose-stepped over clear bottles. Alvi *clacked* all three locks.

"What the fuck is goin' on, Gabby?"

"Hold up." She tossed her bag onto the cot and rushed into the bathroom.

Alvi took the final pull off a Beam and lit a smoke, waiting.

Gabby collected herself in the mirror before squatting on the toilet, assembling a story. She flushed and emerged. "Wasn't supposed to be like this, Alvi. We did it for Erma—this girl we knew—she was murdered. Wanted justice."

"Yeah, I know all 'bout her *now*." He pointed to the timeline of clippings on the far wall.

Gabby approached and admired.

"Why didn't you tell us? Could have helped you guys. Everyone's been worried sick—searchin' for you—readin' the papers—I mean, Vanda's...And now Mongo..." *Faye even.*

"I know—I know. But it's not my fault, alright?" She worked up tears. "Vanda wanted to get money off Satin—not me. Had dirt on him—I didn't know. I'm a victim too, Alvi! You gotta believe that!"

Alvi pursed the cig in his lips, gently unzipping her bag, one tooth at a time. "I dunno what to believe anymore."

Gabby leered as he hoisted one of the bricks. A single tear

jiggled on her chin.

"Justice, huh?"

A hand shot to her hip. "Yeah...well...once, you know...Vanda got it—had to pull something for money to escape. I gotta get outta town, man. You seen what I'm up against. Satin ain't gonna stop 'til he gets me, Alvi—*you* too now. We don't bust out this second, we're done for. Fuckin' *done*."

Alvi socked the window pane. He rattled coffins out the jar, chomping, sweating, thinking of every good memory they once shared in this miserable room, before their big break: her crushing his Oxies at breakfast, him painting her toenails...Now *this*—to bookend it all.

Gabby pulled evidence from out the bag. "Look for yourself."

He turned and grabbed the paper. A photo: *Erma. Satin. Moustasche*—"Who the fuck is this?" He grabbed the Cock-fighting Task Force clip from off the wall and passed both pictures to her. "Same guy—who is he?"

Gabby studied hard. "I-I dunno. Don't matter though." She pointed to a clipping on the wall. "Here's what happened right after Erma took this shot."

Alvi tried to form the link.

"That dead boy you saw back there—his father was killed beside her that night."

Alvi swallowed.

Her arms shot around his soft bones. "Come with me, baby. It'll be like old times. We can start over. Make a good life."

Their lips touched.

Gabby shot a glance to Angie's picture on the wall. "Look—take me to that beach in France you used to tell me about. We'll make it ours, Alvi. Me and you."

"That'll never be *ours*." He ran a hand over his face.

"Somewhere else then—anywhere, long as we're together."

"What about these bricks?"

"I know a guy who can unload it—I trust him."

"Chester, right?"

She smiled, head on his shoulder. "Goddamn lover, you really have been lookin' for me."

29.

One of the punches cracked an orbital. Mongo flinched, eye fluttering, jagged bone poking through like a jumbo shrimp kebob. The world was a vicious blur that she preferred stay fuzzy. Wasn't sure how much info she'd divulged between losing consciousness but sure she'd talked. Five ugly faces surrounded inside the Escalade. A flash of light from a passing car startled her; hand shot up in defense, not sure if it was the Indian's fist again. Her good eye came back into play. Sight out a window brought on a shiver. Across the street—the Lafayette.

Satin gave her time to recoup, focusing on Kang who was speaking with Holt on the phone. He was too ashamed to ask for Rocco's body dump, along with the rest of the crew. Holt *did* say to call with any hiccups. Kang passed the phone to him in the back seat, head shaking.

"He's fuckin' pissed, Ray."

"Yeah—yeah, he'll get over it."

"I dunno this time. Hope so."

Satin told Kang, Marky and Roach to exit and keep an eye out for their couple, then nodded to Sweetbreads. A giant hand grabbed the back of Mongo's neck, popping a vertebra.

She clutched the forearm, thick as a log. "I towed you, she ain't live here no mo'."

"But *you* do—I'm bettin' your boy Rat does too. What room?"

She squirmed, *Fuck*, conjuring an out. Could see Alvi's bedroom light on. Zimba's door was open too. "Awright, shit—lemme go. I'll see if he's dere."

Ray passed the phone, carefully watching as she dialed. Alvi not having a cell finally worked in his favor. She cupped her busted socket, waiting for a connect.

"Hello?"

"Alvi."

"This' Doreen, Mong—wrong number."

"Listen up—*Shit's fucked.*"

"What's up?"

"Where you at?"

"Zimba—boys got another keg. Alvi ain't here though. What's the 'mergency?"

"Just sit tight, okay?"

"Brawlin' or what?"

"Mm hmm. I'll meetcha there in five minutes."

"We'll be ready."

Ray reached for the phone.

Mongo hung up before he could grab it. "'Kay, I know where they both be at."

Holt scooped salsa onto a foil wrapper. Tangerine sign above him read, Macho's Tacos. An escort patrol car was parked on Vermont. Two officers awaited his return. Succulent bites filtered through the 'stache, careful not to drip on his paisley tie. Before he could finish, one of the cops (McCorkle) called out. Steaming chicken splattered cement. He raced over.

"Reynaga?"

Sandoval nodded from shotgun, handing over the cell.

He swallowed taco bits. "Mayor—this' gone too far. Satin's not only reckless, he's incompetent to boot. Now, I've had it—" He listened as Reynaga commiserated, regurgitating mistakes made on their end, proposing a new plan. Words sang into his ear, washing a sly grin. "Now *that* makes a whole lotta sense. I know it's a bit earlier than we planned but it has to be done—" He laughed. "Well, you won't have to worry anymore, sir. I'll take care of the situation personally."

The phone slid into his pocket. "Sandoval, radio back-up to gather Satin's stiffs and meet you two in the park—new spot— same deal—can burn these ones though. Have to be fast with it, another issue needs immediate attention." He exited the vehicle. "Long night ahead, fellas. Pick me up when you're done. Gonna grab some more dinner."

Sandoval grabbed the receiver as McCorkle lit berries and gunned it up the block.

Ronnie gripped a bat, tip wrapped in barbed wire, peering out his apartment's front window. Maribel was on the line with Doreen in the Zimba.

"Anything yet, Ron?"

"Nah."

He was careful not to draw the curtain too far. Car across the street had dark tint, restricting what else they were up against. The stooges buzzing at the bumper didn't raise alarm; Ronnie could take them out himself. Rain started up again. A car window slid down, and the bumper boys began to move.

"Here they come, Maribel. Don't look like they're armed. Tell 'em to do just as I said. I'll grab 'em on the way out."

Maribel whispered into the phone as if the bad men could hear.

Ronnie motioned for her to stay put as he headed out towards the street.

They left the lights on and crouched behind the bar. Doreen and Lexi had their pepper sprays ready. Elvira clutched stilettos. Footsteps tapped louder and louder outside. Vargas and Noodles manned fire extinguishers, barricaded by couches, twitchy as the men strolled in.

Everything was a little too quiet for Kang. He carefully paused in the center of the bar, finger up to keep his boys silent. By the looks of it, cockroaches could be the size of footballs in here.

"Man, fuck this, man. They ain't here, yo." Marky approached the bar, sending a hand over to fish for a bottle.

As Kang turned, he caught the flash of Marky's soles being sucked over the bar. A busty behemoth jumped up, raining blows with high heels. Two others sprung up, shooting something wet in his direction. Eyes burned, choking, he grabbed for the gun at his waistband. A finger barely swiped it before cold metal cracked the back of his skull. Felt like the floor threw its own haymaker. A cloud of white slime masked kicks to his ribcage. Eardrums blared. All he could do was lay there, poorly shielding his pounding head.

Roach stood frozen in the doorway, drinking in the melee. Two punks were turning Kang's face to pulp. But the girls...*Damn*. Couldn't dream Marky's status, behind that bar. Without warning, sharp shoes flew at him, head high. He ducked, turning to sprint back to the car.

Satin took notice too late. Was fixated on that door, wondering what the fuck was taking so long. Didn't catch the hulking menace sneak up the sidewalk with a bat of doom. Roach shot out the store—never saw it coming. His pain had a running start. Ray tried to shout through glass as barbed wire raked into Roach's gut, jackknifing him forward. Kid's eyes rolled white. The hulk's boot stomped Roach's chest, tearing razor barbs out his entrails. Before Ray gave command, Sweetbreads was out on a warpath.

Mongo took heed of the distraction, lunging halfway between

the front seats, punching the horn over and over. Could see Ronnie spin, clobbering the bat into Sweetbreads' roaring mouth. Satin's dry grip bit into her neck. A foot pried him off—only for a second. Her side door was kiddie proof. Ray's forearm now cranked her throat, crashing her forehead into the window.

The liquor store in the distance caught her attention. A man had pulled out front, loading mounds of tabloids into a newspaper stand. Her scream was stifled by suffocation. The man turned to the action across the street, never once panning in her direction. She took in a thin gasp. World began to streak, shake, buzz. Every street lamp became a violent wiggle. She scratched at the hold, eyes on that tabloid stand, bulging for air. *Goddammit, look this way!*

That's when she noticed.

On the cover of the papers—*LA Xpress*—*soft chocolate skin—honeycomb wig—highlights. Had to be. Just had to.* She forced one final focus. *It was...It—*

Ray jerked a last time, just to be certain. His attention went back to that door—the crew. Roach and Sweetbreads were down for the count; the hulk hovered over them, winded and unscathed. No sign of Kang or Marky. *Was there any crew left?* He glanced back at the body, contemplating his next move. In all his years, never once had a corpse looked so content. He climbed into the driver's seat and rumbled the beast to life.

The scene down below chilled their hearts. Initially, those honks didn't have them scrambling. Thankfully, Alvi checked the commotion. Gabby's face was blank, watching as Ronnie slid that giant new guy into the Zimba by his ankles, still writhing, trailing thick crimson tracks. Satin's car remained out front— could only see its roof.

"Come on!" Alvi grabbed the duffel and shoved her out to the fire escape.

30.

Fire engine cries tore through the night. Giant lips of flame lashed upwards across hilltops, spreading rapidly with purpose and conviction, scorching anything dead enough to ignite. A baptism of rain couldn't contain the rage. Holt leaned on the squad car, puffing a Swisher, reflecting on the incompetence of the LAPD. Griffith Park commenced its suicide, sending animals racing for sanctuary.

He spat tobacco flecks, devouring the street scene. McCorkle averted traffic from entering off Los Feliz, creating congestion in every direction. Sandoval peppered flares, closing off the park, sucking a scorched finger like infant to nipple. *Seriously, what kinds of tests were passed in order to wear that badge?* Then again, what caliber of folks did the City expect would show up, answering their call on billboards? These two had to be walk-ins; ex-jocks nursed through high school because they could memorize a few plays, protect the QB. *Thinkers were frowned upon on the Force.* Nevertheless, even the simplest of tasks could be botched when done over and over. He didn't blame them for *this*. Sure they lit the match and piled the bodies…*How were they supposed to know Rocco's corpse would roll down a ravine once barbequed?* Nope, the blade would fall upon Satin this time. He was fully responsible—accountable, for everything. A thought made his 'stache tingle: Ray publicly incinerated like a Zen Buddhist monk.

Cell buzzed.

"Talk to me...GPS came through...Uh huh...Where is he? Okay, keep me posted. On my way to the vicinity—be there in ten."

The cigar hit McCorkle in the vest as Holt shot past in their cruiser.

Sandoval pointed a blistered digit. *"Hey?"*

The Benz creeped, lights off, lurking in darkness as the Escalade sped off. Alvi kept the car burning diesel, couldn't slug it to Chester's—no way. Satin had driven in their intended direction; a new route was necessary. They crept onto the street, rain sperming the windshield. Zimba's door was closed. Gabby wondered what was happening inside. Alvi detoured down towards Wilshire, playing it safe.

Satin cursed the steering wheel, swerving up Beverly, sending Mongo's skull thumping in the rear. The Glock his nephew tried executing him with now sat on his lap. He screeched on a dime in the center median. A gypsy cab honked, swerving. *Couldn't leave the crew like that. Couldn't crawl to Holt like* this. Had never run before, wouldn't start now.

Tires hydroplaned, spinning him back towards the Lafayette. Caught a glimpse of taillights launching out its parking lot; could barely make two passengers. Thoughts of the crew were dropped. Triumph might be back on the table. He fingered the trigger, thinking, *Had to be*, trailing at a distance for blocks.

He cut down shadowed side streets for closer glances of this Mercedes. Profiles flickered at every cross street. The girl could've been Gabby—could've been anybody. It was the driver's tattooed cranium that confirmed all hopes.

* * *

Cold asphalt glistened. They cruised with caution, Gabby petting his thigh. Streets were eerily quiet. No burrito wrapped bums. No streetwalkers. Felt like the city was in freeze-frame. Alvi remained alert. *Only a few miles to go.* His mind was sound on survival until the rearview brought back floods of hell.

The Gaylord Apartments beamed emerald tubes high above, letters forming an evil grin. His mouth went dry. Had avoided this stretch for years. Their current predicament had forced the notion deep into his brain. *How could he forget?* Tried to pry his eyes from the building—could swear the menace began to breathe. He focused back on the road, blinking for clarity. Shots of Angie clipped the eyelids.

A beast with a downtown heart…

He popped a smoke.

Streets are arteries…

Gabby brushed his arm. "You okay, lover?"

Before he could nod, a crash sent them flying into the dashboard. Alvi's head slammed the wheel, cigarette like an accordion. Gabby had a gash below the eye, slowly seeping red beads. She swabbed the tears with her shirt.

Tires screeched behind.

They turned and saw Satin's broken headlamps. Maniacal eyes met theirs as the car growled for another smash. Where did he come from? Gabby screamed as Alvi punched the gas, trying to minimize impact; bumper cars this time. The clip gave an added boost, pinballing them between palms.

The frantic pace was too much for the Benz. Sideswipes jarred the world, sending buildings into their path at weird angles. They grazed parked cars, lopping off rows of side mirrors. Alvi cranked the wheel, regaining control for brief moments.

Veins, Veins, Veins…

Neon teeth chomped from rooftops, piercing the windshield, trying to swallow them whole: Bryson/Asbury/Royale Wilshire.

Alvi flinched as the concrete monsters closed in, spitting sparks at every shrill Satin crash. Gabby gripped the dash and ceiling, best she could, bracing each impact. There was no out. Alvi thought fast, smartening up at MacArthur Park, both feet slamming the brake.

Satin shot past, tires gripping wet road. The Escalade spun violently, crashing up the sidewalk of the park's bridge; a jutting gutter snapped its front axle, sending the rear smashing into a statue of General Otis. Ray was unfazed, leaning out the driver's side window.

They saw white flashes before hearing bullets smash around them. Gabby screamed. Alvi pressed her head down to her knees and gunned it towards the Escalade. Windows shattered as they careened past, over the bridge. Gabby's head rest exploded fluff innards. The Benz fish-tailed a left at Alvarado. Their heads popped up once shots simmered.

Alvi felt for wounds, heart fluttering like an abandoned puppy. "You okay?"

Gabby nodded, blood tears streaking the cheeks.

A line of patrol cars flew past in opposite lanes, their berries twirling without siren screams. Ghetto bird blades thumped overhead, turning them spastic in their seats. Alvi slowed to the speed limit, as if the Benz wasn't in shambles. The choppers' searchlight cast behind them, white light freezing its prey. In the distance, could see Satin's busted car completely surrounded.

A block out from the Paradise Motel and the hilltops grabbed Gabby's attention. "Alvi—get a load of that!"

He leaned in for a better look out the fractured windshield, catching surreal glimpses between cracks and wiping blades. Griffith Park was ablaze. Homes roasted, glowing like coals as heat licked the Observatory, headed for the Hollywood sign. Hoards were out on Sunset, fleeing their cars, crowding sidewalks, watching, pointing—white knuckles on loved ones as

Satan blazed his city to the heavens. Alvi wondered, *Would it be contained or feast till every last celebrity turned to ash?* He took one more glance. "So long, my love."

They pulled into the purple fog, parking out front. Frantic knocks were met eventually. Chester was in boxers, doped up; the sight had him slap his bruised cheekbone.

"Gabby—that you?"

They pushed past, inside.

Alvi locked the door, peering through curtains as Gabby embraced her other man, clobbering his blue cheek with lipstick and blood. Coast was clear.

"What the fuck, Alvi? How'd you find her—what happened?" He dabbed the fresh wound on her face and rummaged for Band-Aids.

"Long story, man—ask me later. Right now, we need a solid."

"Sure—what?"

Alvi placed the duffel on the bed and pulled out bricks. Gabby grabbed one and handed it over.

"Need you to move these, Chestie—tonight. Can you make a few calls?"

"Where the hell'd—"

Her fingers pinched his lips. "That's not important, baby. Can you or can't you?"

"Can't wait a few hours—'til mornin'?"

She shook her head, pouting a lip.

"Okay, sure—my guy could prolly move it."

He tossed the brick back and forth, gauging weight. "How you even know this' any good? Could be cut to hell for all we know."

"See for yourself," said Alvi.

Chester lit up, sending a palm out to caress Gabby's face, heart growing thick. Remembered the last time he felt this happy: *Letty's darling picture.* "Yeah...yeah, sure thing." He paused at the bathroom door, gazing back in disbelief. "One helluva sight, sweetheart."

Gabby blew a kiss. "Hurry up, daddy."

The door shut.

She headed straight for the mirror, sprucing up best she could. Alvi lit a smoke and watched her analyze every inch: hair frazzled, nails chipped, blood crust on her chin. Only now had it finally sunk in. All his time spent, and there she was—in the flesh. *Persistence paid off*. Wished Mongo could see this. Hoped she and Faye were somewhere safe. Happy thoughts: *they were tough, no worries*. That conversation with Mongo earlier popped into mind.

Told you what she said…Don't believe me?

I want her *to tell me*.

Gabby caught his spaced-out stare and approached. "You okay? What's the matter, lover?"

Ritual instruments were strewn, accordingly. Chester cranked his neck before lighting the candle. *Just a taste, maybe a pinch more for the connoisseur—a real high-brow hit*.

The caramel aroma perked his senses, nerves panting like a pooch for biscuits; that lovely *hisssss* over flame, bubbling hypnotic, could listen for days; the plastic *crrrrunch* of fresh rig from wrapper; then a final *sizzzzle*, goods sucking up to barrel. Few forearm pumps and he was geared for sacrifice.

Didn't spurt the wall this time—few dots on the floor. Caught a glimpse in the mirror, leaning back for the ride. Course was quick. Chin to chest as it peaked, too soothing to smile. Stuff was tits, alright. *Damn…damn…too good*.

A ghost wall sprung up through linoleum, smacking him in the face.

His head snapped into the shower curtain, eyes leaping the skull. Faculties went void, everything grinding to a halt. *Was this still bliss or had the ride finally gone off the rails?*

* * *

The Escalade sat diagonal on the bridge sidewalk, geyser spouting at the moon beyond.

"Suspect remains in the vehicle, sir. Appears to also be an unidentified male in the rear—deceased."

Holt nodded to the officer, watching as a team commanded Satin's hands out the window, guns drawn. Perimeter was blocked. Flatfoots diverted any oncoming cars. No pedestrian activity. Holt approached the passenger door, unlocked it through the shattered window and climbed in. Cops held ground, lowering guns.

"The fuck's this all about, Holt? You got no idea what's going on right now! This bitch—"

Holt noticed the Glock on the console. "Shhh—get your hands on the wheel."

Ray complied. "Gun's empty. Listen—dirt that girl Vanda tried to blackmail me with actually surfaced, for reals. This other bitch knows everythin'! Was on her tail when your guys took me down!"

"By the looks of this car, took yourself down." Holt craned into the back seat, tilting to admire Mongo. "Who's this?"

"One of this bitch's friends, ay. She's still on the streets with some other dude—we gotta find her—names' Gabby Wang—"

"Shuddup—you're telling me there's more blood to be let?"

"Little bit—that's it."

"Where's the rest of your crew?"

Satin shrugged.

Holt scoffed. "You wouldn't have lasted this long down in Mexico—let me tell you. As a runner—I had incentive to deliver. If standards weren't met, repercussions were dire—this shit just wouldn't happen. You fucked the Mayor over bad, Ray. Should be strung upside down under this bridge, minus a head—but you're lucky—this is L.A. Now that's too bad about your men but listen, you know why I'm here—"

"Wait."

"City's done wiping your ass, Ray. When we went into

business—thought things were clear on both ends. Past few days have been a strain on the relationship—the delivery crash, bodies on top of bodies—you realize you're a few bricks short this week, right?"

"*Mira*, that's small nuts compared to what we got going, man—you gotta bear with me, bro."

Holt rubbed an eye. "Trail trickles up, Ray."

"Listen, you in that photo too—"

"Don't give a shit. I know you're desperate, but even if I'm incriminated with you for that night with your brother—I got Reynaga and the whole fucking city at my back. You had that too—not anymore. Should have come to us with this—like you were told. How good's the help when they can't take fucking orders?"

Ray shook his head in disagreement.

"Look, I'm not here as a mediator today, okay? The contract has been terminated and I'm here to see to it." Holt pulled a matte black piece from out his jacket.

"Wait!"

Windows flashed orange, surrounding officers re-aiming weapons.

Satin choked words, thin stream draining out the chest.

Holt cleaned off his prints. "This wasn't supposed to be enjoyable, Ray—just business." He waited for the final gasp before exiting, tossing the gun to the closest officer inching towards the vehicle.

31.

Features on her face were foreign, hard. Whatever Alvi once saw in them, a beauty reminiscent of Angie, had completely vanished. Couldn't remember her overbite being so sharp, teeth so crooked, eyes like swamp water piercing him after floating those long aching words. *Just wanted to hear* her *say it.*

She gave an appalled routine, denying such ridiculousness, hurting at the thought of such an act. "I love you *sooo* much, Alvi—how could you even think I would do you like that? Because of the break-up? Look—*now* I know that I want to spend the rest of my life with you. Isn't that enough—"

"Save it, okay—Mongo told me everything."

She iced, could almost hear bones cracking.

"Why d'you lie to me, Gabby?"

Her mouth went slack but no words.

A loud *thud* came from the bathroom.

She rushed to open the door. "Fuck!"

Alvi grabbed Chester, slapping him silly, searching for a pulse. *Not again! How long had he been out?* "Gotta call him an ambulance!" His cry went without response as he cranked a familiar cold shower.

Drawers slammed open and shut in the bedroom.

Gabby tried remembering where he kept it, last time she borrowed for the gig. She grumbled, "Know you're in here."

Alvi placed Chester gently in the tub and went to see what was happening.

"Bingo." Her fingers raided a Barbicide jar, filled with rolled up bills. "He's dead, Alvi. Can't unload the bricks—ambulance won't help us either." She fanned nine hundred, pocketing it. "You comin'?"

He grabbed her by the shoulders. "Can't just leave him like this."

"Watch me." She pulled the remaining bricks out the duffel and tossed them onto the bed. "When they find him—be an open-shut case. Your hands are clean now—have a nice life."

He spun her back.

She saw passion boiling in his eyes, knew what was coming next.

"*Why did you lie, Gabby?* After all we had…you owe me an explanation. *Give me a reason!*"

She smirked.

He slapped it off her face.

Her head snapped back. "*I don't owe you a goddam thing!* I needed cash, and you supplied it. That's all. No love— *nothing.* Already got two girls of my own back home—and a husband…Anything else you wanna know, *dear?*"

He choked air, eyes glued on her playful face. Before the blow could sink in, another came his way.

Gabby shoved a knee into his crotch, doubling him over.

Alvi fell to his knees.

She raked nails through one of the bricks, scraping a hefty pinch.

He coughed vomit, lunging at her feet.

She leapt from his grasp, throwing a cloud of heroin at his face before sprinting out the door.

He writhed on the ground, burn trickling through eye sockets, roaring as it took hold, body herky-jerky, slower and slower till fading into a blackened sea—Great White nightmares circling around.

The screams had motel guests averting attention from burning hilltops, roaming violet fog to gawk the scene in room fifteen. Gabby kept on down Sunset, blending with the onlookers, asking about the fire, hailing an idle cab on Beaudry.

"Union Station."

She sniffed the binky in the backseat, never once looking back, vowing only foreword from now on. *Good riddance.* No glory left in Los Angeles.

The squad car rested in darkness under a 101 overpass. Tears bombed off Holt's 'stache, soaking his chest and collar; an endless river every time, always followed by laughter. Adrenaline dump: an old friend.

Last time it was this bad, happened in broad daylight, outside a cantina. Tijuana. Once all was settled, those blank stares on filthy Chiclets kids forever branded the brain. That time it was self-defense, three of them, associates—friends. Saw them coming in the barroom mirrors. Savages, spraying death throughout: busboys, barkeeps, whores, whoever. How he made it, still unclear—just a week before this current stretch of living. Never had he known getting that shipment busted in Long Beach could turn out like this. At least things turned out; his dark prayers answered. He lingered in positivity, *Satin dug his own grave*—snot belting hanky, collecting himself for the call.

Reynaga.

"The problem has been solved—I've gone and sent twenty men to the casita, taking over activities, making sure none of the hiccups have stirred our customers. It would be in our best interest to move on to Phase II of the operation..."

He scribbled deets onto a memo pad.

"So, everything's in motion—Fitzie's is ready for re-opening too?" The pen died, concentric circles spawned rebirth. "No, we're still short on those bricks but I'm working on it—you said the next shipment arrives midday tomorrow, correct?" He wrote quickly as the Mayor rattled off instructions. *Every casita under their control—every one a distribution hub—major increases in volume—county wide.* "Sounds like we're on track, sir. If I may give a suggestion as to the bodies of Satin and his men—I say go the *hero* route, commending them in the public eye for their Cockfighting Task Force duties—reiterating the severity of this ongoing problem, vowing justice on those responsible— blah, blah, blah—retaining this diversion for the operation." The Mayor's laugh washed a smile. "Thank you, sir. I—what was that? No, I haven't heard the latest on any fire...Really? Alright, I'll steer clear."

Lights flashed the car to life, awakening tunnel dwellers piled by cardboard. He gave a deafening chirp before gunning back into the trenches. Barely one block out and a call came over dispatch. Buzz words.

Heroin—blocks—shooting gallery—Paradise Motel—two bodies—one deceased—one critical...

He skidded a u-turn, opening the engine, piercing night.

White lights, weak limbs...

Punches to the heart, plastic over mouth, warm air into lungs...

Commotion—cold hands—shouts of strange men: stat, cc, one-two-three lift!

Goddamn you, Gabby...

Protect me, Angie...

Ceiling knife marks began to move, wheels squeaked beneath. Outside—an ambulance strobe disco, ash and soot dancing through night chill.

More sharp pricks.

Ma...

Your son is slipping...

Warmth enveloped, from toes to neck, dragging Alvi back into abyss.

* * *

In the distance, helicopters bombed hilltops with reservoir rain as Holt walked into room fifteen, dismissing detectives for a moment, sliding leather gloves. Body in the bathroom had familiar bulging peepers. Bricks on the bed confirmed his thoughts—their H—ones missing—too pure for the public. Ambulance crew had the second OD stable enough for transport, wheeling him out the door.

He swiped a duffel off the ground, pouring contents onto the table. Women's clothes—punker garb. *No woman was reported on scene.* A crumpled piece of paper stuck out a jacket pocket. Made sure no one was watching before he unfolded. The sight of his own face was a thumb in the ass. *Satin's blackmail photo— wasn't blowin' smoke.* He re-sifted the garments. *Who was this girl?* The dunce's words rang, pre-death: *This other bitch has it...Name's Gabby Wang.* He pocketed the image and quickly loaded the bag with bricks.

Ambulance doors crashed outside.

He bolted towards them, re-opening.

"Close the doors—we're losing him!"

Holt jumped inside. "Step on it—need this one alive."

FOUR

Damn This Soul

Final 'Bust...

Albuquerque, New Mexico—A Monday, 6:06 a.m.

The train yawned upon its stop. Passenger commotion awoke Gabby from deep sleep—best she'd had in months. She swabbed gunk from the eyes, glancing at her itinerary, knowing exactly which city she'd just arrived. Layover was three hours, then onward to Chicago. Had time to hit Garcia's for a hot bowl of Menudo, buy a warm jacket for the expected wind, maybe even...She reached into a pocket, sniffing at the binky, drifting. Had time, wouldn't make contact—just wanted a glimpse. Who did they look like? How had they grown? She sped through the station, eager to cleanse this guilt smudge from the brain.

Four paws clobbered the driveway, skidding dirt to a stop. A slobbering tongue lashed out, clamping down on today's newspaper, tail at full bore, sprinting back towards the porch. Colt gazed at the dog with tired eyes, slurping the day's first cup of Folgers in a bathrobe and moccasins. Sans undies, he cinched the belt tight, butchering that coffee jingle in the brain. Best part of waking up is crisp air on your nuts. Pooch circled around, playfully gnashing the Journal. Come on, Georgie—don't be drenchin' them headlines. He sat at the table, perusing the day's atrocities—purposely skipping anything pertaining to Los Angeles. Didn't care. Became accustom, once she bailed. Midway through the Cowboys' column, Georgie began to holler, frothing at the screen door—something off in the bushes. Colt rose. Must be 'nother one of them coons fuckin' with the garbage again.

He opened the door, giving Georgie first whack, heading upstairs to retrieve the rifle.

House looked the same, a bit larger than Gabby remembered. Dew frosted the lawn, dandelions tall and crisp, floating like a legion of jellyfish. Could see Colt through the window, wearing her purple robe, sipping that cheap dirt she couldn't stand. Girls would be up for school soon. Georgie dashed out the house, straight for her. Shouldn't have parted those branches, shimmering leaves. Before she could rise, the mutt was drooling in her arms. She kissed his bristled head, warm breath sour but welcomed. Knew seeing family wouldn't be easy, but now touching—thoughts of hugging—twisted the ribcage like fork to spaghetti. Could just walk up like nothing ever happened— wouldn't want her back after all this. Too long—too late. Be the last time. Still make that train.

Colton knew it would happen. Role played this day, every day since. All those times hadn't worked him up this much. He released the blinds, erasing her image. Blood boiled, gazing from the doorway—girls' angelic faces, peaceful in sleep. Never deserved this. Never again. He darted into his bedroom. Rifle slid into play, crouching beside the window. She was now in full view—face scabbed—bright teeth, beckoning Georgie to follow her towards the porch. Dumb dog's tail lashed in excitement. Colt scoffed. She prolly pegged him a fool too—expected the same warm embrace. He rose, barrel at his toes. She froze in the driveway, looking up; an awkward palm ascended to greet. He remained stone, chest a balloon stoked by fire. Didn't need crosshairs, no imagination this time—no beer cans. The real deal screamed down below. Barrel rose to perfection. Morning breeze made her hair dance. Held his breath as the world shattered, then her skull, brain out the back like pumpkin innards. Body gave, timbered slow. He rested the rifle to relish her fall.

Screams broke slumber. Blast had the girls crying in fear. Lottie Mae shot out the Barbie bed, climbing a plastic slide by the window. Shasta followed with her plush elephant, too short to see. Mommy! Back from the Angels! Lottie Mae ran out the door, just past daddy's grasp. Shasta crashed into hairy arms, tiny body shaking as daddy flew her down stairs. From the porch, saw mommy sleeping on the lawn—Georgie circling in whimpers—Lottie Mae, pajamas soaked red. Did she spill fruit punch too? Thick fingers shielded her eyes. Cold bit her earlobes; Lottie Mae's cry introduced a new side of life. Daddy's voice: Just 'member, honey—the damned don't die...only them dreamers.

32.

Lips of water glistened in sulfurous sunlight, haze cloaking the entire city. Hillside fire wasn't close to containment. The L.A. River's current had a healthy flow from the night's drizzle. Three young boys skipped rocks across it, loitering on the bike path, avoiding school. Their hands were caked in mud, shirts filthy. One wearing an oxygen mask hurried to round-up more stones. Other two had their shirts over their noses, trying not to breath in lingering smoke. The masked boy heaved half a brick at the water.

"Almost nailed the big one that time!"

A voice resonated beyond.

"Whatcha guys doin'—skippin' stones?"

The children turned to see an older girl walking a bike. A white carpenter's mask covered her mouth. She slid the mask down around her neck and gave a hearty smile.

The two boys lowered their t-shirts, faces rough, missing teeth.

Masked one asked, "You're not a teacher, right?"

The girl set down her bicycle, took off a backpack and grabbed a rock, gauging its weight. "Nope." She winded up to throw. "I study film at—" Before she could complete her sentence, four mounds at the riverbank held her cold. She squinted for clarity, trying to decipher what they were; coursing water stifled each.

One of the boys heaved another brick, this time striking one of them. A wet *thud* made them giggle.

The girl approached another ten feet and instantly knew what they were. Each was hog tied with duct tape, face down in the bank. Her hand cupped her mouth, turning to see the boys sprinting off in the distance. She ran for her backpack, retrieving a cell to dial 9-1-1.

Three of the bodies were unknown but one had Holt blowing kisses. Kang's bloated carcass lay like a beached seal at the river's edge. Holt flipped through more of the crime scene photos in the back of the cruiser, sparking a fresh cigar. The other three bodies were of no concern to him: two dreadlocked skulls and an Indian the size of a grizzly. Kang was the last of the casita boys who could identify him or the Mayor personally, which made his day a tad bit easier. The final transition in their casita takeover was now complete. He tossed the pictures back into their envelope and exited the car.

Beverly Boulevard was oddly serene for an area that thrives nocturnally. Must be the patrol cars lining the block. McCorkle and Sandoval waved from across the street. Holt ignored them, savoring long puffs, scanning the crumbling apartment complex they were standing before. Could barely make out what the age-old paint spelled on the side of the building. *Bath & Showers $2.50?* Alvin Drake's car found at the Paradise was registered here; Vance "Mongo" Mongalez's ID bore this same address. Warrants were issued to search each of their units. Holt had his own investigation going. He tossed the stogie to the gutter and marched into the street.

Ronnie and Maribel stood in the hallway as detectives tore Alvi's room to shreds. An officer barred them from entry, dodging their questions, holding up a warrant. Doreen inquired from her open door, Lexi and Elvira looming behind her. Maribel *shooshed* with hand signals, telling them to stay inside their apartment.

Two more officers approached from the stairwell, trailed by a suit with a moustache. One of the cops nudged Ronnie from blocking the hallway as the suit darted into the room.

Holt stood before the giant poster on the wall, peering closely at the young skater's facial features. The composition of the shot was superb, a juxtaposition of innocence and danger balanced only by grace and skill. The child was defying gravity—universal law. He knew for sure that this was a young Alvin Drake. No wonder this was what became of the bastard—once that grace had departed. *Sooner or later, gravity takes its pull.* He rummaged through a hulking pill jar, popped three Vicodin and chewed till dust.

His attention returned to the opposing wall, filled with damning news articles and documents. Everything thumbed a finger at Drake, didn't matter if he was innocent—looked guilty as sin. The newshounds would have a picnic; an answer to the public's prayers. Was almost too easy. *Pin the tale on the flunky.*

Sandoval approached with a nametag in his hand. "One of our guys found this in Mongo's room, sir."

Holt inspected the badge. Clean Spikes Now. A pretty face for a lousy name—*Gabby, Gabby, Gabby...Where are you, my dear?* He re-entered the hallway. "Which one of you is the complex manager?"

Ronnie raised his hand and introduced himself.

Holt refrained from giving his name, dangling Gabby's badge before Ronnie's face. "Tell me about her."

Ronnie barely peeked at the image. "Never seen her before."

Maribel shrugged beside him.

Holt smiled. "Don't keep track of your tenants, huh? That's hard to believe."

Ronnie deadpanned. "Wasn't my tenant—like I said, dunno the gal."

Holt nodded and noticed a door ajar, down the way. He turned to stare directly, and it slammed shut. "You have ghosts here, Ronnie?"

"Doesn't everybody?"

Maribel gave an awkward giggle.

Holt snapped at one of the detectives. "Call more back-up and seal off the perimeter 'til a warrant for the entire building is secure." He tapped the nametag before handing it over. "She's here, somewhere. Find her."

Ronnie and Maribel roared in protest. Sandoval held them back with his club as Holt hit the stairs to phone the Mayor.

Lafayette hard lucks cluttered the sidewalk along Beverly. Most were in tattered sleeping garments, physically present but mentally aloof. Any reason for this disruption in their lives was beyond them. Doreen, Lexi and Elvira huddled at the stairs, chain smoking menthols, gossiping on Gabby, worried for Alvi, wondering where the fuck Faye and Mongo were. Noodles and Vargas were shackled in the back of a police cruiser; officers found them huffing spray paint in the Zimba, faces silver as cutlery.

Ronnie and Maribel took the girls aside, insuring that their best interests rely on keeping their mouths shut. Not that any heat was coming down on them, but when it came to police questioning, clamming up was always best.

Ronnie: "We make our own justice, 'member?"

They all nodded, thinking of those four fledgling attackers the other night, before returning to the moment at hand. Everybody knew Gabby wasn't inside the complex. Hadn't seen her in forever—just another fallen angel. Since when did the pigs give a fuck about those? This roust was a waiting game, and like every other citizen when it came to the LAPD, they were helpless.

* * *

Every room got ransacked. Looney tenants knew bubkis. Holt could've bet big that his hunch was right. He shook it off. Gabby wasn't here...*She'd turn up, eventually.*

The initial search brought enough dirt on Drake though— still piling. Holt ran fingers through his hair, admiring a lipstick scroll on one of the tenants' bedroom mirrors.

FAYE LOVES ALVI

He'd have one of the detectives look into it. *Could be something worthwhile.* Regardless, Drake had sealed his fate—another screaming cellblock soul. Well, he would be—if he could hang on and pull back through to the living.

33.

Waves crashed, keeping Alvi under; lungs to the brim, tumbling through whitewash. Arms finally took stride, legs kicking to breach the surface. Both hands dug sand on stroke number four. Wrong way. The heart stopped—too weak. His body seized, floating weightless at the mercy of the tide...

Bright light, strong arms. Water choked out the mouth, spraying cold air. Eyes opened to salt burns; Angie—helping him to shore. France. The body surged, grabbing her at the waist, lifting; those eyes were diamonds, cutting the clouds. He walked towards their red striped umbrella, retrieving a towel. She followed, giggling, splashing water. He grabbed the camera as she ran up, capturing the frame forever. She jumped, legs wrapped akimbo, lips smashing as the sand sucked them down...down...

Feet hit cement. She was gone. Under the arm, a skateboard—before him, Malibu Castle. Familiar voices beckoned Ratboy. He turned to see all of them—the old crew. Blisko stood before them, pointing down. Moat was dry, smooth hips, a pristine circular snake run. He slapped tail on coping and dropped straight in. Wind rushed over cheekbones as he flew, effortless—twisting, grabbing, grinding, every trick clean—bolts—bliss. The boys hooted, clapping boards to cement; just like old times. Each graceful launch brought the heavens closer. He reached, longing for her touch, a hand to pull him back up. Instead, he took another slam, breaking through concrete, falling...

Fifteen steps to that rooftop. Knew exactly what lie in wait. She'd be naked under that Ratboy shirt again, cursing Gaylord tubes, blood pooling beneath her into a river of death. He stepped out into silence, city void of restless clamor. Scarlet blotted tissues wafted about—a thousand perfect snowflakes. She was crouched, quiet, fingers between her thighs. He placed a hand on her shoulder. Comforting words were stifled once the face craned his way. Gabby! The world erupted. He stumbled back, too close to the edge, flailing. Buildings breathed fire down Wilshire, windows bursting under neon brains. Above: the Archangel lopped skulls off ascending demons, casting souls back to famed gutters. Whole city was aflame. His balance was almost there—if only there was something to grasp. She approached, cunt smeared red—dripping hands cast out to him. He strained for the gesture, realizing too late that she wasn't offering a gift of life, just applying one final push...

Sweat chills greeted upon revival. Overhead: fluorescent bulbs, caged by honeycomb. Eyes darted from the bed. Clean walls; antibacterial scents masking urine. Hyperventilation brought the tubing into light. Arms were slow, swiping the plastic out his face. He sat up, examining monitors—a crippled senior snored across the way. *Hospital?* He rubbed the back of his head, trying to lift the fog. A portly black nurse rushed in.

"Mister Drake—please lay back." She killed the buzzing machines, paging for assistance.

"Wha—where am I?"

Her hand pinched his wrist, eyeing a watch. "You're at Good Samaritan Hospital—been here for three days. Welcome back."

"Wha—"

"Mister Drake, you've survived a massive overdose of narcotics. Rapid detox was administered. You're lucky to be here. Someone upstairs must still care about you. Please lay back, doctor is on his way." She re-inserted an IV drip.

Images flooded back into the brain, slowly, piece by piece.

The heart raced as the nightmare resonated. A doctor walked in: tall, cold, bloodshot.

"Does Mister Drake know why he's here?"

"I've already filled him in, doctor."

The doc analyzed his chart, barking orders into a recorder before administering meds. "This should help with any pain. We lost you for nearly four minutes, Alvin. We induced the coma once you stabilized—to reduce any more trauma to the brain. Keep that in mind during your recovery. Most patients like you remain dead on arrival." He whispered to the nurse as they breached the door.

Alvi deciphered their mumbles, familiar tingles coursing his system, massaging nerves.

"Have the Detectives been notified?"

"No, doctor—they're in the cafeteria."

He shook cobwebs, waiting for their footsteps to trail before sitting up, attempting to swing both legs to the floor. Right one hit a snag. Blanket off, a handcuff shackle brought palms to his face.

Holt took the phone from his ear and set it on the balcony rail. Views of the sprawling Southland lie before him, a dense orange mass enveloped the sun's warmth from touching any streets. He watched as an airplane ascended over downtown towers, disappearing once it breached the suffocating smoke. Fire hadn't reached the Mayor's compound as firefighters were dispatched accordingly. Holt could see the massive destruction of neighborhoods due west. Might as well been an air strike that hit the hillside. He sipped the final blast out a coffee mug and smiled, reflecting on the phone call. *Another perfect day.*

His slippers scraped down the mansion's marble corridor; walls formed a tunnel of accolades, magazine covers and awards. A giant key to the city guided him upstairs. Reynaga had wanted to re-analyze Alvi Drake's police file last night, now Holt had to retrieve it. At the third floor, he cinched his robe and rapped on French doors.

"Come in!"

Reynaga was in bed. On each side of him, brunettes gave kitten yawns, rolling back to sleep. Another body bobbed beneath velvet sheets, covering Reynaga at the waist.

Holt was unfazed as he approached. "He's come to."

"Drake?"

Holt nodded. "Where's the file?"

Reynaga turned to a nightstand, girl #3 adjusting her strokes with his every move. One of the brunettes was in his way. He flicked a finger at her brow before pushing her aside to reach the documents. "Here."

Holt perused the contents, securing that everything was there.

Reynaga said, "The paperwork on Faye Green is inside too. Withhold her whereabouts to the detectives—they can use her as further ammunition."

"I was thinking the same thing—since the casita has tabs on her."

Reynaga yawned. "Drake's perfect though—everything adds up; our precious little lamb. Tell the detectives to go forward with it. I'd like to make a formal announcement about Drake at this afternoon's C.T.F. press conference—put the city at ease while the cameras are rolling. Any new developments on this Gabby situation?"

"We're working on it. Men have been dispatched to Mrs. Wang's former residence in Albuquerque—still no word back. Now that she appears to be the only loose end in this whole Satin debacle, I doubt she poses any real threat to us. My guess is she's gone, and she'll stay gone."

"For peace of mind then, see if they can squeeze any more leads on her during Drake's interrogation. I prefer *zero* loose ends."

Holt nodded, turning to leave.

"Uh, one more thing."

"Yes."

"Could you hit the Record button on the camera on your way out?"

He spun, noticing a tripod in the corner.

"Thanks, buddy."

The bed began to squeak before Holt had even shut the doors.

His guest house was at the rear of the compound. Holt walked through columns of roses, breathing in sweetness all the way to his front door. The innards were dark, black curtains drawn, omitting any outside light. The walls were bare, no television, no computer—just a small table in the corner; atop sat dark candles, drawn behind a pewter dagger, frayed book and human skull. He tossed Drake's file onto the bed and proceeded to draw a bath.

His red robe fell to the tile; he stood before a mirror, gazing at scarred pink flesh, slapping his hairless stomach. *'Stache could use a trim.* Across his chest screamed the head of a goat: blank eyes, frothing lips, numerals carved in its forehead. He strummed a nipple before retrieving a lighter below the sink and heading towards his altar.

Each hop shot aches up Alvi's groin, shackled leg now scissored, ninety degrees north. The bed trailed, squeaking, inching closer to the phone at the geezer's bedside. One nearest him, removed. He plopped next to the old man, exhausted, both bed's t-boned, cluttering the room. Duffer remained sedate, sweaty. First number he could remember got punched on the dial.

"Come on, Mong—pick up," came under stale breath.

Five rings to a voicemail. He hung up and tried again. No luck.

Blisko popped in the brain. He punched rapidly, met by disconnect tones.

"Fuck!"

He racked. One more option, one he hadn't called in some time.

Brrr...Brrr...Brrr...
Each ring made the gut sink further.
"Hello?"
"*Ma,* don't hang up—it's Alvi."
"*Alvi...*this is your Aunt Rita. I've been desperately trying to get a hold of you—"
Rita.
"You'd better come on home, soon as possible."
"Put Mona on the phone."
A sigh came through.
"Alvi..."
"What the fuck's goin' on?"
"There's no easy way to say this, so I'm just going to say it. Mona passed away last week—I found her unresponsive in her living room. I'm so sorry..."
His jaw unhinged, expelling a faint puff.
"I tried to find you—Mona had your forwarding address but I went there and spoke with a young girl who said you didn't live there—a redhead. The funeral was yesterday—Alvi, I had no other way to contact you..."
Faye: Some lady came by, asking for you...
Mailbox: No letter, no salvation.
He wanted to lose it, tears wouldn't come.
"Are you there, Alvi? Where are you—I'll come pick you up, right this second."
Before he could respond, a hand grabbed the phone, slamming the call short.
Alvi spun: one baldie, one short stack, cheap ties, badges at the waist. Baldie shoved him onto his bed, kicking it back in place. Shorty gave coarse introductions (droll detective gems), then rifled Miranda.
Baldie: "Get comfortable, Drake.
Short stack: "Playtime's over."

34.

A puny television beamed live images of the great fire, still consuming hillside homes—million-dollar matchsticks, sixty percent contained. For privacy, the detectives had him in a break room, cuffed to the table. Cue ball was Carroll, short stack—Brenes. Snack machine was low; a gypped Twix clung to a coil for dear life. Framed profiles of yesteryear physicians leered from every wall. Alvi studied their forced smiles, dead eyes, shaking his head at false accusations. Brenes went full press.

"Heroin you were found with is responsible for a rash of deaths throughout the city. Name Daphne Wrigley ring a bell?"

"No."

"*No?* That's funny—you killed her, slang her bad dope. Rap sheet says she was street meat, but still, blood's on your hands. Was found up in Griffith Park, thumb stuck on the plunger. Rig residue links her to the bricks found in that motel room—*your* dope. Same as your boy, Chester..." Brenes' fingers snapped for memory. "Carroll, what's that fucker's last name?"

"Mims."

"Chester Mims—victim number two. You're being held for both of 'em—formally charged on top of possession with intent. How's that sound, shithead? If only you weren't a failure at killing your damn self, right?"

"The drugs weren't mine! I didn't—this girl stole 'em—

Gabby—"

"Put a cock in it, Drake. Now's the time you sit an' listen."

A knock came at the door. Carroll nodded to Brenes and went to answer.

Alvi tried eavesdropping. Sounded like the detective was being fed orders. Silence fell, Brenes' bubblegum *clack-clacking* away. His eyes were glued to the door. A familiar face flashed, fleeing down the corridor as Carroll re-entered, holding a file.

Moustache Man.

Holt!

Alvi blurted, "Who was that?"

Brenes shushed a finger. "While you was getting your beauty sleep past few days, Carroll here's been reading up on you."

Carroll plopped a file before him. *His* file.

Brenes swiped the manila. "Your past peaks our interest, Ratboy?" He thumbed through the contents. "Your wife—Angelica, was also on the wrong end of a needle some years back, huh? Interesting. Pile that on top of your recent arrest, plus all these minor assaults and petty drug busts you've accumulated over the years—any jury's gonna eat you alive. Now, we could take you in right now, just based on what we've told you—but something else has surfaced."

Carroll approached with an envelope containing photographs. "Upon executing a search warrant for your apartment, we saw everything, your walls—the clippings—photos."

Alvi swallowed as each picture fell: Erma, Hector.

Brenes took over. "The case for these two has gone cold in past months and, needless to say, all recent evidence says it wasn't an isolated incident."

Four more pictures: Vanda—her mom, dad and sister.

"We *know* you know her," a finger tapped Vanda, "Erma Rios' best friend. Lived in the same building as you. Ate the big one up in Sun Valley, big rig turned her into pudding on the 5 north—rest a her family has vanished, presumed deceased."

"Hold up," Alvi said.

Carroll cut him off. "Two more have gone missing recently, also neighbors—both friends a yours."

Photo: Faye.

Brenes watched Alvi go flush. "In Ms. Green's apartment we found lipstick scribbled on her mirror, suggesting you two were romantically involved. DNA is pending on bed sheets from both her room and yours. Can you see where this is heading, Drake?"

Before Alvi could think, an *LA Xpress* slapped the table.

Mongo.

Carroll tapped her seductive pose. "Streets say you two were buds—worked the boulevard together. Vance Mongalez hasn't been seen or heard from since last leaving the Lafayette Hotel...with *you*." Anger tickled his esophagus, sparking a pause. "Now, this amount of killing..."

Brenes' voice sweetened. "Where are they, Drake? You're the key to all this. What have you done to 'em?"

Alvi choked on words, only sound resonating was the refrigerator's *hummm. Where to start?* One thing burned his skull. "—Gabby!"

The detectives leaned in.

He watched Brenes' mouth move, but everything went mute. Doctors on the walls now had beady eyes on him. The room squeezed, juicing his brain. *How had this happened? Only wanted to find her, help Mongo, help himself.*

"It was all 'cause of Gabby—"

Carroll whispered something to Brenes, pointing towards the door.

Brenes nodded. "Said that just now?"

"Yeah—as he gave me the file."

"Gabby what?"

"Gabby Wang. Said this guy might have more info on her. Run with it. He needs to know where she is."

Brenes punched the table. "Gabby Wang! Tell us everything you know about her, Drake! Where is she?"

Wang? He stammered.

"Come on, Drake—save your sorry ass!"

Words began to flow, their coherence hinged by the coursing meds. Alvi regaled past weeks, the search, distancing himself from all wrongdoing. Names flew, connecting dots, best he could. Gabby Gretsch peppered throughout. The truth and nothing but.

Carroll's pen danced like a magician's wand.

Brenes wasn't buying it.

Another glimpse at Mongo and Faye halted Alvi's song. A crushing thought weighed in; blood dribbled out his nose onto the patient's robe, seeping like cocktail napkin rings. *Gabby hadn't put* them *in danger*—HE *did*. His need for closure from the girl had them missing—or worse. *Why didn't he stop, think, heed warnings?*

Blisko: "Hope you ain't still tryin' to save every gal comes 'round..."

Mongo: "You still thrill seekin'...Some bitches just perma-fucked..."

It was all him. He *chose* to be *here*.

Brenes kicked a chair, shouting back on mute.

Or did he? *Were there choices in Los Angeles after all?* He drifted further. Those final moments with Angie preached wisdom. *A never-ending cycle of damnation, fueled by eager participants—across the globe.* Could see it now, her crazed logic rang true. *The City: The Beast.* One couldn't prevent being devoured. *Right?* Easier to think that way—made him feel better than those pretty little coffins.

Three pages slid before him: a full-blown confession, typed. Carroll's pen bounced off his forehead, skidding on the table. Validation was warranted, in name and blood. Sour mugs suggested it be done of his own volition—or else they'd help out. His eyes were blank, those beautiful blinking tubes spelling it out for him—

D-O-W-N
D-O-W-N
D-O-W-N

Stubby fingers pulled him up, fist hammering the ribcage. The walls jeered each aching grunt. Brenes' face boiled violence. Carroll awaited his turn. Alvi's lungs went void, dry heaves crumpling him to the floor, arms cranked to the table. One kick to the temple had the body shut down. Pain was shielded by total darkness, strange warmth evoking subconscious...

Angie's voice in whispers...

"Forgive them; they're trapped in darkness. We know the light: innocents who sing as this wasteland burns. It's not our fault, Alvi. The downtown heart beats, flooding hungry streets, flirting wild desire to devour its children. Behold! False neon halos! We need them—they need us. Can you see 'em now, glowing, buzzing—beckoning, loving? Do not tremble, child. The veins of the Los Angeles—they're our veins too..."

Epilogue

A crisp breeze swept down the boulevard as Faye sat at a bus bench near the Sunset Free Clinic, staring across at Micheltorena Elementary, strumming her navel, marinating in thought. The clap had cleared up, some good news for once. Blisters were new, but no day was perfect—not here, not ever. Her bus slugged to a stop, doors parting with a welcoming *swish*. She lumbered aboard, shuffling past rows of confetti print seats, avoiding eye contact with both the elderly and the crazed.

Her gaze out the window was empty, numb. A creep's *pssst* over the shoulder forced her eyelids shut. When they creaked back open, the streets gave a neon greeting; a giant palm radiated bright white, SPIRITUAL HEALER pulsing purple beneath. Could have sworn Alvi's face washed in their glowing reflection. *Fucking bastard.* Wondered what would finally become of him, then refused to care. All those lectures her father had given echoed in the ears. *Reckless...Naive...Careless...*She pulled a grainy ultrasound from out her purse, studying the image again, biting the inner cheek till it bled. Knew what to do, just not when. She wiped tissue and blew snot. The Stop Request bell went mad.

Through Echo Park, she studied well-lit homes, crumbling but cozy, searching for families at dinner, memories on walls. At a stop near the lake, an ironically dressed man leapt from a front porch, guitar slung over the shoulder. Before he could reach a cargo van filled with howling dudes, a tiny scream hammered the night. Faye watched as a kindergartner flew across the lawn, wailing for one last hug. Mother was behind, arms crossed. The embrace lingered as the bus glided on; her voyeurism cut short.

A meaty black girl waved from the sidewalk before boarding at Temple. Faye made a sad face, soon as she sat down beside.

"No way, girl."

Faye handed the photo. "Sixteen weeks, JaTonya."

"Well shit, least you ain't been at da casita dat long. Know who it be?"

She nodded, remembering his awkward face, soft inside her.

"What ya gonna do?"

She shrugged. "Got no choice."

"Gonna handle it?"

"Gonna make a run."

"You can't do dat—too dangerous!"

"You said it's better than before. Maybe they'll just let me go? I mean, what are my other options?"

"It be betta fo' sho, but dey still got a file on you, girl. Best believe much harm gonna come of it. Listen, few months back, girls be disappearing all da time—bitches gettin' shanked left an' right. Couldn't leave da 'partment to see my damn kids— just down da way. Now, dey let us come and go—I take my girls to school in da mornin'. Dere's a reason for it too, know we comin' back every night...or else." She handed back the pic. "We makin' awright money, ain't so bad."

Faye's brow crunched. "JaTonya, this ain't no way to live. No way I'm gonna! Makin' my move soon—tonight maybe. Longer I wait, harder it'll be," a palm rested on her gut, "for us."

That ominous rooster hovered up ahead, swelling, block by block.

"You ain't afraid, girl?"

"My dad's a Marine, has a buncha land up near Portland. Once I make it there, no way anyone can harm us. Can't be scared of 'em anymore, 'specially now that I know for sure. Gotta give him a fair chance in this world—let him follow his own dream."

"*Him?*"

"Yeah, doctor was pretty sure."

JaTonya smiled, nodding. "Whateva you need, girl. I'm here to help."

Faye choked as JaTonya's arms squeezed around. Bus windows glared the last drop of sun sinking into night. Rooftops began to howl, neon sirens teasing new flesh. She ignored them, caressing her womb, welcoming new light into forsaken dark days.

ACKNOWLEDGMENTS

First and foremost, thanks to Eric Campbell, Lance Wright and the team at Down & Out Books for taking the chance to republish *Neon Lights*; cheers to Tom Pitts for the recommendation. Many thanks to all those at publications who believed in me along the way: Todd Robinson and Allison Glasgow (*Thuglit*), Anthony Neil Smith (*Plots with Guns*), Tony Black (*Pulp Pusher*), Steve Weddle (*Needle*), David Cranmer and Elaine Ash (*Beat to a Pulp*), Kent Gowran and Ron Earl Phillips (*Shotgun Honey*)—along with all those at Los Angeles' Biggest Music Publication, the *L.A. Record*. Without them, this novel would not have been possible. A big thank you to Richard Lange and Frank Bill for their guidance and support. Chris Wibberley / 8th grade English: Thanks for crashing a podium through the blackboard of my brain. Tattoo Mike Suarez: "Wipe your nose, kid." Raven, the lost angel behind the spark for this book: rest in peace; you are not forgotten. To those who championed *Neon Lights* on its first run: Jim Ruland, Steph Post, S.W. Lauden, David Nemeth, James Pate and Jen Hitchcock at Book Show. To all my family and friends, thanks for the love and support. Jenny Jay, T & C: my loving gang affiliates. Lastly, to Los Angeles. I wear your birthmark. With your beauty, intrigue and filth as my fire, I am complete.

NOLAN KNIGHT is a fourth generation Angeleno whose short fiction has been featured in various publications including *Akashic Books, Thuglit, Crimespree Magazine, Shotgun Honey, Tough* and *Needle*. He is a former staff writer for Los Angeles' Biggest Music Publication, the L.A. Record, and currently resides in Long Beach. *The Neon Lights Are Veins* is his debut novel.

www.ingramcontent.com/pod-product-compliance
Lightning Source LLC
Chambersburg PA
CBHW020140310726
48970CB00006B/1961